PUFFIN BOOKS

DODGEM

For Simon Leighton no⟨...⟩ the same since his mother died. His father, Alex, ⟨...⟩ble to function properly in everyday li⟨...⟩r but he hasn't worked for ⟨...⟩ught with problems for Ale⟨...⟩'s got to look after Alex be⟨...⟩

Despite his good in⟨...⟩o take action. They send Alex into hospit⟨...⟩e.

In the home Simon meets Rose – a resourceful ⟨...⟩ girl who works the fairgrounds with her uncle. Effecting an escape that is both brave and ingenious, the two hatch a scheme that changes Simon's life more than he ever thought possible.

This is a moving, intensely exciting story of a young boy trying to cope with problems that would tax people of all ages.

Bernard Ashley

DODGEM

PUFFIN BOOKS

Puffin Books, Penguin Books Ltd, Harmondsworth, Middlesex, England
Penguin Books, 625 Madison Avenue, New York, New York 10022, U.S.A.
Penguin Books Australia Ltd, Ringwood, Victoria, Australia
Penguin Books Canada Ltd, 2801 John Street, Markham, Ontario, Canada L3R 1B4
Penguin Books (N.Z.) Ltd, 182–190 Wairau Road, Auckland 10, New Zealand

First published by Julia MacRae Books, a division of Franklin Watts Ltd, 1981
Published in Puffin Books 1983

Made and printed in Great Britain by
Richard Clay (The Chaucer Press) Ltd,
Bungay, Suffolk
Set in Monophoto Plantin

The author would like to acknowledge the generous help
given by the showman, Henry Botton, and his family,
by Fred Fowle of 'Fairground Art', by Pierre Portugal,
and by Laurie Stibbards, E.W.O.

for Iris

I

The word above the school gate, cemented in seventy-year-old brickwork, said *Boys*. But for Simon Leighton, going in on his nervous toes, it might as well have said *Them*, because this was another world he was forcing himself to enter: their world: and he was as reluctant as a man crossing a frontier into alien territory. He went because it was a crossing he had to make, a calculated move. A sequence of red diagonals was needed in that register to interrupt the long line of black noughts, or he knew for sure now that he'd be in serious trouble. They'd both been told, him and his dad – and this time they meant it.

He went in, and he looked round at this strange world where people thought having friends, or scoring goals, was more important than what there was for the next meal; he listened to the foreign language of easy greetings; and like an immigrant he set his face to pretend to be familiar with it all. Five minutes to the bell. Five long hours, more like.

Instantly, his way was barred. It was almost unbelievable, how predictable a situation could be.

'I don't believe it! It's Leighton!'

''Ello, little Leighton. You come to see what the inside of a school looks like?'

Simon smiled. 'Yeah,' he said brightly, 'that's right.' You always agreed. It was best to agree, especially with these two. He wasn't so much of a stranger that he didn't know right now in his rolling stomach that Jackson and Clark were the last pair you wanted to run into on a morning like this.

Clark's hand moved quicker than the head of a striking

7

cobra, but low and grabbing. Simon jumped back, knowing the sick pain before it ever came; and when he looked up Clark was already scratching his head, an innocent sneer on his pale face.

'Wassup, Leighton? Don't think I'd 'it a little titch like you, do you?'

Recovering, Simon tried to keep his face from saying either yes or no: it could go against him whichever it was.

'Any'ow,' Jackson's shoulders heaved at the humour to come, 'with your dad, Leighton, who'd 'ave the guts to go out nights if they done anything to you?'

Clark collapsed against the wall in a pretence of helpless laughter. Simon didn't react. You didn't react with these two: he knew that as well: everything got turned round, nothing pleased. Besides, he'd had all this about Alex before, and like someone with a funny name or different features, Simon was well used to not letting it show when it got to him.

''E's come for the prize-giving, 'aven't you, Leighton? Biggest number of days off.'

Clark cuffed his dribbling laughter. 'No. 'Is dad wants 'im out the 'ouse while 'e digs up the kitchen floor!'

This time they clutched each other, laughing, and Simon saw his chance. He shot off, zig-zagging on his trainer tips across the yard. It was big and crowded, and these two never chased after anyone – they were suddenly just there – and he could lose himself till the bell went if he kept his eyes open.

What they weren't going to do was force him to run out.

A crowd watching a kid striking matches gave him the cover he wanted. He quickly wriggled himself into the group, but he didn't bother getting to the front. He wasn't watching any fire raiser. His eyes were out for Jackson and Clark; but already his mind was back to that morning; and instead of the spurts of flame and the tossing hand, he saw his dad's pathetic waves goodbye from the house. He saw himself turning round every ten or twelve steps down the street, waving, hoping each time he turned that his dad would have gone from the window. But he saw each time that he was still there, and he knew that the corner of the street would have to make the final break for them. He gave a long, confident wave he didn't feel, and he set his face for school. On good days, when he was only going to the shops, his dad stood back sooner. This morning, though, it was as if Alex sensed that today was going to be especially bad in some way.

Well, God knew it wasn't going to be easy. The longer you went, not doing something, the harder it got even to go through the motions. But it had to be done. What they called a test attendance was a test attendance, and a couple of weeks solid now could mean they'd think extra hard before they took him to court. They fell over backwards to give you every chance, the welfare man had told them that. So, a bad day or not, there was no other way but to face it out. The big thing he had to remember was, this stretch could buy him six more months at home with his dad before they bothered him again. And the way things were, that wasn't just a good idea. It was more like a matter of life and death.

The bell rang and Simon hung back before following a group from his class through the left hand door. Things seemed to change when you were away a lot, so every move had to be thought out: you couldn't do anything automatic any more.

'Oh, 'ello, Leighton, where d'you spring from?'

At least the girl smiled, giving him a sense of belonging. But he couldn't remember her name.

'You 'aven't 'alf missed a lot. We've started cooking this term . . .'

'Have you?' Oh well, if that was all he needn't feel too much out of it, he thought. He did cooking all the time.

'You been ill?'

'Yeah . . .' It was usually quicker and easier to lie when this question came.

'You been seen out, though . . .'

'Oh yeah?' All the usual stuff – best ignored.

'She's moved your place, Miss has . . .'

That didn't surprise him. He'd expected at least that to have happened. This last year coming to school had been like the first day after the holidays every time.

'She don't bother calling your name no more. She won't 'alf 'ave a shock, seeing you.'

The girl whose name he couldn't remember looked at Simon hard, as if she were seeing how he took to the idea of not counting for much any more. He shrugged; but he felt far from nonchalant. Never mind teaching them cooking, Miss What'sername'd make a right meal of him coming back this morning. She always had before, with her remarks about him honouring them with his presence; and putting him back down the reading scheme.

'Yeah, what a surprise!'

But the surprise was Simon's. Miss What'sername was watching out for him, and when he turned the corner by the matador picture, the Buffet, she smiled at him and she took him by the arm and walked him into the classroom to a desk where there were new books set out, and a new ballpoint pen and pencil. He said nothing. He'd grown out of being shown a welcome, so reacting to one was hard.

'A fresh start, Simon,' she said. 'A good, fresh start. Half a term before the Easter holidays, a nice time for a bright boy like you to catch up. Break the circle. Get interested again, and catch up.' She squeezed his arm before releasing it; and with a long 'Mmmmm' she walked back to her own desk at the front.

Simon frowned. Everyone was staring at him, and one yob blew him a kiss. It had only helped to throw him, her friendly approach. Completely out of character. Prepared for one thing and getting another, he didn't know how to take it for a minute: until he saw her give the hand that had held him an involuntary wipe on her skirt: and he knew then that this was all part of something planned. They were trying something out: helping him to break the circle, as she put it: and there was no doubt any more that this was his final chance.

The morning still stretched ahead when the Educational Welfare Officer tapped with his car key on the headmaster's frosted glass.

'Come in, Denny.' The headmaster went on swiping at an annoying fly with a child's record card.

'Morning, George. How's Sir this morning?'

George Rogers fixed Denny Adams with a meaningful stare. 'Fed up with being a ruddy social worker. The sooner Social Services stop protecting the freedom of the individual . . .' – swipe – 'and start worrying about the kids, the quicker I shall be a teacher again . . .'

'Go on, you love it. All these young mums crying on your shoulder . . .' Denny Adams sat down and took the rubber band off a little black notebook, watching with interest while the other man tried to lull the fly into a sense of false security by looking the other way. 'I called on young Leighton Friday night. Is he in today?'

The headmaster nodded. 'Yes. I checked first thing. Well done, Denny. And our Miss Baker's doing well in the classroom – she's giving him her spiel about a fresh start. Good girl, putting herself out a bit . . .'

The E.W.O.'s elderly baby face wrinkled up. 'Glad it worked. Mind, I laid it on a bit strong for them. Told them the score. It's this, I said, or we go to court for a care order. Well, the boy's got to be educated, whatever trouble there is at home.'

George Rogers nodded, the fly forgotten. 'What did

Dad say? Did you get through to him, or is this coming back all the boy's doing?' He lit a cigarette from the packet of Senior Service on his desk. 'You'd never believe the change in that man. Taught him years ago. Talented painter, old Alex was: stable: nice fellow: not a hint of all this . . .'

Denny Adams shut his notebook. 'It's like talking to that wall, George. The man should be away. Just sits and stares. You can shout at him, do what you like, you get no response at all. You end up doing all your talking to the boy . . .'

'Well, thank God *he's* got his head screwed on. Otherwise he'd have no chance at all . . .'

Vibrations from a loud electric bell suddenly sent the fly diving through the layered smoke towards them.

'Peace over,' said the headmaster. 'Morning break. Now the trouble begins. Now we see what sort of a weekend they've had.' He lifted the record card again at the fly on his net curtain.

Denny Adams heaved himself up and opened the door. 'Then I'll leave Sir to it. But keep in touch over young Leighton. One word from you now and we can start proceedings. Then we'll see how quick Dad comes out of his trance when the boy gets taken into care . . .'

'Will do.' George Rogers looked beyond the fly and out into the yard. 'But don't go far from your phone! With the best will in the world I don't give him more than a fifty-fifty chance. Not after all this time . . .'

Denny Adams waited while the headmaster poised himself for the final swipe. It was as if he had to know the outcome.

Whack!

George Rogers smiled, and there was a murmured, 'Well done.' But when the record card was lifted the curtain was clear; and both men watched helpless as the fly buzzed past them, and out of the open door.

The bell was a disappointment to Simon. It sounded the end of a peaceful couple of hours for him, a period when he hadn't had to worry about anybody else. Now he was going to have to move about again, and face more people.

He'd been put next to another boy who was finding Market Junction School a strange place to be – a Pakistani who'd just flown in and was too busy being bewildered to worry about him – so he'd been well left alone. And the work had been easy enough, the only real problem that empty notebook labelled 'News', where he was supposed to write about some family event which had happened over the weekend.

Stupid idea! he thought. So what the hell did *he* write? Couldn't she see it was different for him? Did she really want something like, '*On Saturday my dad, Alex Leighton, picked up a paintbrush again, and broke it in half, and threw it in the fire?*' It was news all right – but what would she make of it? Or, '*On Sunday I went to see my Gran and Grandad but they wouldn't open the door any wider than it took to say "Clear off"?*' What would that get? Some spelling mistakes or a high mark for being original? No, it just wasn't the same for him, and that wasn't being soft, that was a straight fact. No mother, and a father who'd changed after she'd died from being the best signwriter around – a real artist – into a zombie who sat and stared at the wall, and picked at his fingers, and had to be bullied into eating enough to keep himself going. And him the one who was doing the keeping going. No, there was a difference, even between himself and the other kids in trouble; and if she couldn't see that, she was stupid . . .

But as if she'd realized, just before it was too late, Miss Baker had given him something else to do, and both he and the kid from Pakistan had lost themselves in Maths, and only between the lines of the exercise did thoughts of home continue to nag.

Thoughts like, if Alex turned the gas fire on, would he remember to light the flame? And, was he still up, or was he huddled back in bed, pretending to be asleep?

For the most part, though, Simon had got on, and when the bell went he knew it was for break, and not the sound of an ambulance at his house three streets away. He was beginning to feel more relaxed already, and for the first time he really started to reckon he could manage a fortnight here. Easy, he thought, providing he could work something out for these dangerous break-times. He'd be all right then.

Alone amongst the others he let himself be carried down the stairs, smaller, lighter on his feet, bouncing like a rubber ball in the middle of the others' clatter. At the bottom he psyched himself up to look as if he hadn't a care in the world. Optimism was the name of the game for him. When he gave up hoping that really was the end, he knew that.

The first thing he had to decide was where to go in the yard. There were always territories, and a calculating look around told him that they were all as dangerous as they'd been before. Aggravation everywhere. The amount of give-and-take was at the same low level he remembered, when an accidental knock of someone else's football meant a kicking, or at the very least an angry mouth formed up in an 'f'. He could see that each of the netball pitches had coats down for football – he'd avoid those – and where the angles of the tall building provided dark recesses, small groups plotted, so he'd avoid those, too. And he'd ruin his inside sooner than go near the lavatories for more than the quickest visit. That left an uncertain area by the gate, or the ring of security round the teacher on duty. He looked at her: a young woman already uptight and screeching at two kids who'd lost their rags. No. Not there. So he ran quickly, as if it were part of some game, to the gate. There were only a few people in that space, and nothing organized going on. Surely he could lose ten minutes amongst them without being pestered by questions or hounded by the arm twisters. As long as he kept an eye open for Jackson and Clark. He got over there and suddenly stood still, trying to look as if he'd been there all the time. This should be all right, then, he thought, over by the gate. You could see all round from here. He sighed, began to relax. A bit clever, one jump ahead of the game, that's all you needed to be. On your toes.

And then who came in from outside in the street with the perfect timing of the clever ambush but Solly Clark and Toss Jackson – smiling widely at him as if it were only ice cream they were hiding behind their backs? And it was a hundred years too late for him to do anything about getting away when they showed their hands and their tight knotted scarves.

'West Ham', 'The Hammers'; the scarves which were waved in victory, shaken in challenge, or swung like maces in aggression, were just hanging there for the moment, threatening.

'Well, well, well, it's Leighton.'

Why did the worst aggro always start off sounding more innocent than *Sunday at Six*? And how did these two know he'd come over here?

'Going 'ome, Leighton? Done your stint, 'ave you?'

'No.'

'Time for Daddy's shots, is it?'

'No.' They were trying to wind him up, and they'd got him where no one was going to take much notice – the place he'd chosen himself for its quietness. Already, Solly Clark's mouth was wet at this chance; and Toss Jackson's eyes were wide open with the same huge enjoyment. Two cats and one mouse. He didn't stand a chance.

'Been putting in a bad word for us, 'ave you, Leighton?' Jackson's knuckle whitened its grip on the scarf.

'No.' The frown was genuine.

'All "no's", i'n it, Solly? Can't you say nothing else but "no", Leighton?'

'Yes.' Play them along was all he could do. He looked round at where the teacher had been. He couldn't see her. But how long before that whistle went?

'Only we don't want no lies, Leighton. You've been 'aving a go about us, 'aven't you?'

Jackson took a half step nearer. The moment of sudden violence was very near; and now Simon knew for sure that things were going to happen before ever the whistle went. 'No,' he said, but neither of them was listening.

'So 'ow is it your ratbag teacher 'as a go at us about talking to you, then? Gave us a right rollicking as we went in, didn't she, Soll? She ain't your mum or something, is she, looking after you like that?'

'No!'

'No, she wouldn't be. Wouldn't take that chance, would she, after what 'appened to that other mother you 'ad?'

They laughed, and everything stopped for Simon: breathing; heart, even, it seemed; he felt his head begin to drain of whatever there was inside that kept him behaving normally. Who the hell were they to dare to even mention his mother? A picture of her, *the* picture of her, flashed at him. The pigs! Starting on like that, it was like having someone's dirty hands groping inside you.

'Accident on purpose, wasn't it, Leighton? Anyone'd act barmy to stop doing a stretch for what he did . . .'

Simon's inside was coiled tight and taut, wouldn't take much more pressure before it gave. He could usually take a lot, but this was different talk. These two were winding him up too far.

'Still, Solly, don't they say she only got what she deserved?' Toss Jackson stared Simon in the eye and spat his insult at him. 'Bit of a tart, your old lady, weren't she, Leighton?'

The spring suddenly gave. The case shattered. Pieces

flew. In a sudden lash of blind fury Simon's foot drove hard into Jackson's crutch.

The kid grunted, clutching himself, doubled up: then his voice rose to a surprised yell of anger and pain. Simon stood his ground, his eyes blazing. There was no running now. And he didn't want there to be any running any more. This was where he wanted to be, giving it and taking it for the good name of his mum.

Clarke hit him in the side of the face; but it didn't hurt. Simon kicked again to get the other one the same as the first; but Clarke caught his foot and twisted him onto the ground. His head hit the asphalt, hard; but still nothing hurt; all he felt was the faint prickle of grit, with the smell of the tar, and the hot taste of blood from his nose and teeth.

The boot came next, and the hob-nailed swearing. Get up now, and go in again! But at that moment the kicking suddenly stopped, and there was only the screech of the woman.

'I saw that! What's your name? You asked for that! You kicked first. I saw that. I saw that. Get upstairs, you. Serves you right! Go to Mr Rogers and tell him *I* saw it. Tell him that. Go on! Go on! I know! These two aren't always to blame, I've said that all along. I happened to see that with my own eyes. You nasty little oaf!'

Simon pulled himself up and looked at her. Her eyes were alight behind pink glasses, her mouth was twisted worse than Clark's and now her hands were tugging him towards the steps. In his mouth there was thick blood and dribble. He couldn't talk. There was no point in trying to talk.

He took two steps, pretending submission, before he suddenly broke free. He twisted his own look at the woman, and he went: not to the steps, not to the head-master, but past the man who stood in his way and out through the gate into the street, where his trainers ran him fast from the alien place.

From the entrance marked *Boys* they watched him go: the woman; the other two; and Denny Adams, who sighed and pulled the notebook from his pocket, to make an entry which he underlined.

At least when Simon went to the corner shop he came back with something in his hand: some shoppping to show for it, even if it was only five fish fingers. There it was for Alex to see, something to jolly him about, to provide some contact. But running in from the school today was an empty return, with nothing to show but a throbbing face and a bloody shirt: nothing to talk about but the terrible way everything had gone wrong. Simon was only glad his father wasn't around, was upstairs, because seen like this he was just a kid again, not the man any more, as if that other world had put him back in his place with a thump. No, he definitely didn't want to meet Alex for a while.

He shut the front door and went straight to the small living room, to the chimney-breast and the thick-painted, layered portrait of his mother. He wanted just a minute or two here. It was a good picture, one of Alex's best. It caught the light different ways at different times to give several views of the girl Alex had been going out with – sometimes looking out with quiet, uncertain eyes and a firm mouth, at others with serious eyes and a faint smile; black hair on bare brown shoulders, her arms crossed modestly across herself. This morning he saw her looking sadly at him in the dark room, it was her in real life, as he'd known her; he could almost hear her, sympathizing like a big sister because he'd been set on, about to open her arms and hug him to her. And suddenly it choked him as he hadn't been choked since the first week after that terrible accident.

He leant in the doorway and kept the bad side of his face away. If he turned that towards the picture he'd weaken too much, and cry: and he hadn't done that with Alex around for a long time now.

A bedroom door closed slowly, and Simon pulled himself up. Alex was on the move. No, not yet! Why the hell couldn't he have given him another ten minutes? Simon stood and waited for the familiar measured tread of a man with nowhere to go. A shoe banged on the skirting – he'd been to bed in his shoes again – and the landing banister creaked as Alex leaned upon it heavily.

It was pointless saying anything till he got down. Alex wouldn't call out. Nothing was ever important enough for him to call out. He'd wait till he was up close, and murmur something on his feeble, drugged breath. Creak, creak, creak, down he came, resting on each stair, his mouth open and noisy. He didn't exist fully enough even to breathe deeply.

Alex stumbled off the bottom step at Simon, shirt out, wrong buttons, and he frowned at the injured face. What am I supposed to do about this? he was asking. Another insurmountable problem.

'Had an accident,' Simon said thickly in the blood. 'Don' worry, it's all right, Alex. Sent me home. Gave me a mark, sent me home . . . sick.' He pointed to his mouth. 'Not much. All there still. Rinse out, s'all . . .' He eased past Alex and went up the stairs towards the bathroom: and he'd got right to the top before he heard the faint 'Oh?' from below.

Simon swilled and spat. 'Put a kettle on, Alex. Cup of tea.'

No reply.

Rinse and spit. 'You fancy one? I do.'

A grunt.

'Will when you see it. Put the kettle on . . .'

Alex shuffled off and Simon heard him bang the kettle on the tap.

The Vaseline was almost empty. Simon smeared it thin

on the puffy rawness of his cheek. It didn't look as bad as it felt; and he couldn't make up his mind whether to be pleased or not. The worse it was, the more the welfare man would have to sympathize when he came round: he'd see what he'd been up against, and that might help. On the other hand, all the time till it was better Alex would keep frowning at it like it was one more worry on his shoulders.

Simon dabbed at it and felt himself breathing faster again, the anger reviving as the smarting eased. Animals! Those two! They'd done for him; ruined it all; probably finished it all for good by making him run out.

He stared at his face until it was a stranger he was looking at: a pair of stinging grey eyes, a mat of wet brown hair, and the lop-sided shine of a face. Marvellous, wasn't it, what this creature in front of him had done? After a weekend gearing himself up to going back to that place, not sleeping with the worry of it, not stopping talking or hoping about it, he'd blown it all in a fit of temper, run away from it; and made everything a million times worse than it had been before.

Now it would all happen very quickly, whereas six months would have really sorted a few things out, with a bit of luck. Warmer weather and a long campaign might have melted the old people just a bit; time to get them opening that door wider than a crack – a whole half-year to have got them less frightened of accepting him again, paving the way for Alex. Who knew? Perhaps even getting to see he needed a bit of help instead of hate. And Alex himself, with the odd dinner coming round from them, and another chunk of time to get over things some more, perhaps he'd have been able to begin to accept what had happened, and see the need to pick up his life again. In six months Simon could have gone a long way towards getting paints and brushes back in his hands, and then they could have talked, had it all out in the open, answered that big, final question Simon needed to put.

But now? If Simon had to go, and Alex was left alone, he'd end up not eating, or setting his bed alight; or, much more likely, getting put into Stonelands like the old people wanted. And when that happened, that *would* be the finish. The end of the end, Simon reckoned.

He made the effort to focus and see himself again. And all the mad ideas of Friday night came back: the two of them running away to a cave in some lonely part of Scotland (were there caves like that any more?). Or getting across the Channel and going on the road, moving about all over Europe like the travellers in the stories. Could you still get away with that without being picked up?

Simon slammed the bathroom cabinet shut. He thought he knew the answer to that question! He used the lavatory and yanked at the chain. Wasn't there any freedom anywhere in the world? Who did these other people all think they were, to tell him what he had to do? How did any other person have the right to split him and Alex up? Who dared to have the neck to say what was best for other people? He spat red into the torrent.

A loud clatter from the kitchen suddenly held him still and listening. Hard to tell what it was with all the water going, but it sounded like saucers, probably skidding across the hard kitchen table and shooting off onto the floor. It had happened before when Alex made a cup of tea.

'All right!' Simon shouted. 'Coming!' He raced down the stairs to rescue Alex from his upset. He'd be standing there staring at the damage as if the broken crockery was another death: there was nothing in-between with Alex any more: everything that turned on him was a major tragedy, even a couple of broken saucers.

But Simon was stopped in the doorway by what he saw. There was Alex all right, standing in the middle of the kitchen with sharp pieces of white china round his feet; but it hadn't been saucers that had broken, it had been two plates; and instead of having his hand pressed to his face Alex had them clutching what he'd saved from hitting the floor, a jam Swiss roll, squeezed as thin as a tube of toothpaste in his anxious grip.

'Hey!' Simon stooped to the china; but he wasn't looking at the floor; he was staring at his father. Plates? Swiss roll? Alex had never got cake out before. He'd manage a cup of tea, but that was it: even getting out a packet of biscuits was beyond him. Today, though, he'd gone to the cupboard for the Swiss roll; Simon's favourite.

An end of the cake fell from Alex's grip and rocked a piece of china to and fro. It was absurd, the throttled, breaking cake and the uncertain face of his father, looking as if he were a dog caught with the Sunday joint.

'Cake's off then,' Simon said. He looked into Alex's eyes. It was impossible to expect him to smile: anyway, who wanted to smile today? But somehow that wasn't the important thing. The point was, for the first time in nearly a year Alex had done something off his own bat, for him.

Simon put a fingertip to his sore cheek. Perhaps it was the sight of the wound had made Alex do it. Or guessing what had happened at school. Anyway, whatever the reason, it was a move: definitely a move in the right direction.

Simon carefully slid the china into the kitchen bin.

The only trouble was, it had come at the wrong time. Picking up the pieces in this house had started too late to please the people who thought they knew best.

A bell you've been expecting shoots you up a lot quicker than a surprise ring. For a start, you haven't been relaxed, you've been on edge; and you're bound to have had false alarms to keep you in a state of tension. Simon could remember the same feeling from happier times, like birth-day parties, waiting for the first kid to come. So when the sudden call came that evening, the adrenalin squirted and his stomach seemed to spin. He knew that wasn't a Jehovah Joe with a message, or someone selling soap for spastics. This was the bloke from the School Welfare again, come to tell him how he'd let himself down, and what they were going to do about it.

Alex turned his head from the shapes on the television screen: but only for a moment. He never got near to the door any more.

'I'll go,' Simon said. He'd have much rather ignored it, let the man ring till he gave up and went away; but the uncertainty in him made him want to know for sure how they'd taken what had happened, and what allowance they'd make for his injuries. He didn't like being in the dark one bit.

As he got up he rubbed at the graze on his face and he gathered the memory of the blood back into his mouth, ready to talk painfully. It was the only card he had left to play now, because they wouldn't understand about the cake. And it was important: it would all turn on that. He'd made his mind up sitting there. If he got one more chance to go to school he'd jump at it. Never mind how he felt about the place. Up Jackson and Clark! After the cake there definitely seemed a bit more to hang on for now . . .

Denny Adams was a man who knew how to get across a threshold. He stood easy in the porch, his blue eyes twink-ling, his broad brow creased like a big rubber doll, and his mouth turned up in a relaxed grin. 'Hello, son. Can I come in and have a word with your dad? Thanks.' And he was along the hall and turning into the living room before Simon had the door closed. 'Hello, Mr Leighton. Don't get up. Remember me? Mr Adams.' He sat in Simon's chair and flapped his blue raincoat off his knees.

Simon followed him into the room and stood with his

wounds between the man and the picture on the chimney-breast.

'Well, we didn't do too well today, did we? None too clever, was it, Simon?' He crossed his legs and a cracked but highly polished black shoe swung in front of the television screen. Like a hypnotic's, Alex's eyes couldn't leave it as he pick, pick, picked at broken skin on his palm. 'What happened, son?'

Simon gave every gram of sincerity to the kind, grandfatherly face. 'Two of them had a go at me,' he said. 'Said a load of really rotten stuff . . .' He was sorry Alex was sitting there; he should have talked to the man in the hall, because he couldn't tell the full story now, not without putting something else between them. 'I couldn't let 'em say the stuff they did . . .' He tried to convey some special meaning with his eyes, but the welfare man was turning the pages of a notebook.

'It's a pity, that is, Simon. I told you, you had to show everyone you could settle down in school if you wanted to go on looking after your dad: and school's like that, people saying aggravating things all the time . . .'

Aggravating things! Simon tried to take a deep breath. What they'd said hadn't been aggravating, it had been something shoved right into an open wound. If he could get the man on his own he could give him some idea . . .

'With regular attendance you learn to cope with all that without hitting out and running away. That's what we mean by "breaking the circle". That's what I was trying to tell you you had to prove . . .'

That's what *she'd* said, all neatly worked out between them as if he was some clock that only needed regulating. Suddenly Simon thrust his bloodied cheek further down into the man's line of vision. 'They half killed me!' he shouted.

Denny Adams winced. 'You certainly took a pasting, son,'

he said. 'But it doesn't help Mr Rogers if you don't let him sort it out. Running out doesn't solve anything . . .'

'But . . .' Simon waved a frustrated arm that was meant to bring in the woman teacher who'd gone for him so unfairly. He looked at the man, at his dad. He had to get it across. If anyone in the world would understand he thought this man would. 'Alex,' he bent to the bent head. 'Alex, cup of tea, eh? Put the kettle on?' If he could get him into the kitchen for just a minute he could give the man some idea what they'd said about his mother. He'd know how upset any boy would be about that. He didn't have that closed-up face some of the doctors had. Simon's eyes urged his father to get up out of that chair and leave them alone.

'Don't worry about tea for me, son. I've got a couple more calls to make . . .'

But Denny Adam's voice trailed away as the boy's father unexpectedly started to respond. He was still pick, picking at his hand, but his frown had changed from one of apathy to one of concentration, and he was pulling himself up out of his chair. He shuffled over to Simon and all at once he grabbed Simon's head in a fierce, trembling, grip. He took the boy off balance as he twisted his head in his hands and pushed the injured cheek into Denny Adams' face. 'My . . . son . . . doesn't . . . go . . . to . . . school . . . for . . . that!' he exploded weakly. 'No! Not any more!'

As suddenly as he'd grabbed him he let Simon go, and he collapsed back in his chair, gripping the wooden arms and rocking himself backwards and forwards, his eyes staring their anger at the blank television, his breath hissing through his teeth.

'O.K.,' Denny Adams got up. 'O.K.' He buttoned his raincoat. 'I do understand how he feels, son. I do know how you feel, Mr Leighton – but what we've got to do is work it out for the boy.' He turned square to Simon. 'We've got to do best by you. It's your interests I've got to keep in mind.'

The man saw himself out, because Simon stayed to grip Alex's shoulder and stop the angry movement. Oh, Jesus! It was all hope, this anger Alex was showing, all hope. And because of it everything was hopeless now. It just wasn't fair. Life wasn't fair, he above all people knew that, but he'd had the strength to cope with it so far. This, now, though, was something different.

After a minute or two he went to the kitchen to put the kettle on himself, and to bury his face privately in the damp roller towel. But, strangely, the tears wouldn't come, now he was ready to let them. Instead, he found his mind had too much to work on to give in just yet: too much to work on because there was still so much he desperately needed to know, and Alex suddenly seemed a step nearer giving him an answer.

2

Denny Adams stared at the Alsatian, and the Alsatian stared back from the end of its chain as if it could see the white scars halfway up the man's right forearm. A caravan site like this was always approached with a care born from bitter experience. Being an Education Welfare Officer meant more than just sitting in other people's front rooms, and an active background in the naval dockyards wasn't at all a bad preparation for what this job sometimes had in store. He knew the yard well. There were two caravans there these days, through the small door in the double gates: the bigger one they lived in, and the smaller of the two, boarded-up. With the tarpaulin-covered ride and the big, blunt lorry there was just about enough room to manoeuvre – when the dog was out of the way.

'Good boy,' he said, 'good boy.' But his voice lacked conviction against the growling of the hostile dog. He said it again and the growling increased as the dog tried to stretch its chain. 'There's a good boy.'

There was a light in the main caravan and the occasional shadow. Carefully, keeping his limbs on his own side of the invisible barrier, Denny Adams bent to find a stone in the mud. The growling subsided, as if the animal saw something else in this low shape, something more like itself. The human hands felt about, but the eyes never blinked an instant from the staring dog.

'Tempest! You got someone there?' The caravan door had swung out and an oblong of watery light fell shallow in the yard.

The dog barked, a single bite of sound. Denny Adams

straightened up and called across at a trilby-hatted figure in the doorway.

'It's me, Mr Penfold. Mr Adams, Education Welfare.'

'Can't you come back tomorrer? I'm up to my eyes, 'ere . . .'

' 'Fraid not, Mr Penfold. It's my leave day tomorrow.'

The man in the doorway swore. 'Come on in, then, if you've got to. Tempest! Get back 'ere.' The dog hesitated for a moment, as if it wasn't sure – as if instinct and training were pulling against each other, like being called off a kill. 'I said, *come 'ere!*' The man jerked the chain viciously and the dog scuttled back beneath the caravan. The yard was too small for more than one master.

Denny Adams walked cautiously towards the light, side-stepping as if the puddles were his real concern, and not the dog within whose chain-length he was walking.

Old Man Penfold had gone ahead and was sitting at a tassel-clothed table when Denny Adams stepped inside. He still wore his hat, his hands lay motionless on the table like driftwood, and his brown eyes stared the other one out. There was no one else there. This time the E.W.O. didn't sit down: there were no more chairs, and the seat in the caravan's bay was piled high with bundled newspaper.

'Rose about, Mr Penfold?' The small caravan was all in one; there were no other compartments.

'Out.'

'I see. Are you expecting her back tonight?'

'She'd better. She's got the 'and cart, picking up paper . . .'

Denny Adams opened his notebook and sounded very business-like. 'I don't suppose I need to tell you: but in spite of my warning last time she hasn't made a single attendance at school. She's obviously not ill if she's out working.' He looked round the caravan. 'And you still haven't made proper arrangements for her to sleep in a separate room . . .'

The driftwood found new shapes, but the eyes remained firm on Denny Adams. 'No need; she's family.'

'Family or not, it's not good enough. She's a big girl. Even a daughter of her age should have a separate room, let alone a niece.'

The old man shrugged. 'That's only what you say. I've told you, our ways are different: different, mind – not wrong.'

'I'm not making judgements. I don't make the rules. But I have told you what they are, Mr Penfold, and I have told you what we'd have to do if you didn't comply with them.' He put on a man-to-man voice, lower. 'When does your season start, Charlie?'

Old Man Penfold wiped his nose on a red hankie from his waistcoat. 'Week before Easter,' he said. 'Month an' a half, two months?'

'Local?'

'Dunno yet awhile. I'm waiting on the *Fair*: see who wants what I got . . .'

Denny Adams' small eyes creased over. 'Well, I understand that, but why can't you play the game like the others do? We won't chase you to the ends of the earth while the season's on, but the least you can do is get her into school while you're laid up. Denying a kid of her age a bit of schooling just won't hold up in the modern world, Charlie. I'm surprised a man like you can't see that.'

'Schooling never done me no good,' the old man said. 'An' I'll still be paying my way long after you're drawing your pension . . .'

'Could be.' Denny Adams's voice remained even. 'But will it be you or young Rose paying your way? It looks to me like she's the one doing the grafting tonight.'

Old Man Penfold stood up, quickly for a man of his age. 'Who the hell d'you think shifts that lot when it's bundled?' he asked. His hand waved at the heavy news-

29

print. 'I'd like to see you lift one o' them bundles, Mr Welfare . . .'

Denny Adams looked at the top pile, bitten into quarters by thick, tight, string. His free hand strayed to his abdomen. 'Well, I'm not here to argue with you over that. But whatever you say, it still doesn't put you above the law . . .'

Old Man Penfold stared at Denny Adams for a full ten seconds. His unshaven Adam's apple rode in his throat. He pulled his tough frame taller. 'Listen Mr Welfare, no one's above the law in this world who 'as to work for a living, so don't kid yourself about that. We're as right and proper and law abiding as any. In our own way, with our own laws.' His head turned involuntarily towards the stacked-up ride outside. He frowned. 'And one o' them's the law of what people want. Now you go and do whatever you've got to do; but don't come pushing into my trailer with your council talk. *My* time's too precious.'

Denny Adams made a disappointed, misunderstood face from the many creases at his disposal. But he said no more. The dog was barking outside at the raised voice.

'You know your way to the gate. And I'll still be here when you come running back with your law . . .'

Denny Adams shook his head. 'All right, just as you like. Thank you, Mr Penfold.'

Going back he made it from the step to the gate in six strides. But the dog didn't budge: and neither did the girl who was crouching there holding it. Only when the man had slammed himself out of the yard did the chain shift on the ground, and the girl pushed herself in through the door of the trailer.

'So what did the Welfare want?' she asked.

'The usual!'

'Taking me in, are they?' Slight as she was against the old man, there was the commanding ring of the woman in her voice.

30

'Only till Easter,' he said, 'if we get ourselves on the road.'

'Thank God for that!' She turned and shut the door. 'Be a break from bloody paper . . .'

Simon and the girl couldn't possibly have sat any further apart in the Transit van. She climbed in quickly and went straight to the back, staring out through a side window, while he took a seat at the front and waited for the places between them to fill up. But the van pulled away almost empty: there were no more to come: everybody else, it seemed, had gone away from the court with the people who'd brought them. Only Simon and the girl had been taken out through the double doors into the yard, to the transport, and into the care of the Social Services.

Simon felt numb. It was like the night they'd told him about the accident, when it wasn't the enormity of it all that had registered but all the small stuff – like having to choose between ham and cheese in a sandwich, seeing a dog running off where it wanted; noticing the paint flaking on a shop-front Alex had once done; small things that he'd never forget occupying his frozen brain.

The van jolted and bumped him in his seat. It found one hole in the road deep enough to make everyone shout: but they each stayed silent and shut-in with their thoughts – Simon, the girl at the back, the Social Worker by the door, and the driver. The van was held up once or twice in traffic and people passing glanced in and looked away, as if there was nothing extraordinary about a council Transit taking a couple of kids somewhere, it was happening all the time. Simon looked out at them and remembered seeing the police Black Marias going through the streets, and the isolated faces staring out through the barred windows on their way from court to prison. He remembered wondering what they felt like. Now he knew. They felt like nothing very special; just numb.

It was a long journey and in the end, when something did get at him, it was the distance. As the van took them further and further from the court, first the houses getting noticeably bigger, then the gardens getting bigger than the houses, and finally the spaces in between getting bigger than both, he became more and more aware of what was happening. They were really separating him and his dad. And it wasn't the going away from Alex that got at him, it was the distance they were putting between them. They were taking him a long way from home.

Simon looked round at the girl. She was still staring out with her fixed stare. He looked at the Social Worker, a young man with a weak moustache; he was still sorting out papers in a cardboard folder. He looked at the driver; he was relaxing a bit now they were on the dual carriageway. Only Simon seemed to be feeling tense. Where the hell are we? he thought. Getting back to Alex wasn't going to be easy from right out here.

He looked for landmarks but they'd never been pub people in their house, so the huge *Thatched Cottage* – 'No coaches' – didn't mean a thing. Nothing did, and his mind went instead to thinking about the man and what he'd said when he'd come to collect him from the house. Had it all been a con trick for Alex in his chair? Or was the Welfare as shocked as he was at what they'd said in court? 'Supervision Order', he'd reckoned: a Social Worker to keep an occasional eye on things at home while Simon kept up a good attendance at school. That's definitely what they'd ask for, Mr Adams had said in the waiting room. And what had happened? 'Into care at Darenth Lodge Assessment Centre' had been the decision when they'd finished reading the reports: and while the man had gone out looking like a losing lawyer – a bit put down, but thinking about tomorrow – Simon had been guided into a small room with a closed door.

Anyway, his mind reverted, he could ask the way back

once he got out. People on the edge of London always knew where Market Junction was. And with that fiver from the housekeeping down his sock he'd make it home all right, no sweat . . .

Simon clung to the seat as the Transit swung in through pillared gates and Darenth Lodge gave them its gravelly welcome, like just about every country mansion Simon had ever seen in films. The van pulled up in front of the red brick building and they were there, with the engine switched off and the key dangling. It all felt very final.

'Right, folks, here we are.' The Social Worker came to life. 'Come on Simon; come on, Rose.' He jumped out of the van and stood between the house entrance and the gate, smiling – and clearly blocking anyone's way who fancied running.

Simon got out. He looked round about him and up at the house. It was all very quiet here: only the buzz of traffic on the road, no children about. He could see into plain bare rooms; there were no curtains at the ground floor windows, and those upstairs were a uniform blue, short, skimped, and clearly not what the house was used to. The door was open, and the hall was a disappearing vista of polished brown lino and red buckets of sand. The outside walls showed the rub of trees cut back, all of it giving the double-fronted Victorian mansion the look of the Welfare, a place where fireplaces were always made smaller, fancy plaster was made smooth, and banisters were boarded in. Simon had been going in and out of places like this for the past twelve months, collecting the supplementary benefit, applying for a clothing allowance, being turned down for a rate rebate. And he'd never failed to picture them with their families in them, in the days before the living rooms were offices.

'Come on, if you look sharp there'll be some dinner.' The Social Worker rubbed his hands.

Simon looked at him quickly, a hard swift glance before he put on a more amiable face. Too generous of them, that was – forcing him to come here and then making a big deal about feeding him. He walked into the house, not at all certain whether he could stomach anything, anyway.

'What's it to eat?' The girl behind him spoke for the first time since they'd got into the van. Simon looked round. 'I'll eat your'n,' she said, staring back, as if she'd read his mind.

The Social Worker sniffed the air. 'I don't know, love. Smells like greens and something . . .'

Her face was pale; tired eyes; tangled fair hair, too long for the style; and a mouth which looked as if its muscles never worked the way of a smile. She was the sort going into care was about, Simon thought, not him.

Someone cleared a throat.

'Hi.' A man had appeared at the door of the first room on the right. He was in thick-soled, silent shoes, with a voice to match. 'I'm Rick.'

The Social Worker smiled. 'Hi, Rick.' Then more publicly, 'This is Simon and this is Rose.'

'Hello, Simon, hello, Rose.'

The man's gold identity bracelet jingled as he made a point of shaking hands. Momentarily confused, Simon shook with his left.

But beyond Simon's polite smile neither took much notice. Already Rose was staring at the other doors; and Simon knew he wasn't going to be there long enough to worry about who this bloke was.

They'd laid-up for half-a-dozen in the Recreation Room: it looked as if the magistrates hadn't sent as many as they'd expected. The two of them ate alone, with Simon picking at his; every mouthful long to chew and hard to swallow. He couldn't stop telling himself how badly he'd handled things to lead to him having to abandon Alex. What was Alex doing, he asked himself bitterly, while

34

he was being fed? He wouldn't be eating, that was for sure. He'd be back in bed, or standing still in the house somewhere, staring at a wall.

Simon stole a look at the girl. It was strange how cut-off you could be behind a plate. She seemed completely unaffected by what was happening, head down, eating with determination, looking neither happy to be there, nor unhappy: just there, and getting on with it. She looked up once while he was starring at her: and she returned to the next mouthful as if he weren't at the table at all.

The room was fairly large with enough tables and chairs to suggest there'd be a lot more there for tea. A cream-coloured hatch had been knocked into one of the walls, and the painted mantelpiece on the opposite wall held clusters of salts and peppers and bottles of ketchup. With a soft singing and some clatter from the kitchen everything seemed set for a larger onslaught later.

Simon had the tip of a tasteless forkful in his mouth when Rose spoke again. 'You gonna want your afters?' Simon looked at the stewed apple and cold custard. He shook his head, and the girl slid her plate away and gathered his with her arm. Without another word she started on it. Simon dropped his fork in his plate. How could people wolf away on a day like this?

Rick, the warden, put his soft-bearded head through the hatch, perfect timing as Rose pushed the second plate away. 'Er, usually there's a rota for washing-up,' he said, 'like in a youth hostel. But we'll do yours with the pots today. Hand them through, will you, and Ruth'll show you where your rooms are.'

Without speaking, Rose got up and put her plates through. Just her own, not even Simon's plate that she'd eaten from. She went over to stand looking out of the window, her back very straight in its silky frock, her arms folded. Simon scraped back his chair and cleared what was left: the salt and pepper to the mantelpiece, the rest to the hatch.

'O.K.? Let's go, huh?' A girl in a shirt and jeans had appeared in the doorway: short, dark, hair in a scarf. 'I'm Rick's deputy, Ruth . . .'

Rose came over from the window and walked past Ruth out of the room; Simon followed. She hardly said a word, this Rose, he thought; just ate everything in sight and did as she was told. More than likely she had the same idea as he had – give no trouble to anyone then bunk-off out of the place at the first opportunity.

He walked behind them up the wide stairs.

Well, not the first opportunity. The first opportunity would be tonight, and they'd all be on the look-out tonight. No, tomorrow night would be the time: when they'd relaxed a bit here: and when Alex, at the end of a couple of days on his own, would be more ready to do as he said and come away with him. Besides, Tuesday was allowance day, and they'd need that money if they were going to get a train out of London, get away to the country and lose themselves somewhere. He had to wait for that. And he had to know the geography of this place, and the running of it. And be aware of things like these creaking stairs. He couldn't afford for anything to go off at half-cock.

'Er, right, Stephen . . . Simon . . . yes! This is where you'll be.' Ruth the deputy opened a door at the top of the stairs.

Phew! Gawd! Two bunk beds and the smell of socks! Simon went in, breathing as shallow as he could. It was rough-tidied, the sort of clear-up he knew so well: clothes piled but not folded, covers pulled over, not tucked in; spare shoes and trainers kicked under the beds. There hadn't been even the swiftest of adult hands in here. It was his room at home, but bigger, with others in it. And there were no bars on the window.

He could see his place before Ruth pointed it out: the

lower bunk behind the door, where the stripes of the stained mattress showed a vacancy.

'I'll give you your linen in a bit and you can make it up. You can make a bed, can't you?'

Simon nodded.

'And you've got no pyjamas or change of clothes, have you?'

'No.' The court didn't allow for that. It was like going to prison, the way they did it. You weren't allowed to go along prepared, like going into hospital.

'We've got plenty. We'll kit you out. Hang on here while I show Rose where she'll be . . .'

Simon waited to hear them creaking on up another flight of stairs before running across to the window on his toes. He looked around the frame. It seemed the sort that would open; a sash window like the ones at home. Down below was an untidy patch of bushes. He could hang by his fingers and let himself go into that. It'd jar him, it was still a good drop; but it wasn't too far to risk.

He turned his back on the window and looked round the room. What were they here for, the other three? he wondered. And who were they? How old? What sorts? Was there a Clark and a Jackson amongst them? The heaps of clothes gave few clues; only the shoe sizes said they'd be about his age, some a bit older; but empty shoes always looked unreal; a bit sinister; a reminder of a death . . .

What about this Rose, then? Think of something else when you got choked. What was up with her? She looked as if nothing much had anything to do with her: sort of unaffected by things. She never smiled; but then she looked as if she never cried, either . . .

Kitting out Simon with the bare essentials didn't take long: a couple of sheets spread awkwardly on the bottom bunk, a hard pillow dropped into a pillow case; some pyjamas, a toothbrush and a towel; and these were the limits of his personal world. Almost as if she sensed this impoverishment Ruth hurried him downstairs to the Recreation Room. There she spread kitchen paper on a table and produced a tray of poster colours from a cupboard.

'How about a picture for your room?' she said. 'Something to make a corner of it yours. Or there's plasticene somewhere. It'll be a little while before the Transit comes back with the others . . .'

He was on his own. God knew what she'd got that girl doing. Behind the hatch there was the clang of heavy pots now, and still the singing. But in here he was on his own; and on the table were thick poster paints, and large brushes . . .

Brushes and paints. He stuck his hands in his pockets and saw Alex at the kitchen table; messy yet orderly; circling a brush on a palette, a blob of worked paint woken into a glistening life, then laid on the hardboard, surely, and yet hesitantly, and stroked and tempted into going where he wanted it. Alex could have painted that matador at school, the bold, blue figure, bringing it to life. Could have. Once. Just as he could letter someone's name and bring a shopkeeper to life. Once upon a time . . .

Simon picked up the brush and flicked dried paint out of the bristles with his thumb. He smelt the jars of poster colours. They seemed all right, and the colours were rich. He dipped the brush in the scarlet, without any idea of what he might do. The colour clung there, shining, thick, as if it were refusing to come off the brush till it was where it had to be, on the oblong of white paper.

He stroked it on. It ran smooth and creamy, surface bubbles popping, broad and strong until the bristles showed at the end of the sweep. He dipped again and took the line on; and then he brushed another above, and below. The broad sweeps fizzled on the paper like red sherbet, or bubbling blood, and he worked more vigorously, faster and faster, dipping, stroking to fill the paper, keeping it all alive and wet until he'd done and he could lift the brush high and plunge it into the black, circling it on the seething red in a large, bold outline of a face: any face: eyes, nose, mouth, hair, ears. Just a face – primitive as a wall-painting, the black running into the background along the lines of the paper's weave.

He stood back, and he was panting, out of breath. He sighed, let his lungs catch up, and he looked again. Just a face, he'd done: a face which had turned out to be Alex.

'Hey, that's not bad!' Rick was at the hatch. Simon hadn't even heard it open. 'Anyone special, is it?'

Simon looked at the picture with his head on one side, wrinkled his forehead in a frown for Rick. He wasn't expected to answer.

'Great! You can put that up. I've got some Bluetack somewhere. Just let it dry. Gonna do another one?'

Simon looked at the paper, and the paints, and his hands where the red was drying and cracking in the folds of his skin. 'No, not now,' he said.

He cleaned his brush and put the paints away, the discipline of the painter he'd observed so often. He peeled the picture off the table. Not much good, he thought, as a painting. And it would always remind him of here and now, this room, if he kept it.

He still hadn't decided whether to keep it or crumple it when Rose walked into the room. He saw her looking when it was too late to hide it, and he frowned because he didn't want her to make any comment: although he was strangely disappointed when she didn't, when she walked past him to stare out of the window instead, as if the room were empty.

When she said something at last it could have been to him, or to no one.

''Ere comes the roughs!'

Simon looked past her, the painting still flimsy in his hands. The Transit van was there again, but crowded this time, with a woman Ruth's age in the front and a mixture of faces – of eyes – at the windows. Simon studied it carefully. These were the kids he'd been sent to live with. Which of the boys had the beds in his room? he wondered. The little one who jumped first, with the aggressive face daring anyone to hold him back? The tough skinhead who spat as he slouched down? The nervous-looking kid with the eyes everywhere? The boy with the Afro hair? It was going to be a weird night, shared with three strangers.

He backed further into the room and looked for some-where to put his picture – he had suddenly decided to keep it – but the girl didn't move from the window. People didn't seem to affect her the same way they did him. He was wary, nervous: she was as sure of herself as you like. She'd stare them out as they looked in while he wanted to hide his picture. His stomach tightened as they clattered into the hall: he suspended his breathing till the voiceless noise had gone up the stairs.

He slid his painting down behind a storage heater in the alcove between the fireplace and the window and he made sure the cupboard door was shut on the paints. None of them knew anything about him here. He didn't want to be an easy target, the way he was in school with Jackson and Clark.

The girl had turned from the window, and she was staring at him; not inquisitive, very matter of fact, looking at him and then at the cleared table, where there was nothing to show. 'Waste of time, weren't it?' she said: and she walked out, as if she'd accomplished just as much doing nothing.

Simon stared out at the rough garden. It was beginning to get dark, that time when you felt low enough without anything bad happening to you. He saw his own reflection in the glass, small in the big, empty, room. He thought about Alex, alone in their house; and Alex's picture shoved away behind the heater. God, if only it was this time tomorrow, he thought. If only it was nearly time to get out of here and back to his dad.

The little one, the first from the Transit, was the first into the Recreation Room. He came in through the open door like a swinging puppet, fast, backwards, all arms and legs. Without seeming to steer himself he avoided everything, the table corners and the chairs, running round Simon, staring at him, before throwing himself up onto the storage radiator, warming his hands flat on the top and kicking his heels behind him on the wall. He made a string of strange noises which was a song, and he eyed Simon like an animal in a circus cage, ready to bite if there weren't a whip in the other's hand.

Simon stood holding the back of a chair, still and very tense. He knew all about false moves, and he wasn't going to make one. He wasn't going to say anything and he wasn't going to leave hold of the chair until he felt sure about what would happen. It wouldn't take much to trigger this kid, he could see that.

The staring continued, but now the younger boy changed his tune. His feet kicked a different rhythm and his mouth twisted seriously round high words like 'Ba . . . by' and 'go . . . a . . . way . . .', as if they were important, and Simon listened hard for some significance. Was he singing to himself or was he trying to get at him with the words? It wasn't a song Simon could recognize. 'Long . . . w . . . ay . . . from . . . yew . . . ew . . .' The eyes said he was wanting some trouble, but the words were sliding out innocently enough.

'Wanna fight?'

Till then. The snarled question sent a cold knife straight into the gut. The singing had stopped and the kid was standing up on the heater now, leaning out of the corner, his right hand holding on to the mantelpiece, his left clenched towards Simon.

'Yeah, come on, then.' Simon stood up, let go of the

chair. A good stroke that, he thought. Call him here and now and someone would be in to stop it, quick: this way you didn't look chicken and you didn't get hurt.

'Right, mate.' The kid sniffed aggressively. 'I'll fight you.' He leapt off the heater, everything stretched, to land stumbling in the centre of the room. He knocked his back into a chair, but he didn't seem to feel it. He stood up and faced Simon. Feet apart, Simon stood ready for the first attack. Let the kid come at him, he decided, then he'd be telling the truth to say he hadn't started it. And it'd be a foot first, he was sure of that: the way the kid moved was all feet first. If he could catch the first foot he could twist it over and throw him back into the chairs – that'd make a noise loud enough to bring someone running . . .

The kid's brown eyes glared up at him. 'Not 'ere,' he twisted out. 'Tonight.' He gave an almost comic smile of aggression, as if to emphasize for some huge theatre what an opponent he was going to be. Then he sat up at a table for his tea, singing again, his feet swinging clear of the floor.

'Right,' Simon said. He sat too, trying to be as confident himself. He looked again at the little figure, to draw some reassurance from his size: but all he could think as he stared was what a terrible man this kid was going to make one day . . .

The hatch slid back behind him and unzipped Simon's spinal nerves.

It was Rick. 'Oh, er, Lee, put out the sauce and salt, will you?' He looked at Simon. 'Um, you can see how it's done, O.K., er . . .?'

'Yeah.' Simon put on his pleasing smile. There wasn't much to show about putting the things on the mantelpiece round the tables, he thought. And what brilliant timing, umming and aahing through the hatch when it was too late to prevent the real aggro going on!

A pile of plates was slid heavy on the servery and the

smell of toast wafted in from the kitchen. A hand-bell rang briefly in the hall. Come and get it now, it seemed to say, or miss it.

Lee hadn't moved for Rick. He'd stayed where he was, tipping back his chair to the final millimetre of balance. 'On that shelf,' he said to Simon. 'You 'ave to put three on every table.'

Simon walked nonchalantly to the window, where he looked out at the dark, then over to the mantelpiece, ringing his hands round a cluster of salts. Casually, he put them round the room, one on each square formica table top. A cutlery tray was crashed onto the servery. Chairs scraped back as the rest of Darenth Lodge came in for tea. Suddenly, it was all noise and movement.

They all stared at Simon as he went on round, but there were too many new faces for him to take in; although the boy with the skinhead – and an ear-ring – was there; and a table of girls, black and white, with Rose on it; a couple of much older kids talking in gruff voices; and lots of younger ones.

Tomato ketchup, salt and pepper went round to these faintly inquisitive stares. Meanwhile Simon's place was taken by a little girl with a dog-eared teddy-bear, so he found a table with just one other on it, the quiet-looking black boy who'd hung back getting out of the Transit.

The noise was still more feet than mouths: there wasn't a lot of conversation.

A cook's head appeared in the hatch. 'All right, that table,' she said, pointing at Lee's. Lee was waiting for it, as if they always chose him first, and in a long yelling slide he careered sideways to the counter for his food. One by one the other tables went up, with Simon's – furthest away and half-filled – the last.

He was at the hatch, asking for one slice of baked beans on toast instead of two, when the boy with the ear-ring suddenly raised his blunt head.

'Who done the sauce, then?' he demanded, already staring at Simon. 'You, weren't it, Titch?'

Simon steadied his plate with two hands and nodded. 'Yeah . . .'

'So what's up wi' this table. Got the pox, 'ave we?'

Simon looked at the table. Salt, pepper, but no tomato sauce. He thought he'd done the lot. 'Sorry mate . . .'

'Yeah, so'm I!' The boy turned in his chair and jerked his head at a fat girl on the next table. Without a word she left her meal to sidle over to the mantelpiece.

Marvellous, wasn't it? Simon thought. The Welfare thought one of the reasons he wouldn't go to school was he couldn't face up to the bullies. So they send him somewhere where it goes on all the time. They put him in the aggro here to make sure he goes to school to put up with the aggro there. It seemed a crazy sort of thinking.

'Hey, you lot, anyone lost this?'

The girl who'd gone for the sauce was at the heater by the mantelpiece, the tomato sauce in one hand while she fished something out with the other. Simon stared, unbelieving. It was his painting. Of course. Today it had to be! She held it up. It was stiffened by the heat, crinkled, and the colours had gone off. In its wrinkles Alex looked older, slightly bizarre with his eyes staring and his mouth parched open. Simon looked down at his baked beans. Take no notice. Deny it. Don't bring Alex into this.

Ear-ring gave a derisory yell at the art work. It was the signal for others to laugh safely.

'What's that? Some loony?' someone asked.

'Some ape, i'n it?'

Lee was already wound-up to go over the top. 'Some fat pig!' he shouted, dripping beans and kicking his legs.

There were cheers and rude noises.

'Well, 'ave I gotta stand 'ere all night?' the girl asked.

44

'Does anyone want it or don't they? 'Cos it's gonna catch on fire down 'ere . . .'

Simon looked up again and stared at the back of Rose's head. She was the only one who knew. Keep your mouth shut, he was willing her: because if you can keep your mouth shut, I can keep mine, and that girl can tear it up and done with it. I don't want any more out of any of this lot. The picture doesn't matter. Just don't . . . say . . . *anything* . . .

The beans clogged in his throat as he watched her straight back turn to give her a look at him. No! he was frowning. I'd have said by now if I wanted the picture, wouldn't I?

But her expressionless eyes stared into his. He tried to shake his head without moving it. I gave you my food. I was all right to you. Now you be all right to me.

'It's your'n, i'n it?' she said; and she fixed him before she looked away.

The room swivelled. Because Ear-ring had laughed at it the thing had taken on a ridiculous importance.

'Oh, yeah,' Simon said. 'Must've forgot . . .' He stood up to take the picture from the girl. He tried to shut his ears to the hollow cheers, to Lee's obscenities and Ear-ring's scoffing. But he couldn't sit down again. He barged out of the room to the privacy of the corridor and leant, miserably clutching his picture, against the scarred panelling. And for God knew what reason he found that he was crying.

Crying! Over this! After all he'd been through and kept control!

Too soon, Rick was there, and Ruth. 'Hey!' They eased the picture away and took him into an office. They sat him in a chair and said soothing things to him. They told him how everyone felt strange and upset like this at first. But he'd get used to it, they said. He'd settle.

Simon didn't hear them, though. He was too choked,

and he didn't really know why. Was it him being laughed at, or having the mickey taken out of his picture of Alex? Was it Alex? Was it being here?

He stared at a flat square of carpet, the paint all over his hands and smears like woad round his wet face.

And by the time they'd finished being kind to him he thought he knew what it was. It was all those other things, everything that had built up, it had to be. But something else had made it worse: two things really, but linked. One was the careful watch they'd be keeping on him after the way that girl's action had made him behave: he could almost see Rick marking it against his name; Simon Leighton – runner. The other was the fact that she'd done it. The let-down, after he'd done no harm to her.

Yes, a lot of this upset was down to that girl. What was her name? Rose? Well, for the short time he'd be here Rose was someone he was going to have to steer clear of like the plague.

3

Simon sat on the edge of a chair facing the crinkly glass. Next to him Rick fingered the frayed ends of his scarf, and then there was Rose. All around them were the sounds of the school settling to a new day: the rise and fall of adult voices, the rapping of chalk on boards, the rhythmic chink of a milk crate. Simon watched the silhouette of Mr Rogers crinkle in and out of view: he wondered who was in there all this time, but idly; he was used to waiting for people to see him. Rose sat swinging her legs, looking at a wild-life wall chart opposite. Rick asked, 'O.K.? Won't be long now, I don't suppose . . .' He stuck his legs out and hummed a little tune.

It had been a fast-moving twenty-four hours for Simon; so many changes had occurred. The day before at this time he'd been waving an extra-special goodbye to Alex, making his going look like a very short-term affair. And in some ways, of course, it had been: because here he was already, back in the school where his recent troubles had begun. But in between times he'd fallen foul of this dangerous girl, Rose, he'd spent the night in a room with a weird little kid who fell asleep and woke up singing about the fight they were going to have, and he'd been on a tour of the district in the Transit, dropping kids off at different schools till just he and Rose had been left here with Rick. Dinner money had been handed out like a pension, and pocket money had been promised for the end of the week on the condition that they were sensible for four days. And now he was waiting for a warning talk from the headmaster. Simon shifted on the hard seat. Things changed; and yet they didn't. He'd be on about the same things as the rest; how stupid it would be for either of them to try to run off. Well, Simon knew what *his* plans were; although there was no way anyone could tell what went on in that girl's head. He yawned. It caught him suddenly, like a hiccup does. God, he felt tired. It had been a long time after Lee's last threats before he'd been able to go off to sleep last night. He'd heard several creakings of the door as they'd gone on checking on him into the small hours: the checks that had put off the big fight, which would make the break-out difficult if they did them again tonight; and for what was left of the night he'd seemed to be thinking – or dreaming – of Alex.

Of Alex walking round the darkened house, striding from room to room and doing nothing when he got there. Of Alex painting the picture Simon had done, and putting it up in place of his mother's on the chimney-breast. Of Alex running out into the street and being the one who was backed into by the Ford Cortina. Of Alex just being on his own, with all the dangers of electricity points and gas and too many sleeping pills. Simon had woken up needing to see Alex just to put all that right in his mind, quite apart from his plan. He yawned again. He couldn't take another night like that.

'Leave it with me, Mrs Bean, I'll sort it out this morning.' Mr Rogers was in the doorway standing aside for a woman: a big woman who was huffing and puffing her way out, looking far from satisfied. 'Ah . . .' Like a shop assistant, his attention switched to the next customer.

Rick stood up slowly. 'Mr Rogers? This is Rose Penfold and Simon Leighton. I'm Mr Bayne from Darenth Lodge . . .'

'Ah, yes. Hello Mr Bayne. Well, Simon I know: Rose I don't: but we'll soon put that right. If I said I'll take her, I'll take her.' A fair man, as good as his word, he led them all into his room and found them seats. He settled himself and toyed with a Senior Service packet. 'Now listen,' he addressed himself to the window, to the ceiling, and finally to the two of them, 'let me tell you how I see things. And then you tell me if you don't think I'm right. Now, your temporary home is Darenth Lodge; and Mr Bayne is acting as your guardian and is going to make sure that you come to school every day . . .' He looked at Rick, almost as if he were one of the children, and Rick nodded. 'That's his job. My job is to make sure that you get a reasonable education, and you know, Simon, there's every opportunity for that here. Now *your* job . . .' he fixed them both, quite severely, '. . . is to make the very best of that situation.' He took off his stare and smiled at them, like an uncle. 'It's not letting out any secrets to say that both your home backgrounds – just at the moment, we know – aren't able to give you the chances you ought to have: so society is giving you a chance. Whatever else is going on around, society is saying, we're going to look after these two. So, make the most of it; work hard; come to me if you have any problems; and then we'll all get along fine.' He threw the cigarette packet flat on the desk with a little smack and he frowned. 'But don't be stupid and run out, or anything like that. We don't have policemen at the gates, we can't stop you. But you'll be fetched back here in no time at all, and nothing's gained by it, only a lot of needless worry and unhappiness.' His telephone buzzed but he ignored it; and then he suddenly waved his hand towards it. 'You know, none of us is free to come and go. I have to come here every day; Mr Bayne has to be at Darenth Lodge; or we'd both be out of jobs. We're none of us free agents in this life, above the law, we all have telephones to answer, rules to live by, whatever our problems and our unhappiness. Remember that – eh, Simon? You think of that – even the headmaster isn't free to forget the rules . . .'

There was an uncomfortable atmosphere in the room, a longing for the door to open or the telephone to buzz again. Rose was pulling her frock straight under her; Simon was staring at the man's sandy moustache, where he'd noticed it was stained darker on one side by nicotine.

He remembered how his mother had always held her cigarettes at arm's length, at the very tips of her fingers so they shouldn't mark.

'Now, Simon, it'll be you back in Miss Baker's class; and Rose, you with Miss Temple. And both of you – a new start, eh?'

The headmaster stood up, and they all stood up. Rose had to smooth her frock all over again. And it was then that Simon noticed her fingers: those on her right hand quite openly smoked yellow. Her own boss, she seemed. She did everything they said, and still went her own sweet way. Dropped him in it. Smoked her fags. Didn't give a toss for anyone.

Freer than most, she seemed; and dislike her as he did, Simon couldn't help but wonder what her secret was.

A light drizzle kept them in the building all day and Simon spent the school hours without any further sight of Rose – or any sight at all of Jackson and Clark. Miss Baker took him in with a grudging sort of tolerance – she made a small effort without going to town like before – and once more he got through the simpler work he was given without too much trouble. He didn't let himself care about getting one or two things wrong which the Pakistani boy was now getting right. His real concern was going over his plan for that night. About that he had to think precisely; because that was something he knew he had to get right first time.

Coming in to school in the Transit he'd tried to learn the route. Actually, it was simpler than he'd thought: left out of the Lodge drive, follow the main road back to the big pub, do a left turn there to the railway bridge and then he was in a pattern of streets which he knew. It was a long way all right, but straightforward, and the main road, wide with plenty of hedges, meant he could keep well out of everyone's way. No, that bit was going to be easier than he'd thought. The awkward bit was going to be getting out of the Lodge. The quiet kid he'd eaten with, Barry, was on the lower bunk near the window: there wouldn't be any bother from him when he went: but Ear-ring was on top, and getting past him was going to be like creeping past a leopard in the night. It wouldn't take much of a sound to bring one of those paws shooting out at him. And that was only after he'd managed to get out of his own bunk without shaking Little Lee awake on top.

Simon heard Miss Baker reading a story, but it was just a murmur of meaningless sound to him. All he could really hear were his own thoughts, going over things in words in his head, as if he were repeating his instructions to himself until he knew them. 'Keep my clothes on, somehow, and put my pyjamas on over the top. And keep my trainers on, too, or put them back on when I'm lying in bed. *Definitely* don't trust the creaky stairs: it's going to be the window or nothing. Get to the window, open it a bit beforehand if I can, double over and roll onto the window sill. Let myself down till I'm dangling, then drop into the small bushes underneath. Get away from the building first – don't bother about taking off the pyjamas till I'm clear, then if I'm caught I'm only sleep-walking! And forget the coat – it'll be too much fuss, trying to get it off the peg in the dark. I can run to keep warm, and there's a better coat at home. But the thing is, the thing is, I've got to go when it's really late. They mustn't know I've gone till the morning or they'll be waiting for me at the house. So leave a lump in the bed; and shut the window, if I can . . .'

Simon looked up at Miss Baker, who was looking at him, with all the weight of the class behind her. 'Well, so did he do right, then, Simon?'

Eh? Was she talking to him? Simon put his head on one side and smiled, the polite sign for being hard of hearing.

'I said, did he do right, Simon? Taking so much notice of what the passers-by said?'

Simon put on a puzzling face. 'Er . . .' He hadn't been listening; but could he remember the word 'donkey' braying somewhere in the room? Must have done, he thought; he wouldn't have dreamed it up. He couldn't think of the story, though . . . Take a chance. Someone who'd taken *so much* notice; that sounded as if it ought to be a no. 'Er, no, Miss.'

'Yes, quite right. But why not, Donna?'

She'd moved on. Pressure off. Simon suddenly thought of Alex's joking advice, once in that other life. When it comes to questions in class, if you don't know the answers start blowing your nose. They never interrupt someone having a good old nose blow. Simon felt a pang of sadness. He'd been so different, then, Alex, telling him things like that when his mum was out . . .

A few more minutes were spun out by questions before the bell rang for home-time and Simon went out on his orderly toes to the yard. Find Rose, Rick had told him, and wait for the Transit by the gate: it won't be long. Simon looked around for the girl; he'd better know where she was, at least; but once again the sharpness of his eyes was for Jackson and Clark. A quarter of an hour might not be long to a Transit in the traffic, he thought: but thirty seconds could be a lifetime in the street when someone was going to kick you in the head. He kept to the sides of the yard, where the fence at his back gave him a sense of security. He put his hands in his pockets and whistled, all breath and no note. There were plenty of people about, but there was no sign of any of the people he was looking for. No Rose, no Jackson and Clark.

No! The nerves in his stomach stewed with a sudden thought. Rose hadn't done a runner herself, had she? She hadn't been putting on that go-along-with-anything act while she was planning a crafty break? God, she could have gone hours ago – asked to go to the toilet or something, and taken off. She could be miles away by now . . . And that really would put the tin lid on his careful plans!

Suddenly depressed at the thought, Simon pushed with the others at the gate and poked himself out impatiently to look for the Transit and for Rose. The Transit for safety now. Rose for more freedom tonight.

She was there, thank God, leaning against the fence in the drizzle with all the old front in the world. Slowly, she turned her head to look at him. He was aware of it, and he stared ahead. He didn't want anything to do with her.

'They friends of your'n?' she asked.

'Eh?' She made him look at her: made him hurt his neck in his spin back to see where she was nodding. But he knew who they were before he saw them. He knew who they *had* to be: Jackson and Clark, the old gang, grinning through the drizzle like two thugs in a dark dead-end.

Simon spat, to show them how much he cared.

'Well, if it ain't our little friend Leighton . . .'

Somehow Simon smiled: you always smiled first at these two, even though the next thing you were going to do was try to kick them in the crutch: however out of it you were, that was one of the first lessons you learned at Market Junction school. 'Wotcha,' he said, evenly.

''Olding the fence up for Mr Rogers, are you, son? You an' that ugly female? Stopping the school falling down?'

The pleasure on their faces was intense, like the look of thirsty men savouring a drink, holding it off while they went through the preliminaries. Simon stood off the fence and looked at Rose: but her expression hadn't altered: she might as well have been stone deaf.

'Your girl friend, is it, Leighton? The Wife? Gawd, you don't 'alf pick 'em, don't you? Your women . . .'

Simon didn't blink. They had come in closer, and now they were standing squarely between him and the kerb.

53

He couldn't see anything but their mouths, wet and open with taunts. He'd been here before, hadn't he? he thought. It was obvious they were only a few jibes away from insulting his mum again. But he didn't blink, and he didn't look down.

'Yeah, one load of ol' slag for another, i'n it, Leighton?'

All Simon wanted now was to put his fingers in his ears; but that would have looked babyish. He wanted to shut his eyes; but that would have left him vulnerable. He wanted to turn and walk, but they barred his way. He did the next best thing he could. He told himself it wasn't him they were talking to, and it wasn't his mum they were going on about; he'd be all right if he imagined it was someone else. That was it. Psyche himself out. Pretend he was an actor and they were going on about someone fictitious. Or someone he disliked. Miss What'sername . . . Baker. It wasn't his mum, it was Miss Baker. *Think it was her*, he insisted, and who knew? he might even join in himself . . .

'Stone the crows! A cross-eyed mum and a boot-faced girl friend! Ain't you the lucky one, Leighton?'

Simon smiled. They were moving away into general abuse now; and because it couldn't be true it couldn't hurt him. His mum had the straightest brown eyes going. He looked at Rose again. She was still staring flatly ahead – but boot-faced she wasn't. No, hard luck, they weren't getting at him today . . .

'That's right, i'n it Leighton? She was cross-eyed, weren't she? Well, she must've been, the way she was always looking at other blokes. They called 'er Lucky-look Linda Leighton, didn't they, son?' Their eyes didn't leave Simon's as they probed him further with their serrated words. Their mouths smiled but their eyes stared. And Simon knew they were starting to get to him. They were wounding. 'Watch out, girl, or 'e might do to you what 'is 'ol man did to 'is mum!'

Simon's hands felt the wet fence behind him. How could your heart thump so fast without bursting. Your lungs run out without collapsing? Your head spin red without passing out? Simon tasted blood, salt; he had no voice; his legs and his back were like water. But he was still trying to make it not work. He was still trying to tell himself how this wasn't affecting him: how this was Miss Baker they were going on about. Lucky-look Linda Baker.

Linda Baker, Linda Baker, Linda Baker . . .

But, it wasn't Linda Baker! She was a Ruby, and this was his mum. No, his trick didn't work because they'd used her name, her Christian name, Linda. Linda Leighton, the name that had suddenly looked like a film star's on the little brass plate . . . They'd used her name, and they'd dirtied her, *wasted* her by their foul suggestion.

Simon swallowed the phlegm of his misery. He opened his eyes to the blur of them going: arms round one another, giggling, 'See you tomorrer, Leighton,' one of them shouted. ''Ave a ball with Boot-face!' Simon slumped against the fence. He cuffed his nose. The tears were rolling down his face.

'Stupid, you are,' Rose said to his sobs. 'Cryin' about someone.' Her voice was filled with contempt. 'They didn't even touch you.'

The mist cleared. Her stupid words brought him back to the stupid situation he was in. In care, with a load of people who couldn't care less! Suddenly all the mucus and the tears had gone; just a shaking of the legs. Ignoring it like a drunk, he drew in a street of wet air to his lungs: and he walked forward as steadily as he could to the Transit which had just drawn up. Jesus Christ! he thought, the whole world has gone mad! Turned upside down. Someone should be helping him to clear up what people like them were saying, for his own peace of mind, if they were supposed to care. Not put him in with this lot who thought that nothing decent really mattered. For a moment he was tempted to run off there and then, get away from all that and back to the real world at home, to put up a barricade. But some sort of common sense stopped him; and he got in instead. He was going tonight, wasn't he? No point in spoiling a better chance now. Don't let them run you, he told himself.

Rick was driving today, with Ear-ring by the door, leaning over and sliding it open. No, it would have been stupid to run then. They could follow him in the van and catch him in no time at all.

He got into the steam of damp coats, doing his best to keep his eyes on the floor. He didn't want any of this lot to see he'd been crying. The wet from their shoes shone on the ridged rubber. Everywhere was miserable, he thought, not a bit of comfort anywhere.

''Ere, wassup with you, Titch? You been cryin'?' Ear-ring was staring into his face accusingly.

'No. It's all right.'

'You 'ave. You been cryin',' Little Lee called out.

Rick jerked the van into gear. 'We'll sort it out later,' he said, while Simon lurched and landed in an aisle seat.

'You 'ave, 'aven't you?' Ear-ring turned to Rose ''E 'as, 'asn't 'e?'

Why couldn't they leave him alone, for crissake?

Rose stared out of the window. 'Two kids.' It was very matter-of-fact.

'Did they beat you up?'

Simon wanted to pull a hood over his head: there was nowhere away from the idle stares. 'No, it's all right. They didn't . . .'

Ear-ring shrugged and turned away: but suddenly Little Lee was on the move; out of his seat and swinging round a bar to slide down the aisle to Simon. His arm flailed towards him. Simon held up a palm to parry it. Not now! Tonight they'd fight, and by God there was going to be murders! But there was no blow. Lee's arm snaked round

56

Simon's neck and pulled him close. The small boy bent his head and rubbed cheeks. 'Never mind, son,' he said. His grubby hands were all sweat, and his breath was liquorice. 'I'll come over your school dinner time an' 'elp you.' His face twisted belligerently. 'You show me who they are . . .'

It was a strange, surprising moment; Simon letting himself be cuddled by this kid; all uncomfortable, but suddenly not wanting to pull away.

'Lee, sit down somewhere,' Rick called. 'You're distracting . . .'

Lee squeezed in next to Simon, pushing a little girl closer to the window on the inside. Hungrily, he talked of the warfare to come, he and Simon against the two; he promised thumpings, and kickings and knifings: and when he'd driven the self-pitying puffiness from Simon's eyes he quietened and eventually went back to Ear-ring to tell him about it.

It was all very bewildering. So were they mates now, then? Simon wondered. But why should that be? Was it because Lee had seen him weak? Or because it was always Darenth Lodge against the rest?

There was no question of any fight between Simon and Lee now. Lee had taken Simon under his fierce little wing. When the Transit dropped them he pulled him up a tree in the grounds, dangling a fragile friendship from branch after branch.

'What you in for?' The boy crashed about in the budding branches, his face lost in the fading light, an anonymous loom of arms and legs.

'Not going to school.'

'That all?' His voice was all contempt. Obviously, that sounded very tame to Lee. 'My dad's in the nick.' He shinned to the slender tree top, bending it with his weight, as if to show his own daring by contrast. Simon didn't mind: the less anyone knew of him the better. He re-tightened his grip and waited while Lee monkey-dropped down the tree.

'Come on,' he said. 'That's 'ow you get down.'

Not to be unfriendly Simon swung a bit from the lowest branch and let go.

It was a big mistake. He should have done it his own way. He missed his footing, hit a root and went over on his ankle. Oh, no! He tried to stand up straight but it gave under him again. God, it hurt! And what a stupid thing to do.

'I'll teach you to do it good tomorrow.' Little Lee ran off into the house, a dynamo of sure-footed energy, while Simon hobbled to hold onto the tree trunk. Great! he thought. Just what I needed! He swore. Being friends with Lee had left him worse off than if they'd had the fight.

After the meal – a more peaceful affair than the night before – and after Little Lee and a crowd with costumes had been taken swimming, Simon limped into the television room to watch whatever was on. He was tense and restless, and the television would give him an excuse in this place without privacy for sitting without talking, and for thinking. Like reading a book when you're pre-occupied, you could keep your eyes away from everyone else's and let your thoughts chase all over the place. There was a lot to be said for television, he realized, where everyone could sit round and be together, and still be on their own.

He was worried stiff about Alex. This was the second night now, and he'd be in a state, Simon knew that. He wouldn't have eaten, wouldn't have washed; he'd be living every minute listening for a knock, not knowing what to do till Simon got back to tell him. Every minute would be an hour for Alex; he'd be like a caged animal, but with the intelligence to know how slowly time was passing; how long Simon had been away. And in his depressed state, who knew what he'd do if he thought Simon was never coming back . . .?

'Yes, it's "Up the Creek", the quiz game where only the right answers can paddle you out of trouble . . .' The television shouted at them and then applauded itself.

'My fav'rite . . .' murmured a quiet little girl from round a wet thumb.

Simon heard it all, but what he was thinking about was how quickly he had to do something for Alex. Which wouldn't worry him too much, being this close to doing it, if it weren't for the ankle. It wasn't broken, only sprained; but he reckoned it would be another day at least before he could trust it. It seemed impossible to think of, another night, another morning, another day at school – this same length of time all over again before he went. By this time tomorrow they should have been out in the country somewhere down in Wales, finding some old deserted cottage to shelter in; not still here in London.

Could he afford another day before he got back to Alex?

It had to be a good four miles from here to Market Junction: however would his ankle stand up to that – dodging across the verge when cars came and hiding inside gates? And he'd planned on going without his coat, running to keep warm. Well, that'd be out now, wouldn't it? He tried to turn his ankle this way and that, twisting the toe of his trainer in painful arcs. It might stand a bit of walking, but not too much; and it certainly wouldn't stand the drop. And all this time there was Alex, sitting at home, probably with the same television programme passing in front of him, his head in his hands, wondering where Simon was.

No question about it. It was urgent, getting back; to persuade Alex, to draw the allowance, to get out of the district before they came-to here and to go up the coach station and get on a coach to Wales . . .

And yet his stupid ankle said he couldn't! Blast Little Lee and his friendly climb up the tree!

'What time you going tonight?'

The numbness scaled Simon's spine. This was no daft question from the television. 'What?' Bolt-eyed, Simon twisted in his seat. It was Rose standing next to him, all calm and matter of fact again as if she'd been asking the time. She hadn't even bothered to lower her voice.

'You shut up!' he hissed. He looked urgently at the others in the room. How the hell did she know? Was it written all over him, then? Had someone pinned a sign on his back? He hadn't whispered his plan to Little Lee or anyone.

With the first, slightest hint of concern he'd seen in her, a quick look round, Rose bumped herself down next to Simon.

'You're bunking off tonight all right.' She had lowered her voice a little, but she was still defying him to deny it.

'Who says I am?'

'Oh, come on, who d'you think you're fooling? Look at your face. 'Cept when you was upset you're smiling at everyone, being a good boy, doing what they say, just like they all do when they're gonna run. You're all the same: you think you're being clever, wait a day to let them think you're different, then off you go. I've seen it 'appen more times than you've 'ad 'ot dinners . . .'

Simon felt ashamed, being cornered by the truth like this. He felt as bad as he had when a kid had seen him slip a bubble-gum up his sleeve in the corner shop, reaching across for a comic. It gave him a shiver, finding out he wasn't half as sharp as he'd thought he was.

'What you on about?' he bluffed. 'You don't know what I'm thinking . . .'

'Don' I? You was thinking of doing the run when you was cryin', wasn't you? But the van come along and stopped you. I can read you like a book.'

Simon folded his arms and stared intently at the television. But he might have known that wouldn't drive her off. 'What's it got to do with you anyway?' he asked.

'Fags,' she said.

The word stubbed out his own worrying. 'Fags? I haven't got any fags.' He'd had a few puffs at various times; but he'd never like it.

'When you go out you can get me some. I'm dying for a fag.'

Her voice was still too loud for his liking. He lowered his own to a whisper, hoping she'd follow his example. 'Listen, I didn't say I'm going out, did I? And even if I was, I wouldn't be coming back in here with a packet of fags for you . . .' He had another go at ending the embarrassing conversation by turning back to the quiz show: but it was only a gesture, really, and he knew it. Rose wasn't the sort who'd just get up and walk away defeated.

'Please yourself, then. What I'm saying is, when you go out, get some fags, and smoke 'em yourself if you don't come back. But if they do catch up with you, you've got 'em on you to give to me.' Now she did lower her voice. 'Only, I can help you get out, if you want. I know this place, see . . .'

The sudden mention of the getting out brought him back to his own problem. The drop from the window was probably impossible with his ankle the way it was. Help in getting out he could definitely use – not that it would do her any good; he wasn't coming back.

'Well? You on or not? I ain't got all night.'

Simon looked at a woman showing off a stereo on the quiz programme, similar to the one at home.

'Go on,' he said. 'I'm listening.'

Rose sat back in her chair. 'You tell me how you was gonna get out,' she demanded.

This was the open admission now. All pretence would have gone. It balked him because who was to say she wouldn't do what she'd done over the picture – let him down by saying something?

'Come on, kid, stop mucking around . . .'

Kid! Bloody cheek! She talked as if she was twice his age. Who did she think she was?

'The bedroom window, of course. It does open, you know.' He wasn't as daft as he looked. He'd done his homework.

'Does it? Right – for one packet of fags, then. It don't open. It looks like it do, but it only goes about six inches, for a crack of air. Your floor's all the same 'cos you got front an' back stairs for fires.' She stared at him. 'Even you can't get through six inches. So, 'ow d'you get out now? Front door?'

Simon shook his head. 'Locked, bound to be,' he said.

Rose was back at the quiz game. 'Wrong,' she said. 'Can you read?'

'Yeah!'

'Then you read them fire drill notices. They tell you a lot you want to know. They go like, "Get out by nearest stairs and nearest door. Wait on front grass." Something like that. How can you do that if the front door's locked?'

Simon shrugged. Perhaps Rick came and opened it, he thought.

'You push it, that's all. It's got a special catch. You can't get in from outside, but you can get out from inside.' She turned her head right round to him, and it could almost have been a smile she gave him. 'That's two packets of fags.'

Simon frowned. That meant going down those creaky stairs, then. Surely, you'd wake the dead with them. 'Think of them stairs next, don't you? All old and creaky. 'Ave you noticed? And the banisters've got great knobs on 'em every couple of feet. You can't slide down them, not without ruining your chances. So, that's got you stuck.' She waited for a second to let the hopelessness seep into him. 'Know what to do?'

'No.' It was as well out quick as slow: this would be three packets he owed her, if he was ever coming back . . .

'You can trust the banister; it's good. Cock your leg over it and go down the outside. Or keep your back right against the wall on the inside. It's the middles do all the creaking; any burglar'll tell you that . . .'

Simon was sitting back now, drinking this in. She'd been right. He'd never have got out without her. Three packets of make-believe fags was no price to pay.

'Now you've gotta get back down Market Junction, right? Must do, or you wouldn't be down that school . . .'

Simon nodded. She'd got it all sewn up, this weird girl.

'But your ankle won't get you there, right? You done it in, jumpin' down that tree, didn't you?'

Good God what was she going to offer him now? A bike for a carton of fifty? It'd be very handy, a bike, he thought.

'I'll show you where they keep the clothes. They've got boots and everything in there, nine-hole lacers, some of 'em. Do yourself up tight in a pair of them and it's like a splint. That's what we do. Can't afford days off, us lot.'

Her lot? What were they? Simon wondered. Her previous remark dug itself up. Burglars, were they, not creaking stairs in the dark?

'They never come chasing in the night, this lot. They might give the Old Bill a ring, but they don't start chasin' round at night. They know where you'll be, your sort – back 'ome.' She snorted. 'They won't be watchin' no airports and docks for you! So the thing is, get 'ome, get my fags first thing, and keep 'em on you where they won't get seen till you get back.'

Simon just stared. God, what a lot went on behind that blank face, he thought.

'Well? You ain't gonna back off are you? 'Cos if you are . . .'

'No, 'course not.' And he meant it. He knew only too

well how she could spoil it all for him if she wanted. Besides, it was all in the mind. He wasn't coming back, was he?

'Four ways I've 'elped, right? That's worth a few packets, then. Spread 'em out, though, not all lumped up in one pocket. Nicked or bought, don't matter which.'

'Yeah, O.K.' It was easy to agree. However right she'd been up to now, she was wrong over one thing. He'd never see her again. Later on, of course, he could always send her some, in a parcel, anonymous. Yes, he could definitely do that. And it made him feel better, that thought.

It was a private, fleeting promise, interrupted by the music playing on the quiz show and the sight of the evening's winner, some smug woman who'd worked her way point by point to her outlandish prize.

So, someone had had some luck tonight. And after a bad start Simon had fallen in for some, too. Now all that remained to be seen was what surprises the rest of the night held in store . . .

4

The two men sat in the pub like stall-holders on a Saturday night, wrapped in their overcoats, their legs apart and their hands in their laps. On the small round table their pint glasses were going down equally, inch by inch, the time passing in mouthfuls of ale.

Old Man Penfold raised his glass and spoke into it. 'Every year I say it's the end of the road,' he said, 'but God help me this year I reckon it is.'

His partner's eyes didn't leave the slope of his drink. He was a younger man, but old in the ways of beer. 'It don't get better, that's for sure.' He wiped his moustache with the back of his hand and returned to staring straight ahead.

'Mind, I don't look to have it cushy, that's never been my way; but it's when a man can't work who wants to, gets me . . .'

The other looked at him. 'Scrap paper done for, Charlie?'

'Not worth the 'umping about. You need so many tons to make a tenner, without young Rose I'm done for. They oughter take that into account when they cart your family off . . .'

There was a long rumination. 'What about your ride, then? Your round-and-rounder? Drop o' good weather's not far off . . .' His eyes had sharpened.

'No one wants it no more, only fêtes of a Saturday, and they don't pay your diesel these days. Out of date, they say. You're not in the reckoning 'less you're into space rides or steam organs. The big fairs don't want you without some modern gimmick' – he said the word with the 'g' as in George – 'an' if you you don't 'old the lease to the

65

ground you don't get took. It's all sewn up nowadays.' He pulled a folded *World's Fair* from an inside pocket. 'Look at that.' A broken fingernail found the column. ' "Tommy Cotton and Sons, Easter week, South London Flats, tenants with space age rides required." They're all like that. There ain't no casual rolling-up with the "Autodrome" no more.'

The younger man shook his head.

'Oughter be edged in black, this.' The old fingers struck the showmen's paper. 'Really depressed me, this has: no work for me in it . . . and the deaths . . .'

At the mention of death the other glass halted in a sort of respect.

'Look 'ere, 'Arry Driver's gone – heart attack last Christmas – old mate o' mine, 'e was: and Sid Flowers, done everyone's fancy painting for years – don't know what they'll do without 'im . . .' He took a long, melancholy sip. 'Terrible thing, time is . . .'

There was a long silence while the Space Invader blipped behind them.

'Yeah, give me the good old days any day . . .'

'Well, at least when you was poor you could beaver away an' do something about it . . .'

'You've said it. Not gone for long, your Rose, has she? They can't keep her for ever, can they?'

Old Man Penfold looked round the bar, frowning, as if he wished he hadn't mentioned his troubles in a public place. 'No,' he said, briskly. 'They've only got 'er till I've done the other trailer out for 'er. It's only the living space they're on about. I've got it, just haven't been using it while she's been no more'n a kid . . .'

'She's a good girl, your Rose. Mind, she's independent . . .'

'Wouldn't be called Penfold if she wasn't.' The old man spread his hands flat on the table as if they were playing cards. 'No, the family's kids are the family's business, never any question about it. We try to look after our own. None of this land-'em-on-the-rates out of choice . . .'

'And then I s'pose she'll come into the business . . .?'

The old man picked up his hands and put them out of sight. 'That's a long way off.'

'Well, I hope she's out for Easter – if you can get yourself a pitch. You do know I'd give you a hand myself with your caravan – but between my old lady and the hospital I don't get a second's peace if I exert myself . . .'

'Oh, I shall have it done, never fear. And even if I don't, local authorities won't be no worry to me if I can get on the road. Rose and me don't exist to these people once the season starts. No, something'll *'ave* to turn up. Now, you gonna buy me the other 'alf? This drop's gone flat all of a sudden . . .'

'My shout, is it? Certainly.' The younger man stood up with every regard for his bad back. 'Might as well go the whole hog.' He collected the two glasses and, as if he were remembering, limped cautiously to the bar.

Old Man Penfold watched him go and shook his head. He rubbed at a pain of his own – but his hands were back in his lap by the time the other returned.

'Good 'ealth,' he said; and they started on another hour of ale and painful conversation.

Although there were four of them in it, it was Ear-ring's room. What Ear-ring wanted, went. All the time Ear-ring wanted to read his war comic, the light stayed on; while Ear-ring wanted to talk, the others had to answer him; and when Ear-ring wanted to sleep, they had to join him in a shrouded silence. Even Little Lee fell in with things after a fashion: although he wouldn't have shut up for anyone else.

Simon had welcomed Ear-ring's bragging talk: it had been a way of keeping awake until the house was quiet.

Not only that, the muffled conversation must have made everything seem very normal, when Rick or one of the other men had put their heads round the door. Simon guessed he was being watched tonight – if Rose had got things worked out, then so had they – and he was ready to go along with anything that seemed normal. Everyone had a point beyond which keeping awake was a real effort, and he wanted the staff to give in happily when theirs came, while he resisted his own.

Gradually the voices in the dark deepened and slowed, their sentences were left to be finished by others, or just to hang among the blankets; any croaked answers that were made came after long, deep pauses; and finally no one was answering at all. The body's need for rest had taken three of the four off into their private dreams, and it became a struggle for Simon to stay awake. There was so much in favour of the warmth and comfort of giving in and going under.

But that would be to drown: and Simon was a survivor, he decided: he had to be, for Alex. Besides, he still had the long boots on, and the trousers. He was stuffed over-dressed in bed, like a guardsman snatching five minutes, and it wasn't too hard for him to remember that he had some purpose besides sleep.

He listened for the creak of the stairs, watched for the chink of the door as he was checked; but in the stillness now his mind kept wandering to his mother, as it often did, and what those two had said about her.

They made her sound as if she'd been the sort who ran around with loads of different men. But his mum wasn't like that. Just because she smiled a lot, touched you when she talked to you, liked to look good and go to dancing classes, that didn't make her like they made her sound.

Simon wriggled his toes. His left boot, gripping the swelling, made his foot feel numb, his toes cold in the hot bed.

It was because Alex didn't go to the dancing with her, that was it. He was too busy with wood and paints in the kitchen, just occasionally leaving a sign to dry while he ran her to the hall in the car. That was what it was – all because in dancing you had to have a partner and Alex wasn't the one.

The back of his leg just above the boot was starting to throb. It was a dull, deep beat and he eased his hand down towards the boot, but swaddled up tight in bed he couldn't get near it. It was like getting at the truth.

It was only natural one of the men should bring her home after the dancing class: and she'd laugh if Alex frowned. 'In for a penny, in for a pound,' she'd say. Anyway, sometimes a couple came, men and women, and there was nearly always a cup of coffee in the sitting room, with Alex leaning in the doorway with a rag in his hands, or carefully passing out cups. But that was what people always turned their heads at – someone in a car with someone different, and *laughing*. People always seemed to see something wrong when they saw someone laughing.

There had to be a big question mark over how his ankle would hold up. Feeling as numb as it did now, it was hard to imagine how Rose could be right: just lace it up tight and walk on it as if there was nothing wrong. And it wasn't as if he'd put any weight on it yet. He'd squeezed the boots on in the confusion of everyone undressing and shot into bed when no-one was looking. So whether the boots would get him back to Alex at Market Junction had to be in doubt until he got out of bed and actually stood on them. All he wanted to do now was find out. Well, the house was quiet at last, and it had been a long time since Rick had last checked the room. He'd give it a few minutes more because he couldn't afford to be seen. Having his pyjamas on top was one thing; but there was no way he could pretend he was sleep-walking in Doctor Martin boots.

Alex wasn't an idiot, whatever everyone was saying. Before the accident he'd run his own sign-writing business; sold a few pictures, too. He'd have known if things hadn't been right, wouldn't have let them come to the boil. They would both have known, Simon thought. He wasn't so daft himself that he wouldn't have suspected if things had been wrong between the two of them. *But he had to know for sure.* There was no smoke without fire, people said, and, God, there'd been enough smoke. Jackson and Clark were only part of it. All right, Alex had gone to pieces after what had happened: but wasn't that just proof that it had been an accident? Wasn't it?

He pushed it from his mind. Action! That was what was needed now. He stopped breathing to listen again. Outside the room the house was silent. Barry, the quiet kid across from him, was snoring loudly, and if Ear-ring and Little Lee were lying awake they'd kept up keeping quiet for a very long time. Yes, this was the moment. Now his dead ankle would come to the test. And now he'd find out if the rest of Rose's advice about getting out was any good.

Handling the covers as if they were crackling foil, Simon peeled them off. He squeaked a spring by shifting his weight – froze until he was certain no one had woken – and swung his legs, the good nudging the bad, so that he could sit up, his head bowed beneath the untidy saggings of the top bunk blankets.

His foot felt good on the floor; a sort of throbbing life returned to the ankle; but standing up on it would be the real test. Steadying himself on the cold iron framework, Simon pulled himself up. So far, so good; he was on it, full weight. But first the pain barrier of the pins and needles, and with no stamping it out quickly! He put his head back, screwed his eyes up as it gathered strength, and shouted inside his head. It was excruciating: and it took its time. He turned his head this way and that, he tensed the muscles in his arms and let them shake, he pleaded for it to pass, and then, very slowly, the pain began to fade. If that was what coming to life was like he'd have sooner it had stayed dead.

There was still no threatening sound: not even a troublesome cough anywhere that might call for attention. Simon put his good leg forward, then the bad. The heavy boots were thick-soled and quiet. He was all right. The ankle felt fine: stiff – he was sure he was going to limp for a while – but otherwise fine. Like a wire-walker crossing a circus ring, Simon balanced his way to the door. He was a long way from safety now. If there should be a slip he hadn't the safety net of a good excuse; not for the clothes under his pyjamas and the boots.

Why did secretly turned door-knobs always go the wrong way first? A fresh grip was needed, and vital seconds wasted. But at least he knew to pull, and not push. The heavy door came, and he looked round it.

Would Rick be standing silent outside? It was a sudden, chilling thought. But the landing was empty, a low-watt bulb keeping a faint night-watch. The light was eerie, flat without shadows. Simon closed the bedroom door, and stepped across the open space to the head of the stairs.

'The good to heaven, the bad to the devil,' Simon remembered his grandfather telling him, in the days when they'd talked, how the nurses taught you to go up and down the stairs with a pair of crutches: good foot first, going up; bad foot first, going down. And Rose, what had she said? Keep to the side by the wall, where the stairs don't creak. That meant there was no banister to hold; but her advice had been good so far. Now, like the first man stepping onto the moon's surface, he launched himself off, one hand flat to the wall, the other stuck out for balance. Tread by tread and slowly he descended the stairs, dot-and-carry, but his bad ankle was holding up well. The front door might seem miles away, but he was getting there, step by step. Of course, Rick could suddenly come from anywhere; Simon could fall and wake the house; but it hadn't happened on that step, and it hadn't happened on this one. One at a time, so far, so good . . .

The cat nearly did for him. It came from behind, a black shape suddenly shooting past – sure-footed and silent but ringing every alarm bell in Simon's body. He had never realized before how hard you could grip a flat wall to keep your balance. The cat stopped at the front door and turned to look at him. It mewed to be let out, loud and impatient, and Simon speeded up, forgot about his feet, to get to the door. Desperately he fumbled at the special latch, pulling the heavy mass towards him – all front doors opened inwards, didn't they? – and it came. Immediately, as soon as there was the slightest gap the cat competed with him for it, and before he knew it Simon was outside the building, breathing in his first cold shock of night air.

It had worked, the first bit. The gravel crunched like a sound trap but he was across it and in the bushes before the cat had even decided which way to go. Simon crouched there, listening, and suddenly wanted nothing in the world so much as a good pee. But he couldn't stop for that. He pulled off his tight pyjama jacket and ripped off the bottoms when they wouldn't pull over his boots. Sweating now, he bundled them up and pushed them into the heart of a bush.

No lights: no voices: no bells ringing. So go! Bent double, Simon ran to the gate and turned left into the glaring yellow road. He straightened up but he went on running. Great! He was out of Darenth Lodge, no one was chasing after him, and his ankle was holding up in the boot. He'd cracked it! Now for those four miles to Market Junction, and Alex . . .

There was a strange sort of freedom in the night-time,

he thought. Everyone slept, but the world went on. Cats came and went as if human beings didn't exist, as if the world was only lent to people for the day-time; a hedgehog scratched itself out of a secret place and went snuffling into a well-kept garden; and the small noises said that the world was filled with creatures who paid no rent to anyone. The first car to drive past frightened him, but he slowed to a walk as if all he was doing was popping home after an evening at a mate's, and the car didn't stop. It was as if everyone and everything was intent on its own business, and so long as you didn't get in their way they left you to yourself. The way things ought to be, Simon thought. Only the police might bother him, but so long as he kept his eyes open and walked in casually through the first gate he came to, they'd think he was just a kid going home. No: tonight he had the strange feeling that the world was his.

It was a big world, though. What took twenty minutes in the Transit would take two hours like this. Quick mental directions like, 'up to the second set of lights' had him worn out by the time he'd gone through with them; and what he remembered as a straight stretch of road, quickly covered, was uphill all the way and a hundred houses long. But he pushed on, gradually slowing, with occasional jogs to round the next corner, until at long last he was in his own pattern of streets and suddenly the next street corner was his own. He'd done well. No police, no interfering busy-bodies, no group of aggressive yobs to get past. It had gone well – almost too well to be true.

Instead of rushing round that last corner he flattened himself to the wall and put out a cautious eye. If the Transit were there, or any vehicle he didn't remember from home, then he'd know they'd found his empty bed and come to get him back. But what cars he saw there were familiar, and frosted up with long standing. It seemed safe to go to the house.

For the past mile Simon had been fingering the key in his pocket, the familiar smooth ridges which meant he could get in despite Alex never answering the door. He'd kept it safe, through everything, with his fiver, knowing all the time that he'd need it. He went up to the door. The place had the same cold and abandoned look as the cars outside it; but that wasn't new. Alex would be in bed – or sitting hunched by the dead television with no lights on and the curtains drawn. There hadn't been a warm glow here for nearly a year.

Quietly, but deliberately making more noise than a burglar he let himself into the black hall and called, 'Alex!' No reply. He found a light switch and pressed it on: but nothing happened, it was dead. Cautiously, trembling with the cold inside the house, he felt his way in the gloom to the door of the living room. It was open. But there was no sign of Alex in there. Another light switch. Dead again. Simon started to feel a surge of panic. The front curtains were open, the way they'd always left them when they went away, and in the faint light from the street lamp Simon could sense a strange emptiness in the tidy room. There was more than Alex missing. Furniture, was it? His heart thumping inside him, Simon backtracked to the stairs. He had to go up. He was gripped by a tight terror at what he might find, but he had to do it. Was he too late already? Was Alex up there, alone and silent . . .?

Never mind the creaking now. Simon wanted to bring some noise to this deathly house. 'Alex? Alex? It's me, Simon . . .' He felt ashamed of being frightened at the prospect of his own father, the childish fear of coming across him crouched small in a long ago game of hide-and-seek.

The bathroom door was open, the room empty, and another light was dead. The electricity was off at the mains. Had Alex done something to fuse the circuit? Had he . . .?

Alex's room was shut. There was no sound, only the thump of his own fear. Faint in the head, trembling – but no longer with the cold – Simon turned the door handle. Oh, God, what was he going to find on the other side?

Nothing. No one. A cautious look first, and then a full stare. Just an empty bed, stripped as bare as his new bunk had been at Darenth Lodge. The clock was there, but it wasn't ticking any more. Another pair of curtains was drawn open. Alex had gone as if he'd never lived there.

A gigantic shiver shook Simon. What now? Where was he? Surely someone would have told him if the worst had happened?

Quickly now, more to keep going than because he expected to find anything, Simon checked his own bedroom upstairs: it was an empty place, the posters on the wall staring back to remind him of the kid he'd once been, a long, long, time ago. He hurried back down the stairs to the kitchen – another room as devoid of life as he'd expected, the refrigerator open and de-frosted. Just a dripping tap. Simon wheeled back to the empty living room where the first clue had been: where something had told him it had all changed, where there had been more than a normal emptiness. What was it he'd missed?

This time he saw it immediately: the empty space: the dust-edged blank on the wall where the picture had been – Alex's picture of his mum, the one Simon carried round in his head. A bare rectangle that said it all.

Suddenly, the whole world was empty now, and like a fallen bird Simon shrank down on the floor – and for the third time in two days he allowed himself to cry. Just at that moment it seemed there was nothing else to do but let it all come pouring out. There was no one to keep it from here.

But Simon had to know, and the risk was worth it. What in the world else was there for him to do? If his grandparents couldn't tell him what had happened to Alex, there was no one else round here who could. Things were out of his hands again now. It was like the having to go back to school, and he had reverted to being unsure about everything and nervous as a butterfly. He flitted in the shadows from Alfred Road to Parkside and hovered uncertainly in the hedge looking at the double-front of number thirteen.

There were no lights on here either, and no dramas being paced out inside. It was all peace and quiet, the way they always wanted it. Simon could picture them, wrapped up smugly in bed, her in her rollers and him in his pressed pyjamas. He'd seen them once when he'd stayed, long ago: with their individual lights to hand and the tidy markers in their bedtime books. No wonder a scruffy painter in the family had upset their apple cart. No wonder they resented the Welfare ringing at their front door when Simon had started missing school. No wonder they'd tried to make the police take further action at the end. This was a place where you had to watch your manners on the polished tables, where a loofah in the bathroom took the place of flannels and heaven help you if you left pools on the floor playing torpedoes with it.

Now he was going to disturb everything – get their dressing-gown cords in a tangle as they rushed down in the night. But he had to know. It was their peace or his – and there wasn't any choosing in it. He was putting himself at risk, but he'd do something pretty quick as soon as he knew. He pushed the button and set off a discreet chime next to the barometer on the inside wall.

At that hour it sounded loud enough to bring the fire brigade. This had to be done quietly; find out what he wanted to know and away again. He couldn't afford a fourth person turning up. He could out-dodge and out-run these two – but he didn't fancy his chances with some noisy young neighbour.

It seemed as if they were dead to the wide; there wasn't a stirring in the house, not a sound nor a glimmer of light. He pressed the glowing button again, impatient now, and kept his finger on the chiming. Come on! They'd have to come quickly or he'd be forced to lie low in the garden and try again later. He suddenly felt the cold again and once more he wanted to pee. It was anxiety for Alex. He had to know about Alex. His stomach had hardened like a nervous cat. This was worse than the waiting outside the hospital ward.

Without warning the porch light flooded him in brightness. It hurt his eyes, seemed to burn his retina; but he had the presence of mind to stand his ground, not crouch there or cringe. If anyone was watching from the street it all had to look above-board. He drew in deep breaths and watched an inaccessible wisp of cobweb waver in the night breeze. It was just the way he felt.

The hall light went on and there was a shuffle behind the door. 'Yes? Who's there?' It was his grandfather, as cautious as he was.

'It's me, Grandad. Simon.'

'Who?'

'Simon Leighton.' Fancy having to give your second name to your own grandfather!

The door opened. 'Simon! What the devil are you doing? Good grief, boy, it's gone half-past one . . .'

Simon looked up at the tall, erect, old man. He was dressed like someone in a play – smart dressing-gown, smooth pyjama collar, silver hair brushed flat: if he jumped under a bus he'd dress for it! But he wasn't asking Simon in, so Simon squeezed into the house while his grandfather tottered and clung to the door for balance. He didn't wait for the door to close. 'I've come to find out what's happened to Alex.'

'*I* don't know what's happened to your father, Simon.'

The door was shut quietly and the porch light turned

off, everything done methodically. His only haste was in closing off the living room.

'Why should I? It's none of my business what happens to him.'

'He's not at home.'

'How do you know? I thought you were supposed to be in care. Good grief, do they let all their charges run wild in the night like this?'

'I bunked it. I couldn't leave him on his own. I've been worried about him. It's only natural!' he suddenly shouted.

'All right, all right. Don't start showing off. Come into the kitchen or you'll wake Ellen. I'll give you a drink of milk, then they can come and get you.'

'I don't want any drink of milk. I want to know about Alex!'

'Well shouting won't get you anywhere.' The old man walked stiffly over to the kitchen door, put a light on, and took a beaded jug from the refrigerator. 'How should I know what's happened to your father? What on earth made you come here?'

It was unbelievable, Simon thought. Why shouldn't he come here? This was his grandfather, his mother's father. This man had pushed him in a push chair, shown him the ducks over in the park when he'd been little, wiped his nose, even. All right, he'd never liked Alex, but he'd not been as bad as this when Simon's mother was around. Ever since the accident the pair of them had been trying to go back on ever knowing him and Alex.

'It's all shut up at home. All packed up. He's gone, Alex has, and he's not just gone out. *I want to know where!*'

The elderly man shrugged his bony shoulders and continued the careful pouring of a boy's measure of milk.

Filled with a wild exasperation Simon swung himself away, if only to stop himself jumping on that aggravating back. Angrily, he stared through the open hatch into the

78

living room his grandfather had shut off. Where was the telephone kept? he wanted to know. In there? In the hall? He tried to remember. If he found that he could pull the cord out from the wall before the hateful old man went to use it. If he wasn't going to find out anything, he still needed time to get a long way from here before the Transit came.

His sudden shout was of a stabbing pain, a violent anger, of disgust. He fought to breathe out, but he went on breathing in till his lungs were filled ready to burst. *What was that doing here?* That, propped up on the piano. The picture of his mum. His picture from the house!

'You!' he screamed. He rounded on his grandfather. 'Where's my Alex? You old crook! You know where he is. You lying old git! *Where's my Alex?*' He was shouting, screaming, crying, his eyes filled with a haze of tears and anger. He rushed at the old man. 'You tell me where he is! You tell me or I'll . . .'

It was another voice that stopped him: ice-cold and commanding.

'You dare!'

The old man's wife was in the doorway, a bony finger pointing at him from a length of quilted sleeve.

'He's where he belongs. In the nut-house!' She tapped her own forehead hard enough to hurt. 'Your murdering father's in Stonelands – and even that's too good for him!'

'*Murdering?* You . . . old . . . cow! You're an old cow and you're *wrong*.' They were saying it in the open now, were they, what he knew they'd always thought? 'I'll show you! I'll bloody prove it!' And see what else they'd done? They'd waited for him to be out of the way, then got the Welfare to take Alex. That wrapped it all up for them.

Swift on the heels of that thought came another – the certainty of what he was going to do next. Get Alex out of Stonelands, that was a must: so get away from here double-quick and hide out somewhere till he could get to him.

79

Wales they were going to, him and Alex, or the wilds of Scotland, that was the plan: that was the only thing he had that he could cling to. So, out of here, now! Right! Front door was best: it was unlocked from when he'd been let in. Run at the old woman, push her out of his way, and put a mile between him and this place before anyone could get here from the Lodge.

Simon took a deep breath, drew himself up, and ran. He ran and he yelled, like the soldiers did to frighten the enemy, and he charged at the woman in the doorway.

She moved to block his way, but he swayed, shifted his weight to the other foot to head for the new gap she'd left. And on the same breath his charging yell turned to a sudden shout of pain as the quick switch wrenched his bad ankle – and he slithered over on the shining floor, skidding to a crumpled halt against the sink unit.

'You! Let me up!' But on the floor the old man's weight was enough, and the adult hands, stronger than Simon had ever realized, held him in a tight, military grip.

'Like father, like son!' his grandmother screeched.

Shock took all the pain away: but it couldn't take away the bitter hurt of what she'd called Alex, of Simon's disappointment at failing him, and his being forced to stay imprisoned there in the enemy kitchen till the Transit came.

Simon woke to the sound of Little Lee. 'I ran away once,' he was saying, 'but they'd gone and moved all the places round.'

'More like you got on the wrong bus!' Ear-ring scoffed. 'Got on a 235 instead of a 230. You 'ave to know your numbers if you're running off on buses.'

'Where was you going?' Barry asked, sounding surprised to hear that Lee had had anywhere to run to.

'Church Road.'

Ear-ring laughed. '235's go to *Chingford*, not Church Road, you berk. You 'ave to know your letters an' all!'

Little Lee aimed a safe kick at him, one that couldn't reach: and Simon pulled himself up off the pillow to the noisy communal scene, the shared life he was going to have to get used to. Once before he'd woken up disappointed at having ever regained consciousness, come out of a womb of safe sleep where soft dreams had snuggled him, to realize with despair that yet another long, painful day had come for him to get through: that in the daylight his mother wasn't with him any more. And this morning, in all that noise and hunting for lost socks, it took just five seconds for the old life to fade and the raw of his eyes to see the grey of reality.

'Where d'you go then, Titch? Back 'ome for your teddy?'

'Oh, leave it out.' If Ear-ring wanted a fight he could have one, Simon thought. Ear-ring was the least of his worries. Nothing Ear-ring could do would hurt him today – threats, punches or kickings. You had to feel fit in your mind to be frightened of anyone. You had to *care*. Any way, what was bugging Ear-ring all of a sudden? Was it because he'd caused a commotion last night – been the centre of attention after Ear-ring had gone to sleep? Was it because he'd gone through with something instead of just mouthing about it?

'You wanna watch your lip, son.'

Simon said no more but swung his feet to the floor. God, that ankle hurt: and it was all swollen up, puffed and stretched like the skin on bubble gum. It could have been the sight of it, or Simon's attitude, but Ear-ring turned away and started a vigorous tucking-in of his top bunk. Dressing slowly and awkwardly, like someone applying himself with bandages, Simon thought over the last things they'd said in the night – after the bitter shouting at Parkside. Rick's words of disappointment and the silent journey in the Transit – there'd be no school for him today;

and the other precaution, they'd take him for an X-ray if the ankle didn't go down. And, of course, just before the light went out again, all the usual guff about Stonelands being the right place for Alex, not only for himself but as far as Simon was concerned. How could Simon get on with his own life, they'd asked nicely, if he was carrying the burden of Alex?

What they were all too stupid or too blind to see was that Alex *was* his life. With all his problems and in spite of what they said about him, without Alex he was lost. There was no connection here with all the years that had gone before, and Simon didn't want to lose that, didn't want that sort of new start, where you didn't start from scratch like a new baby, but knowing another life. This was like dying and coming back as another person; but *knowing* about the first – like a pauper who could remember being a prince.

He experienced a wave of sickness when he tried to put some weight on his left foot: that twist and fall in the kitchen had made it much worse than before. Now there wasn't a hope of getting anything more than a sock on it; and even that would press like an elastic bandage. He couldn't run away again to save his life. He steadied himself with a hop and gripped at the cold support of the bunk. The feeling passed: but his action suddenly reminded him of steadying himself on that stainless sink unit in the Parkside kitchen: and because of what he'd secretly done, it brought with it a secret thought of Rose.

She'd curl her lip, wouldn't she? She'd been so horribly right, as it happened. He'd been brought back with his tail between his legs: and that Rose had told him he would. She'd been so right it was almost as if she'd set him up – although that couldn't be, because even she could never have guessed he'd be turned in by his own people. He saw her scornful face; and he felt a sudden surge of anger at everyone who'd helped to put him down: Jackson and

Clark who'd got him upset and made Little Lee like him: Little Lee who'd taken him up the tree where he'd jumped and twisted his ankle: and that slime of a grandfather who'd held him in an old army grip till the others had come. Too true, he thought, right back to Jackson and Clark it went – further even! Right back to the stupid dancing which gave them their filthy ammunition.

Lucky-look Linda Leighton!

Linda Leighton. He tried to conjure her up, but all he could get was the picture. He'd lost her voice no matter how he tried. It was terrible how after all they'd done together she'd come to being just the picture now.

The picture! He let out a yelp, audible even in that noisy room. Those old creeps had nicked the picture, and they'd run it round to their place in the car the minute they'd packed off Alex for good. God! How well it had all worked out for them!

''Ere, you in pain or something?'

The others had stopped flicking towels at one another and were staring at him.

'You can say that again,' he said. 'This rotten ankle!' He hopped on his other foot to demonstrate.

'You want your breakfast up here?' Barry had stopped de-fluffing his hair with his comb and was looking at him with a real concern.

Simon considered it. It was tempting. All the Lodge must have heard about his run and his recapture by now. It would save all the stress down there – and one cocky stare in particular.

''S'all right. I'll manage.' He had to see people again, he thought: he had to see her sometime, so why not this morning? Get it over with. And besides, having what he had might make it easier.

A strange, fleeting feeling – like having a name on the tip of his tongue, subconsciously here one second then gone the next – told him that that was the reason he might win out. No matter how he'd just woken, down in the dumps and reluctant to be alive, he was thinking ahead already, being positive. But the thought was gone before he could grab it and dwell on it.

'There ain't no reason why not. I'll bring it up.'

'No. It's all right, thanks.' Yes, he had to face her sometime . . .

As it turned out it was at the hatch, ten minutes later. She was standing there adding to her plate what the little girl in front of her didn't want.

'My doll don't like bacon.'

'Clever little doll, ain't she? Give it 'ere then you won't 'ave to leave it.'

It seemed as if all Rose's attention was on the food. But Simon knew that it wasn't. She'd seen him come in; the whole room had gone quiet for a moment as he'd hobbled in with his fat sock; and she'd looked round with the rest. Typically, she hadn't offered any sympathy, nor demanded anything there – just glanced at him and then back to the plates. But like having a girlfriend at a party, he knew that her not looking meant she was more interested in him than a long stare would have shown.

He should have sat with Barry. Barry had offered to take his breakfast up, and Barry had helped him down the stairs – but somehow Simon saw the vacant places working out another way. There was one place left on Rose's table, and he found himself pretending to see only that. He had to get this moment over with, out of the way, before he could get on with thinking about anything else.

''Ow many?' was all she said through the crunch of bacon. 'All the four, I 'ope.'

Simon looked at the little girl, but she was feeding her doll with a baked bean. 'One,' he said. 'An' that was dead lucky.' The packet had been on the draining board; and he still couldn't imagine how he'd managed to pocket it under the noses of Rick and the other pair.

'You can owe me the rest.' Then she'd dismissed him for the next mouthful.

The food in Simon's mouth wouldn't go down; it was like chewed paper. This was just what eating must have been for Alex, he thought, no matter what was cooked for him. Simon left most of it; but he quite deliberately made sure that Rose shouldn't have it. He'd paid her what debt he reckoned he owed her. He limped to the bin and dumped it, and went on his own to the stairs.

He was depressed, frustrated, and confused.

It was going to be a long time before he got things straight, had any sort of plan of what he wanted or how he'd do it. It was like the middle of a big battle, he thought, as he pulled himself away from the clatter of Friday breakfast and went up to lie on his bed. But it was a battle he was determined to win.

5

The open paintbox grinned at Alex like a mouthful of rotten teeth. The paint-brush leaned untouched inside a jam jar of clear water, its camel-hair point bending at the bottom. The paper, pinned to a board on Alex's knee, seemed almost to be defying the man with its emptiness. Alex sat there in the high-backed chair staring out of the window; behind him was the main part of the lounge where people were smoking or pacing or rocking or sleeping in a fuzz of tablets. Whichever way he faced, though, he was part of that lounge: you had no option but to belong there when you spent your waking day in a pair of soft slippers.

A young West Indian came into the room – tall, with long wrists showing below the white of his nurse's overall. He went to a game of draughts and watched the determined finish: he accepted a cigarette from a man idly fingering old tunes on the locked lid of the piano: and finally he walked across the carpet squares to the window.

'Come on now, Alexander, where's that picture you was going to paint me? I can't tell those trees to keep standing still much longer!' He laughed, and put a firm hand on Alex's shoulder.

Alex looked round at him and shrugged. The nurse removed his hand and crouched instead at his side.

'That ain't so hard, is it? It's been a week, you know that? I've seen *nothing* of this painting Doctor was telling you to do.' He lowered his voice. 'An' you know what they told me, don't you? Yes, you do. They told me when you've done this painting for your boy I can take you to see him, on a Sunday. Now, how about that?' He stirred the paint brush in the water, tinkling the glass, as if the movement would help to get something going. 'The old bribery and corruption! But it's worth a bit of painting, don't you reckon? I bet he's really looking forward to seeing his daddy, eh?'

Alex went on staring ahead, out across the lawns: but his expression had changed very slightly: there was a minute drawing of the muscles around his eyes.

A tea trolley jingled into the lounge.

'I'll bring you a cup of tea to get you going. You got a sweet tooth, yeah? Two sugars?'

Alex nodded, and the nurse went. When he came back the paint-brush was in Alex's hand, his long fingers beginning to feel and shape the point.

'Now don't you go drinking your paint water and dipping the brush in your tea! That's what I used to do all the time.'

Alex shook his head, and the nurse quietly backed away. The cup on the floor was ignored; and Alex looked out of the window again: but a few minutes later he had reached out for the brush, started to stroke the moistened point down a green tablet of paint; and slowly, while his tea grew cold, the colour went on to the paper.

At the weekends Darenth Lodge windows held a fascination, too: not from painters or nature lovers looking out at the grounds, but from residents looking for visitors, for signs of contact with those they'd left. One or two children stood quietly in the bays, their eyes staring out at the drive almost without blinking, until either their visitors came or they decided to give up; while others just kept on passing that way, making excuses for being drawn to the windows, on wild off-chances that a familiar smile might break out in the drive; and the rest turned their backs, did other things so consciously that they, too, were showing the windows' importance by ignoring them. They were bad times, the weekends; no school, everyone around all day, and loads of disappointments inevitable, until by Sunday afternoon the whole place was intolerable. Fights, tears, flouncings-out to the road: it was the time when Rick said he earned his money, with the rest of the week a bonus for his employers: and he hardly ever slept on Sunday nights.

This Sunday Simon was jumpy. The telephone call had come three days before, and he was at that stage where you start to disbelieve good news. The first excitement had gone, and doubt was replacing the elation. They had said they were bringing Alex to see him today, all being well – and those three words 'all being well' had grown in importance to the point where they were cancelling out the rest. All wouldn't be well, would it? Couldn't be well, with Alex the way he was. Anything to do with Alex had been so chancy for so long now that there was nothing left to depend on any more.

The ankle had got better and better – it had only been a sprain – but a week off school had got Simon so used to being around in the home that the outside world had begun to recede. And the trouble was, he knew it was happening, could feel it going away. No wonder people found it hard to get out of places like Stonelands once they were in; no wonder old people like Alex's mother, who he could briefly remember now, had forgotten all about real life and shrivelled and died in her old people's home before Alex could get there to see her. The real world lost its hold on you after a time. And about a week was enough to do it, it seemed. They didn't need to watch him at night any more. He was feeling defeated, and the terrible thing was that he was coming to terms with it. In lots of ways they'd been marvellous to him in the Lodge. Rick had had long talks with him, taken him out in the Transit to collect some laundry, walked in the grounds with him and talked about Alex and his mental illness. The Social Worker had been to explain the situation: the meaning of the 'interim care order' which had put him there till Alex was better. But news of Alex wasn't good – he sounded like someone Simon didn't know any more – and Simon reckoned it was a thousand to one Alex wouldn't make it to see him. It was a losing battle. Already, in those few days, it seemed unbelievable that he'd done what he had – crept down those stairs and out of the door, run home, fought with his grandparents in their kitchen. Why wasn't he thinking like that any more? Because instead he was wondering what they'd talk about if Alex *did* turn up: when casual conversation would be hard, and the things he still needed to ask couldn't possibly be said in front of strangers.

The others didn't help: they were jumpy too. Barry was silent and edgy in a window bay, and Little Lee was high up his tree with unsure optimism, watching for the tops of buses. Only Rose, whose blank face seemed never to expect anything but the next meal, was behaving normally, eating the food the others couldn't and sliding off somewhere for secret smokes.

Simon sat on his bunk, wandered off to lose at table tennis, surveyed the drive, took a couple of surreptitious looks at his painting of Alex.

When the mini did come Simon was in the bedroom, and Rick sent Ear-ring to fetch him. The two of them still hadn't worked out where they stood with one another. Alone with Simon, Ear-ring was quiet rather than friendly, but at least the aggravation had gone. When the others were about, though, he kept making all sorts of remarks to put Simon down, as if he had to keep proving that he was top of the heap. And today, running a message wasn't much to Ear-ring's liking.

'You've gotta come down. Some old twit's come to see you.' He left the door kicked open, definitely wasn't staying to say it twice.

Simon got up. So Alex *had* come, against all the odds.

His eyes filled with tears, but he checked them; Alex mustn't think he'd been crying. He took two or three unsteady steps towards the door, just for a moment as unsure of his feet as he'd been the night he ran away.

What happened next would all depend on Alex, he knew that, deep inside. If a miracle had happened and Alex was his old self then Simon mightn't be far off saying goodbye to this place, and that was the end of that. Even if Alex was the same as he'd left him, with just that little bit of guts he'd shown when he'd shouted at the Welfare, then there was enough chance that Simon would want to do something again. It was only if he was worse – a zombie like the early days – that Simon knew he'd find it too easy to abandon hope and give in to life in this place. He punched his thigh. And that was something he mustn't do, he told himself. There was still a question to answer. Something to prove to that old woman.

There was no special place for visitors: you found them everywhere, in the lounge, in the dining room, in the bedrooms. It wasn't like prison, he'd heard Rick saying, doing his public relations bit, it was supposed to be more like home – and when you had people in at home you could take them where you wanted. But there was a pattern, Simon had seen that. Where kids had said they didn't want anyone to come, where there was a lot of uncertainty, they kept in public groups, clustered in the lounge. No one could show off in there, or start shouting at anybody. But where kids were living for a visit, sure of where they stood, they went looking for quiet places to say their private things.

Simon had worked out that he might tell how Alex was by where he found him. In Rick's room – having special treatment – and he'd be really bad, because the normal Alex never went for privilege of any sort. In the lounge with so many others around and he'd have been led there by whoever had brought him. But sitting up at a table in the dining room and there'd be signs of hope. Alex had always been a hard chair man, businesslike, and that's where he'd be if he were better, Simon knew that.

Well, he'd come, so why not in the dining room? You had to have hope, didn't you? There was a sudden new optimism in Simon's step as he turned into the doorway.

But, no. Simon quickly stamped it into the floor. He wasn't in there. They were serving cups of tea, and Alex was neither sitting at a table nor standing in the queue.

The lounge, then. The obvious place, really, Simon told himself – after all, this was the first time he'd come. But he wasn't there, either. Oh, God, he thought, was he bad enough to be in Rick's office? On his nervous toes again, Simon went towards the closed door. He put his ear to it.

Silence. They weren't in there, then, unless they were all sitting round staring at one another. So where the devil was he? Was this Ear-ring's idea of a big joke? Because if this was a trick he'd murder him tonight . . .

Simon's anger and anxiety must have shown as he stood there in the hallway. 'Are you looking for us?' a soft voice asked from the doorway on his left. Simon turned to see a tall West Indian leaning round it, a long-wristed hand reaching out to grip his shoulder. 'You wouldn't be lookin' for Mr Leighton?'

'Yeah, that's right.' Simon had forgotten this side room with the long table, where Rick held some of his meetings.

'He's in here, waiting for you.'

Simon looked past the man to where a pair of gnarled hands were spread flat and patient on the table. God, that wasn't Alex, was it? He'd never had useless old hands like that, no matter how bad he'd been. What the hell had they done to him, given him some funny drugs? But as the West Indian stood aside Simon saw that the hands were someone else's altogether, someone keeping an eye of his own on the doorway, and Alex, the real Alex, was down at the other end, sitting at the top of the table, working very

hard at a smile, all mouth and tight eyes, trying too hard –
but he was pleased to see Simon all right. He even stood
up, a strange figure in a long overcoat and an unnecessary
scarf, with his hair combed all wrong as if an undertaker
had been at work. Yes he was very pleased to see Simon,
no doubt about that, and he was starting to cry.

Simon ran past the line of chair backs and threw himself
into the dowdy overcoat. ''Ello, Alex.' For a few moments
they were all on their own, patting one another and snivel-
ling at the pleasure, while the tall nurse turned away and
said something about the weather to the man with the
hands.

'All right then, Simon?'

'Yeah; all right.'

'Feeding you all right?'

'Yeah, O.K. Yours all right?'

'Couldn't say; never taste it really.'

'No. Me, too.'

Then they just stood there, conversation exhausted and
unnecessary. They were both all right physically, fed and
clothed, and everything else about them had no need to be
stated. Alex sat down, and Simon drew out a chair beside
him.

He didn't know how much his father had been told
about things since they'd both been sent away, and he
hoped it had been very little: there was no point dragging
all that up now, and he didn't want Alex worried about
the stolen picture. He looked up at him and made a thin
grin which said, So . . .? The sort which puts a brave face
on a bad situation. Alex roughly wiped his eyes with the
scarf, and they sat there, neither of them saying anything.

'Come on now, Alexander, you gonna show your boy
what you brought him?' Alex's companion came down the
room and sat opposite Simon, long fingers flicking the
rubber band off a roll of cartridge paper, making a sound
like small drums in the quiet room.

The old man at the other end got up and went to the door, pushing it wide and standing half-in and half-out as if he wanted to be seen by someone. But as separate as he was trying to be, his eyes didn't leave the paper tube as it unrolled. It was like any unveiling, a ceremony which had to be watched: and today the unveiler seemed to be taking as much pride in the work of art as if he'd created it himself. Unrolling the paper and holding it steady at top and bottom, the nurse suddenly sat up with a flourish.

'How's that for a picture, then?'

Simon stared. It was quite big, about the size of a tray, a view of trees and grass, consisting of flat shapes of colour which made the painting as much a pattern as a view; but the feature which took Simon's first attention was the frame. Painted round the scene in yellow scrolls was a picture of an antique frame as carefully worked as the landscape itself. It gave the whole thing an immediate feel of being totally finished and right, all ready to hang up. In the diffused light of the conference room it was an impressive sight, very much as if it belonged in there.

A good picture, Simon thought. But it was typical that Rose should be the first person to say anything about it. There she was in the doorway, and before anyone else could open a mouth she'd said it.

'Better'n your other one,' she told Simon, even before she said hello to her visitor.

'That's ever so good, Alex,' Simon jumped in straight away, watching his father's eyes. But he was more aware of Rose's at his back.

Alex's eyes narrowed. He didn't say anything, and he didn't look at the picture with Simon.

'That's a real good picture, don' you reckon?' The nurse was still sounding proud and possessive about it. 'Took me three days to get you to do it, didn't it, Alexander, and two more days to do that fancy frame.' He smiled at his patient.

Alex spoke very softly. 'It's for your wall, if you want it. I made it ready to go up.' His voice was flat, almost like a message coming over a mini-cab radio.

'Thanks ever so much.' Simon spoke softly, too, but not to match Alex's tone: more because he didn't want Rose to hear too much about what was supposed to happen to the picture. If he decided to put it away and not have it laughed at by the yobs, he didn't want her going telling all the world what he'd told Alex he would do. 'I'll see to it when you go.'

Even now he was as aware of her behind him as he was of Alex in front. It was bad luck her coming in here when he was having his time with Alex; because no matter what, he couldn't shut her out.

'You feedin' the dog proper?' she was asking the old man with her.

'Yeah, 'course I am, girl.'

'Well 'ow long 'fore I get out of 'ere this time? You got some dates lined up?'

'Oh, I've got me 'opes. Be a couple o' weeks yet awhile, though, afore I know . . .'

There was a short silence.

'What you brought me? Any fags or bars o' something?'

'Yeah, I got you a few bits, Rosie . . .'

'Good. Long as they ain't a picture. Can't eat or smoke a bleedin' picture.'

She'd said that especially for him, Simon knew: he'd heard her voice change into her throat. He gave himself back to Alex, in case the artist had heard.

'Yeah, it's a terrific picture, Alex. Terrific you did it, you know what I mean? Really . . . terrific.' He looked intently at his father. 'So you're all right for brushes and things?'

'Oh, sure thing, we've got all that stuff,' the nurse interrupted, still proudly. 'He's only gotta say, "Chris, you get me a ten foot block of stone because I'm gonna do a statue," and he's got it – no problem!'

Simon still tried to keep his voice low. 'He's a sign-writer; did he tell you? Have you got any of that sort of stuff? He could do any signs you need doing round the place.' Simon had seen a little spark in this Chris, working to get Alex back in the groove.

'No kidding? Great! You can do me a private sign for my room, Alexander. "Staff Nurse C. Beckton. Keep out."'

The group at their end of the table had held the others' attention for a few minutes, Simon knew, because at the other end a silence was suddenly broken.

'I'll be off in a bit, Rosie. I'm gonna go through this week's *Fair* tonight cover to cover, see what I can't find for Easter. Give us a start, eh? Get us out the smoke. I'm gonna read the print off that paper. There ain't a lot for us yet, but something'll turn up.'

'It'd better – I'm fed up here. Another week o' this an' I'll be over the wall and up west, like they do . . .'

Old Man Penfold's hand went to his belt. 'Over my dead body, girl,' he said gruffly.

'Yeah, if you like,' Rose replied: and abruptly she scooped up her presents and walked out of the room.

The old man stood. 'Oh, it won't come to nothing like that, Rose . . .'

'Well now Simon, we'll just carry on looking after your daddy,' Chris said brightly, emphatically turning his back on Old Man Penfold's problems. 'It's only early days yet – and who would have *guessed* he'd be doing paintings like this so soon?'

Simon sat staring at Alex, and Alex sat looking without expression at the table. For a moment the only movement was the nurse's – keeping the painting from rolling itself up on the flat surface.

'You done that yourself, did you?' Old Man Penfold was buttoning his coat, hovering before he made the move to go. 'It's all right, mister: y'can see what it's meant to be.'

Alex shifted his gaze to stare at him, and imperceptibly he nodded, without any sign of pleasure.

'It should be all right,' Chris said, still sounding proud for Alex. 'He's a *professional*, Alexander is.'

'So I see, mate. Yeah, I reckon you done that all right.' And almost as suddenly as Rose, the old man had gone.

Chris allowed the painting to roll itself back to being a tube of paper again and handed it to Simon. 'I reckon we've gotta go ourself just now,' he said. 'We don' want to overdo things on the first day; that wouldn't be too clever.' He put his hands in his trouser pockets and skirted the room to the door. 'Come on, Alexander, say your goodbye an' we'll get us back for our tea.'

Alex stood obediently, ready to be led away. Simon took his arm.

'I'll see you then, Alex. Look after yourself, eh? And thanks ever so much for the picture. It's great . . .'

'No . . .' Alex stared ahead. 'I'll . . .' but he stopped there, and Simon couldn't tell whether he had been going to look forward to being better, or just been about to say goodbye.

Simon walked out to the car with them, and he waved Alex goodbye all the way till he was out of sight, just the way he'd always done when he'd left Alex in the past.

Head down, he kicked his way back through the dusty gravel. He picked up a stone and threw it hard into the air, in the general direction of Darenth Lodge. Suddenly his resolve was back. *He* could do what the nurse was doing. It was *his* job, and he and Alex belonged together; they had things to prove to people. How the hell could he have actually let a couple of weeks go by without still thinking about getting away?

''Ere, who bunged that?'

It was Little Lee, up his tree, and he was coming down,

fast and angry. Simon ran for the house and got himself out of sight behind the door before Lee hit the ground. He ran up the stairs to their room. He'd be lying all casual on the bed by the time Little Lee got inside.

Breathless, he swung into the bedroom, back to where he'd been when Ear-ring had come for him. But it was a different place now. Suddenly he didn't belong here any more, not the way he'd been starting to think he did. Even if he put Alex's painting on the wall this place wouldn't be anything like home for him – nothing like all right till he'd left it behind. He laid down on the bed and waited, but Little Lee didn't come. He'd probably bashed up someone else for throwing the stone. He stared at the fading light in the window, heard the sounds of car doors and feet crunching for buses across the gravel.

And not a mention of his mum, he thought. It had been good to see Alex, in a way: but neither of them had got around to talking about the one who was missing.

He sighed. Well, one bit at a time. They'd sort it all out one day, when they were on their own, feeling free. One day: and not too far off, he thought, if he had anything to do with it again.

Old Man Penfold had fed the dog well. He'd given him a tin and a half of his usual and half a packet of Rich Tea biscuits on top. He'd made a fuss of him, the way Rose did, but all the dog's attention had been on the food, worrying at it like a wolf with a soft carcass, and after a few minutes he'd left him to it, the chain clanking rhythmically on the iron steps of the trailer.

In a stiff cupboard the old man found his wife's glasses and like a man unaccustomed to study he sat himself down in a good light with the *World's Fair* and began his search. Not a line, not a word, not a mark of punctuation was missed. It was as if there *had* to be something in it for him, and like hidden treasure in a familiar house he wouldn't rest until he'd found it. He mouthed every word, as if they'd sink in and mean more that way – words which told him about annual dinners in Yorkshire and Scotland, 'the Showman's Guild and Value Added Tax', the latest rides being developed in Germany, invitations to cross the Channel and spend a million marks. He brought himself up to date with the new French pancake craze – the 'crepes' which would take over where hot dogs left off – but closest of all he studied the small advertisements which meant the most to him, looking, as if the looking could create them, for sites which might not say no to an uncomfortable ride like his 'Autodrome'. Word by word he searched for some way of getting out of his yard for the summer, for the chance of his traditional freedom on the road with Rose. But within the hour he was sitting back exhausted, drinking something small and strong and talking to the heaving belly of the Alsatian on the bed.

'We're dead out of luck, boy,' he said. 'Had it, mate. All my stuff's good for's the junk yard, and it ain't much good for that – all wood and a clapped out generator.' He had taken his wife's glasses off and put them back in the cupboard with her narrow rings. 'Gawd knows what we're gonna do . . .' He refolded the *World's Fair*, all inside out and giving him trouble like a map. 'It's you for the dog's home, mate, and me for the Social Security. And as for Rosie . . .'

The dog, off its chain of duty, only wheezed in its sleep.

The old man stood up and took the trade paper over to a small bundle of waste on the window seat. 'Waste not, want not,' he said, and he started to tuck it into the loosened string.

It was then that he stopped, as if he'd suddenly been caught by an old pain. But his hands went not to his body but back to the paper. Like paws they tore at the pages until the one he wanted came before his eyes again: and without the aid of the glasses, holding it close enough to his face to eat it, he read the words he'd passed over without thinking.

''Ere, 'old on,' he told the animal. 'Listen: "Due to contract unfulfilled" – that's Sid Flower's passing on – "a showman's artist is wanted to paint over or touch-up and varnish various rides and side stuff on site. Own trailer preferred or possibly trailer to let. Good rate paid for right person."'

The old hands tore the advertisement roughly from the page. 'Rosie . . .' he was muttering, 'Rosie . . .' His voice was urgent, down in his throat like the dog's. He started to pace the trailer, two steps this way, two steps that. It took on a squeaking and a rocking, and the dog woke up, bad-tempered. But the old man kept on, banging the thin walls with his fists, impatient to share his find with someone other than the animal, someone to talk it over with. Finally, paced out, he sat down again and poured himself another drink, larger now, and he rubbed the leathery softness under his eyes. A jerky fatigue was twitching his limbs, though, and he didn't sit for long. He found a sheet of paper among the waste and he started on some figuring – a snake of figures which tailed down and down into a tired coil of mistakes at the bottom. It was no good, it seemed, he couldn't get it right; and in the end he laid himself down to sleep. But he woke the dog again with his tossing and turning, and finally he got up and put it outside, to keep an eye on the yard and his property, which had somehow taken on a new lease of life during the evening.

The following morning Simon was welcomed back at school as a new butt for the jokes that had gone round in his absence. At least three small boys in the playground tried him with Friday's: ''Ere mate, what you gonna do for a face when you give King Kong his bum back?' Simon tried to smile indulgently at the humour, but jokes like that weren't for him. They were things you had to hear and pass on, but he didn't know anyone well enough for that any more so it had to stop with him. He might try this one on Little Lee, he thought, when he was in a good mood: but you never knew when you were going to do something wrong.

Before he returned to school Rick had talked to Simon about the futility of running off again, and it was obvious Mr Rogers and Miss Baker knew about what had happened because they didn't say anything personal to him. He guessed everyone was just keeping a careful eye open. He was left to pick up the pieces, fit himself in, rather than be the centre of another great fuss – and he thought that was just about right. At times the working classrooms gave him a good opportunity to think. There weren't so many occasions in his life when it was possible to do that any more. The Lodge was always noisy, and going-to-sleep thoughts got out of hand in their wildness; while at school he could use his healed ankle as an excuse for staying-in at break for a few days, avoiding his enemies, and yet still be near enough to the old life in the streets around the place to think realistically about what he might do.

For a start, now he was back here he could almost work out how to get to Stonelands, something he hadn't been able to do properly from the depths of his lower bunk at Darenth Lodge. A bus with Stonelands written on it passed the school, he'd seen it, and now all he had to check on was whether it stopped at the stop just along from the Girls' gate, or at the other stop around the corner. He'd better check, he knew, because it was very important to know which stop was which, when one wrong turn of direction could waste seconds and make the difference between secretly hopping a bus and being spotted by one of the teachers.

During Maths he decided what he was going to do: and

in Environmental Studies he decided how he was going to go about it. He'd keep up the bad ankle bit till dinner time, then when the bell went for the first sitting – when Jackson and Clark's class should be in the dinner hall – he'd go to the old school gate and check. It had to be dinner time because this gate, and the bus stop, was at the wrong end of the playground for doing it at home time. It wasn't the Transit gate, and he couldn't go off for a casual stroll at four o'clock. Plus, there weren't many teachers about at dinner time, only dinner ladies who didn't know him from Adam, so there'd be every chance he could look like a home dinner and get to the gate without anyone noticing. And that was probably the time when he'd make his break, too, he thought. It'd give him nearly an hour and a half in the clear, a good start, and if he could get Alex prepared they could be away almost by the time the afternoon register was called.

The getting through to Alex bit was going to be the hardest: making contact without Chris the nurse interfering, and then making sure Alec took it all in. Next Sunday would be his chance, if Alex came to the Lodge again, but the way he did it would have to be really well worked out. A walk in the grounds was favourite, saying he had something personal and private to tell his dad: Chris had better not want to push himself into something like that.

Simon kept up the appearance of work by copying a paragraph about pollution out of an encyclopaedia – he reckoned he could keep Miss Baker happy just by looking busy today: and copying didn't involve his brain. That was busy with more important problems than oil slicks in the Channel. He looked out of the window to where a line of squat fruit trees ran down a terrace of back gardens, what was left of an old east London orchard. There must have been more freedom then, he thought, when this was all country round here. Still, at least green was spreading into the trees, better weather was coming, something a bit warmer, bringing more cover as this week ran into next, and there was plenty of rough country still left, not too far away. He'd looked it up. Stonelands was on the edge of Epping Forest, and for hundreds of years people had hid out in that. A trip there one sunny Sunday with Alex and Mum, when they'd left the car somewhere, they'd got quite panicky trying to find it after half-an-hour in the trees. They could have been up the Amazon, so if he and Alex could get off the beaten track and lie low till the sun went down they could easily get a tube round to a railway station and be down in Wales by morning.

Money, they'd need: but Alex probably had money somewhere. They'd have to give him something in Stonelands: and if he knew it was needed he could save some, couldn't he? Anyway, he'd sort that out with Alex when he talked to him. And even if he had to draw out of the Post Office or off the Social, he was used to doing that. It was bad luck there wasn't the car any more – that had been the first thing to go after what it had done – because they'd have been really free with a car. But they'd manage. He'd make sure they worked it out somehow.

But first he had to know about that bus. At dinner time he'd find out about the bus stop; and everything could follow on from that. At last Simon felt settled. To the work on the desk he added a few thoughts of his own about cleaning up rivers – well, not his own, things he'd heard someone say on the telly – and he started to draw a picture. Quite a good one: he enjoyed it. But what he was thinking about was dinner time and making a start . . .

This first part of his plan seemed almost too easy to begin with. When the bell rang Miss Baker gathered up her handbag and the class gathered up their friends and funnelled through the door. Simon remembered his limp and followed them. No one seemed to care where he was going so he didn't need to lie to anyone. He went with them out into the yard, standing cautiously on the steps as they fanned out to their various territories. His eyes almost hurt him with the sharpness he used. The last thing he wanted was a run-in with Jackson and Clark – but while they were at the trough he'd have almost a quarter of an hour to check on what he wanted. And that shouldn't take more than three minutes, he reckoned. He could be safely back inside, reading in the library and waiting for the second dinner bell by the time they came out. Meanwhile there were plenty going home for dinner, which would make it very easy for him to get to the old gate without being suspected. That was good, too, so many going out. When the day came for his run to Stonelands all he had to do was go with them.

One dinner lady was out there, chasing two kids playing football into first dinners. She wouldn't make any fuss. Again, he let the others go first – hurrying, chattering, dawdling – because he didn't want any loud remarks when he stopped in the gateway to look out and check on the bus stop.

It needn't even take one minute. The bus stop signs round there had those grids on them with three or four bus numbers painted up large, and his eyes were good. He could usually make out a bus number as soon as he could see the bus itself, even at the end of the road.

The last little knot strung through the gate, and then the opening was his. He didn't know why he should be surprised, but the bus actually went past as he got to it, a new one, big and square and smooth, coming from his right as he jumped out, close enough to it to turn red in its reflection. He caught a glimpse of one or two people standing halfway down it, waiting for the doors to open, and he drew back. You never knew who might get off a bus: the Welfare man, a teacher. No sense in taking chances. He heard the doors hiss and flap twice, once to open, once to close, and the large diesel roared sweetly again as the vehicle pulled away. But no-one passed the gate. Now he'd look. Now it was safe.

It was a deep shock. It turned his inside over with the sudden worry of what it meant. Had they got the same idea as him? Were these two going to queer his pitch? One of them had got out of school in front of him: and the other one had just got off the bus.

One was Rose, and the other was the old man who'd been to see her the day before at Darenth Lodge. She was lounging back against the fence, the usual attitude; he was leaning forward, going on about something very seriously. Simon kept his head back – he was sure he hadn't been seen; but the next time he looked round it was from close down by the ground where no one would expect a head to be. The old man was explaining something to her, really going on, using his eyes and his hands almost as if he was talking in deaf and dumb. Rose's mouth was open and her eyes were half closed. But for once she seemed to be really interested in what someone was saying to her.

What was it, then? What were they up to? Because if these two were planning for her to run off – and she'd done it before, hadn't she, she'd shown him all the ropes – then that was crucial to him. Like he'd thought the other week, if she went off from the school all of a sudden then his chances of doing the same were going to be down to sweet nothing . . .

Blast! He certainly couldn't wander out and ask them what they were planning. He'd have to wait and see. And even finding out about the bus was impossible while they were standing there.

He turned away, uncertainty churning inside him like some stomach complaint. Nothing could ever go smoothly, could it? Nothing! And somewhere in every one of the upsets, it seemed that Rose was involved . . .

And now his time was up. The dinner lady had started blowing her whistle at him.

''Ere you, you deaf or just being stroppy? You wanna go and stand outside the headmaster's room instead of 'aving your dinner?' She was almost on top of him, yelling at him in anger, ready to blow her plastic whistle right in his ear.

'Sorry,' he muttered. 'O.K., I'm going.' He said it very quietly. He didn't want those two outside knowing he'd seen them.

'I should think you *would* say sorry, too. You kids – God knows what your poor mothers 'ave to put up with!'

Simon ran. There was no answer to any of that, so he didn't bother. His first worry now was getting in for his dinner without running into Jackson and Clark. Finding out about the bus to Stonelands couldn't bother him just now. That could wait, he could do that tomorrow. And by then, who knew? he asked the gritty tarmac as he ran, by then he might be having to work out something else altogether. There was definitely something going on. And whether Rose was bunking off or not, with his luck it was highly likely it was going to affect him. It was a big mystery all right. And he was just going to have to try to be patient till he could find out what it was.

Back at the Lodge after school, Simon chose the television room to be private in. It was always favourite. Nothing was required of you, you didn't have to speak unless you were spoken to, and it was less moody than lying on your bed, or sitting somewhere with a book and not turning the pages. Not that there was much more he could think through till he knew about that bus, till he saw, by what she did, what Rose was up to. So he sat, and like Alex, let the pictures flicker in front of his unfocussed eyes.

Ear-ring was there, uncouth and breaking wind loudly near the door, shouting impatiently for *Superman*: but Simon kept himself out of his line of vision and didn't feel forced to join in the false laughter.

It suddenly quietened when Rick came in to catch the tail end of the news, to make a caustic comment about the names announced in the England team: but he soon went. Unfortunately Ear-ring's performance had been interrupted, and no one was going to get any peace till he'd caught up and got a last laugh before *Superman*. The next thing Simon heard was Ear-ring's voice, and when he looked there was Rose in the doorway: the same thin dress, the same unfussy hair, the same expressionless look of disdain.

''Ello darling. Was the 'airdresser's closed?' Ear-ring's mouth was open, wet with the joke.

Rose refused even to turn to him, but her answer was quick. 'Yeah, mate, it was. They was delousing it after you.'

The others understood that, and it got the laugh Ear-ring had wanted. He jerked up out of his seat, but the girl had moved on into the room, coming to sit next to Simon.

It was all too clear that trouble was brewing. 'Careful, Leighton,' Ear-ring warned. 'Come an' sit back 'ere, son. You'll catch something nasty with 'er there . . .' Ear-ring was a bad loser.

Simon half-laughed at Ear-ring and shrugged his shoulders at Rose.

'It ain't nothing to what you'll catch if I come back there!' Rose retorted. 'Now shut your mouth an' let me talk to someone with a bit o' sense.'

Shut up, Rose, for God's sake! Don't wind him up! Simon's heart sank. Out of nothing these troubles grew. And he didn't need to be dragged into it any further, thank you very much. If only he could walk out, not be there. He didn't want to fall out with either of these two: they could both make a difference to how he got on, just by being for him or against him. There was no room in his life for any more enemies.

The *Superman* music started to play. 'Leighton got

sense?' Ear-ring called above it. 'I've got more sense up my backside!'

Rose didn't *ask* Simon to go outside. She simply pulled him up by the arm and led him to the door, past Ear-ring's lounging feet. 'S'right, I thought that's where you kept your brains,' she said, dragging Simon with her. And they were away, leaving Ear-ring to shout a string of loud obscenities after them.

Simon was led out of the front door and into the grounds. He didn't protest. There was no denying Rose anything in a mood like this – if he'd wanted to he should have done it in the television room: but now, the further away he got from Ear-ring the better – at least until the kid had forgotten the worst of the show-up.

The evening was overcast but dry, and if there was a chill in the air Simon didn't feel it. He wasn't aware of anything as unimportant as the weather. Rose, who seemed to give the up and down days of March as much attention as she gave everything else around her, strode out as if it were blazing June and quickly found a felled tree trunk behind a clump of rhododendron. She sat Simon down. This had all taken on an air of urgency, and Simon had to keep reminding himself that she was up to something – her and the old boy. Like the hospital after his mum's accident, like the juvenile court, the general air of the way people went about things had you halfway there to accepting whatever they had to say to you. He needed to be careful that didn't happen tonight.

Rose wasn't one for beating about any bush. 'Toss Jackson down the school reckons your dad's loony. That true, is it?'

'No, it ain't!' Simon was shocked out of being careful by her very first words. Jackson again! Jackson and Clark. Had they got to her as well, then? 'He's *depressed*, that's what they call it. That's not the same as being loony. No way.' He looked at her blank face and immediately regretted what he'd said. Why tell her that much? She didn't have any right to know anything at all. Tell her to mind her own business to start with, that's what he should have done. Talk like this wasn't worth falling out with Ear-ring over. He had to sleep in the same room as Ear-ring.

''E didn't look loony to me. More like . . . simple . . .'

Was there a difference? Simon asked himself. But he knew what she was getting at. With loony – Jackson's loony – you had a picture of someone running round doing crazy things. Simple just seemed quiet and slow against that.

'So 'e didn't bump your mum off?'

She might just as well have hit Simon, thump in the middle. She'd knocked the breath and the voice out of him. And without the ability to shout at her he wanted to hit her, to swing his left arm round and smash her full in the face over the back of the log. But staring at her angrily he saw again that expressionless face: there was no smile, no leer, not like those yobs at school; just a blank stare at the facts.

'Who said that? Jackson and Clark?'

'An' the rest . . .'

'Well it's bloody not true. She went round the back of the car. He didn't see her. It was an accident!'

'Police didn't do nothing?'

'No! Asked him questions, that's all.'

'An' now 'e's *depressed*?'

'Yeah. Wouldn't you be?'

'An' the two of you was looking after each other, was you?'

'Yeah.'

'An' they put you in 'ere an 'im in the . . . in Stone-lands?'

'Yeah.'

'An' 'e'd gone there by the time you bunked off 'ome?'

'Yeah.'

Rose nodded and stared at the bushes in front of her, as if she'd cleared so much ground and was looking at what she'd done up to now before going on.

'Why?' he asked. He was all hot and flushed. She'd got him off guard again, putting things so bluntly. Delving at him where his own dark doubts had to be till he could prove something once and for all. 'What's it to you?'

But Rose wasn't going to be hurried. No one hurried Rose.

''E's a painter, i'n't 'e?'

'That's right. Signwriter. Does the shop fronts.' He was pleasing her now, he knew, eating out of her hand when he didn't want to; but there seemed to be no stopping that.

'But 'e paints pictures an' all? Like the one 'e give you?'

'Yeah.'

Once more the pause: but this time Simon didn't try to force anything else before she was ready for it. He'd try to be more cagey from now on.

A chill breeze put its fingers round the small of Simon's back. It ruffled Rose's hair and rippled the thinness of her dress across her knees. But she didn't seem to notice and eventually she spoke, slowly and emphatically telling him the truth about his situation.

'An' what you're after is gettin' on your own again with your old man, getting the both of you out the way of the Welfare?'

'Could be.' But it really was much too late for caution now. She knew all right; and she knew it.

'Well, there's a chance ... something I might know about, if you want ...'

Now she was looking at him instead of at the bushes, actually using her eyes to emphasize the strength of what she was saying.

'Aaaaa ... aaaaaaa ... aaaaa!' A cackle of human

machine-gun fire suddenly hit them as a group of three smaller kids came out from *Superman* to shoot up enemies in the jungle. They killed Simon and Rose and ran round the tree trunk to get at whatever was lurking in the rhododendron.

'Clear off!' Rose shouted: but these three were young enough to be immune to older girls. They went on kicking up the sort of racket that killing a guerilla band entails. 'Aaaaa . . . aaaaa . . . pow! Aaaaagh! Aaaaagh!'

Rose swore at them. Just for once she seemed as anxious as Simon to get something sorted out.

'Tell you what,' he offered, for now there was something he had to know, 'Little Lee's tree. That one over there. Get out the way up there.' And he was taking her, leading her, pulling her up into the lower limbs. 'Now,' he said, when they each had two hands and two feet secure, resting and gripping. 'What you on about, then?'

Rose looked at him, close-in enough for him to see flecks in her brown eyes, smell cigarette on her breath, feel the seriousness of her purpose. The angling of the tree's limbs had decided for them how close together they should be, and she was using it for a final scrutiny, it seemed. Whatever she had to say couldn't be taken back, her face was telling him. Whatever came out now was out for good.

'It's someone I know,' she said softly. ''E needs a painter, trav'ling round the country. Someone who could be on the road till October-time . . .'

Simon found a fresh grip on the bark, and bits of it fell into his eye. Did he know who the painter was, and the someone? 'Where, travelling?' he blinked and watered.

'All over. Where the fairs go. Don't matter, do it?'

'Fairs?' So that was it. He'd thought she was from market people, or something. 'You mean like bumper cars and that?'

'Yeah, *fairs*. What d'you think I mean?'

'Doing what?' He pulled a funny face at the ground,

trying to clear the irritation in his eyes without risking a hand.

'Doin' painting. Doin' up the boards and gates on the rides, puttin' Dracula on the ghost train, that sort of thing.' She made it sound very obvious.

'And who's this someone: is it that man who was here Sunday?'

'Could be, yeah, if you must know. My uncle.' She obviously didn't like answering questions instead of asking them. 'We'll be trav'ling, an' we've got a spare trailer; we just 'itch it up be'ind.'

'And that's who the painting's for, your uncle?' He was asking what he had to ask, but he couldn't move a muscle. He was fixed in the tree like the frame of a kite. Every nerve was attending to what this girl was telling him.

'All right, I'll tell you, quick. You go down the fair an' it's all different people with different rides, right? All got together for the week. Some bloke, some big family's got the ground, with 'is own rides: then 'e lets out ground to other people, different rides, all the side stuff, 'ooplas an' that; it's his say who comes on, right?' She looked through the branches at the house, down at the ground. 'An' my uncle reckons 'e can fix up a painter with work for these people. We take our ride *and* a painter, and the painter does painting for these other people.'

'What, travelling round?'

'Ain't that what I said?' She shifted irritably in the tree, shaking it. 'It's better for them, trav'lin'. Else they 'ave to cart their stuff up London to get it done.' She shifted. 'Now I can't 'ang about. I want a quick answer. But I tell you, it's a good stroke, this . . .'

Still Simon stayed rigid. It certainly was a good stroke, a marvellous stroke, Alex getting lost round the country with a fair. But there was just one thing.

'And what about me?' he asked.

''Strewth, you come an' all, stupid. We want a painter

bad. But we can't mess around looking after a l... after anyone all depressed, can we? We'll be busy enough with the ride ...'

'Ah.'

''E done that painting recent, didn' 'e? It weren't something old?'

'He did it last week. Why?' Simon's stomach rolled in anticipation of some disappointment.

'Well, 'is 'ands shake, don' they? 'E's pickin' at 'em all the time.'

Simon hadn't noticed Alex's hands on Sunday. It was something he'd got used to. 'He never shakes when he's painting. Never.'

The girl looked around again. 'Well, that's all right. I'll tell my uncle then. It ain't *'is* business what 'appened with your old lady, s'long as the law ain't after anyone.'

Simon held on tight again. The dry bark was turning wet in his grip. A great chance, this was, it sounded better than anything he could have dreamt up for himself, however crudely she put it.

'They leave you alone,' she was saying. 'The Welfare. They've got enough on their plates without botherin' over fairground people. Probably only too pleased – 'cept we're in 'ere on a court order, an' they wouldn't put this dodge up to no magistrate ...'

Now Simon found himself trying not to smile. It sounded marvellous: dead right. Alex painting all through the summer, with him there to look after him. It'd get him back on his feet. And then time to talk: time to bring some of those doubts out in the open. Talk to Alex about what had happened, hear it all again, have a chance to prove things. Providing Alex would come – and the way he'd looked on Sunday, glad to see him, and with a painting, it could be the best thing in the world for them.

In spite of himself he must have been smiling. 'Right,' she said, 'so you keep your trap shut. It'll be a few days 'fore we know for definite – and then everything'll 'appen quick. We'll get out o' this place one night, meet up with my uncle an' your old man, an' off 'fore y'can say "Welfare"!'

'Right.'

They were just in time. Pleasure for Simon, big or small, could never last for long.

'Come down outta there, Leighton! What you doin' up my tree?'

It was Little Lee. Simon should have known: the machine gunners had gone quiet all of a sudden, at the approach of a real fighting force.

'Tanyard's after you.'

Lee was coming up as fast and agile as a monkey, and even seeing Rose only held him for a second. 'Dirty berk, you up 'ere with that girl?'

Simon risked a lot to get down quickly. He avoided Little Lee's kicking feet by taking a chancy hand-hold; but he took care with the final drop, to spare his ankle. Whatever bother he was in with two kids he wasn't going to ruin his chance of making the final break with Darenth Lodge. He left Rose and Lee arguing the toss in the branches, his money on Rose, and he ran for the house. But once he was inside he knew where he had to go first. He'd got to find Ear-ring Tanyard and say something, try to put things right between them – because he didn't need any aggravation from him if he was going to get away again one night. Rose he needed now: and enemies in the camp he could well do without.

6

The following Wednesday afternoon Old Man Penfold trod the long drive of Stonelands like a tradesman. Perhaps like everyone else he preferred not to look as if he belonged there. He kept discreetly to the side, even though the camber made walking more difficult for him, and by the time he reached the house he was tired, and wet with perspiration where the cellophane lining of his cap met his bald head. He paused for a moment, drew his breath, and shuffled inside, damp cap in hand.

'Who you want?' An aggressive lady in a shapeless dress was standing in the doorway. If he hadn't had his head down he would have seen her watching him come. 'Edie's gone to heaven,' she told him.

'I don't want Edie, love,' he said gently. 'It's Alex Leighton I want. Know him, do you?'

'Don't know no men.' The woman was on the defensive. 'I'm "B" wing. Edie was "B" wing.'

'Yeah.' He looked round for someone else: but suddenly she took his arm, was holding it like a bride.

'Look in the lounge. There's men *and* women in the lounge.' She set her face importantly and walked him through some double doors. There was no one to prevent it happening. If there was any security operating it was lax; Old Man Penfold's step was a little lighter at that.

The large room was filled with other visitors and an open hatch was doing a brisk trade in cups of tea and Penguin biscuits. Alex was sitting on his own in a corner far away from all the activity. The old man withdrew his arm. 'Thanks, love,' he said. 'That's my mate over there.'

The woman let him go. 'Edie's gone to heaven,' she told him again, and she scurried, looking lost, from the room.

If Alex recognized the man who had sat at the other end of the long table at Darenth Lodge he didn't show it. He looked up and then away as if people were drawing up chairs next to him all the time.

'Mr Leighton? Penfold's the name. We was both at the Lodge, Sunday.' He hung his cap on his knee. 'I spoke to you 'bout that picture you done . . .'

'Yes . . .' Alex seemed to remember, vaguely.

'Well now, listen,' Old Man Penfold looked round like a comedian about to tell a rude joke. 'Come straight to the point. I've got a chance of a good "out" for you. Get you away from 'ere, travelling, you an' the boy. Your lad – Simon, eh?'

Alex frowned; he was listening.

'We mustn't say too much, gotta treat it all a bit secret service, but I've got this undertaking – all written an' signed – saying you can go to work doing' some fancy painting, round the fairgrounds. You an' the boy, with a nice little livin'. Now 'ow does that strike you?'

Alex stared at him.

'I fix you up wi' your living quarters, an' you an' the boy get left in peace. Sort yourself out. None o' this malarky 'ere, an' none of that care stuff for the kid.' He paused while a wet tray of teas went past. 'You'll be along o' me, see, an' I'm going' well off the beaten track . . .'

Alex sat up straighter, but still he said nothing.

'Even if it all went wrong you wouldn't be no worse off than you are now. But you're *voluntary* 'ere, see what I mean or you wouldn't be in this place, so it's only takin' the boy back. You're a free agent, yourself, like me. An' it's 'olidays soon, then the summer, and none of us 'as no 'assle in the summer, providing you've got a few school books in your trailer . . .'

'Trailer?' Alex's voice sounded surprisingly firm.

'Caravan. Nice little place. I'll get all that ready for you.' He fanned his face with his cap and put it back on his knee.

Alex was picking at his hands now; then he turned them over once or twice; but there was no knowing quite what he was thinking, how much of what he'd been told in such a rush had gone in. There was a long wait.

'Say it again,' he said eventually.

Old Man Penfold breathed out heavily: but slowly, patiently, and very, very quietly, in short cap-flapping sentences, he went over the plan that Rose had fed to Simon. He stressed the simplicity of it, the freedom, the being together with Simon again, looking after the boy: and, above all, he underlined how neither of them had anything to lose. If it all went wrong, he explained, they'd only end up where they were now: Alex in Stonelands and Simon in care. There was no risk attached, only the gain of being a family again, the getting back to painting, being his own boss, and the freedom: especially the freedom . . .

Alex said nothing for a very long time. The hand picking went on and a lot of staring out at the grounds, the landscape he'd painted. He looked all round the room. He stared hard without blinking at Old Man Penfold. And finally he gave his reply.

'I don't mind,' he said. 'Give it a try if you like.'

Old Man Penfold stayed just as he was: he didn't smile or make any move which could upset the delicate balance. 'Right,' he said. 'Mum's the word, now. Don't go saying nothing to that black bloke, whatever you do. 'E's sharp enough to cut 'imself.' He tapped his forehead. 'Keep it all in 'ere, an' when it's all fixed up, which won't be long, I'll come an' take you out for a drive one afternoon, an' we're away . . .'

He looked at Alex for a few moments more, then he got up without a word and went over to the hatch to buy some teas, like all the normal visitors did. The two men sipped at it in silence and picked at the foil of their Penguins.

'The thing that 'appened,' the old man said at last, in a casual, throw-away voice. 'It was just *accident*, wasn't it?'

The brittle chocolate seemed to catch in Alex's throat. He threw back the dregs of cold tea as if they were a litre of water.

'What . . . else?' he managed, in hardly a voice at all.

'Yeah.' Old Man Penfold unhooked his cap. 'Like you say, what else? Any'ow, don't you forget, mum's the word. An' I'll be in touch.'

He took Alex's hand and shook it, and he went then, turning at the lounge doors and waving back at Alex, the normal visitor departing. On uncertain legs once more he made for the main doors. The woman was still there, staring down the long empty drive. 'Ta-ta, love,' he said.

'Edie's gone to heaven,' she told him again.

'Yeah,' he said. 'Edie an' a lot else besides.' He pressed a crumpled note into her hand. 'Get yourself a nice cup o' tea, eh?' And he shuffled out to start his long walk to the open gates, but this time more in the middle of the road.

At Darenth Lodge it was cold war between Simon and Ear-ring, just what Simon had dreaded. Little Lee hopped from one side to the other, aggravating things like the neutral who always stands to gain from real conflict: in the day-time, when he had the space to run away, he was more often Simon's; but at night when it really counted, he was with Ear-ring, hotly reminding them all of Simon up his tree with that girl.

Simon knew what was up with Ear-ring. In front of everyone he'd come off second best against Rose, and Simon had openly gone along with her. And now it seemed that nothing private between them could put things right. Whatever the outcome was it was going to have to be a very public affair. As it went, Simon wouldn't have minded that so much: he didn't give a monkey's what they all thought of him: all he was intent on now was the plan to get away. He wouldn't even have minded a fight that he could lose: a lot of shouting and a couple of thumps and it could all be over. But Ear-ring was too clever for that. It was as if he knew that Simon and Rose were hatching something; he didn't miss a trick, intercepting every glance before it happened like some jealous boy-friend; and he was obviously waiting for some big showdown that would put the tin lid on everything.

He kept a very special watch at night.

'Not tonight, is it, Leighton? You ain't thinkin' of goin' to meet your poxy girl-friend tonight?'

'Shut your trap!'

'We're list'nin', ain't we, Lee? Put one foot outta bed, Leighton, an' we'll 'ave Rick an' 'alf the 'ouse up 'ere 'fore you get to the door.'

'Belt up! Dunno what you're on about.'

But it was worrying Simon, and the night he genuinely had to get out for a late pee his eyes were opened to the real enemy he'd made. He waited as long as he dared. He tried to tell himself he didn't really want to go, it was all in his mind. He delayed, he drew his legs up, pressed himself tight until it was touch and go whether he'd make it in time, until at last he thought he heard the regular breathing of Ear-ring asleep. Only then, a centimetre at a time, did he move his sheets – slow sheets don't rustle, he learned that – and he crept his knee to the bed's edge as if he weren't moving at all, as if he were still lying there in a deep sleep, so that when he slid out he'd be on all fours on the floor.

But no sooner had his hand and his foot touched he floor than, 'Where you off to, Leighton?' – and Ear-ring was bouncing bolt upright in bed, pinning Simon down in the beam of a flashlight.

'I'm goin' for a pee if you must know.'

It just showed what would happen. Ear-ring was out of bed, the light was switched on, and the door was being held wide open for him.

'Do one for me, Leighton, while you're there.'

Little Lee decided he wanted to go, too, and the whole thing became such a performance that Rick had to come to shut them up and keep an eye on them till the bedroom door was closed again.

'Your sleep-walking days are over, son,' Ear-ring told Simon. 'Don't make no mistake about that!'

And Simon believed him. How he was going to get away with Rose when the time came, the Lord alone knew. Perhaps in the day-time. He was all sewn up in his bedroom, that was for sure.

He visited on Sunday, the old man. Simon saw him walking in, scruffier than he remembered in an old mac, but very business-like, hurrying through the door with a newspaper folded small in his hand. He felt like hovering near to see if he was wanted, to answer any questions the old man might want to put and to hear his reaction to what he'd told Rose about the difficulty of making a break from the bedroom. But he decided against that. He'd kept his contacts with Rose down to a minimum in case the two of them were linked any stronger in Rick's mind – so it would be stupid to be seen talking to her uncle. And there was another reason besides that. Little Lee didn't have a visitor either – the fourth week on the trot – and a bit of friendship with the little kid wouldn't do either of them any harm, he reckoned. He led their game up Little Lee's tree, their look-out post in the war against the enemy spies – the visitors. And brilliantly, Simon thought, he made the tree theirs again, his and Lee's. With an arm round the trunk and his hands rounded into binoculars, he talked a load of war-rubbish – while at the same time he kept an eye on the fair ground pair huddled close in the common room.

★

'It ain't gonna be easy,' Rose told the old man, looking as if she were doing nothing more than inquiring after the dog. 'The kid's got these others on 'is back, an' 'e's never gonna get out of 'is room without all 'ell breaking loose.'

'What about you?'

'That ain't none too clever, neither. One o' mine wets the bed, an' they're in to pot 'er whenever they wake up. Nice for 'er, but it don't give no peace.'

The old man supped at his cup of tea. 'Nuisance, that,' he said. 'It's all goin' a treat outside. Got the painter eatin' out o' me 'and. 'E's right ready to go. All I'm waitin' on is the word from Tucker. Spare trailer's comin' along lovely – an' I've took our name off everything. Now all I've gotta do is give the word to Stonelands I'm takin' the painter out for an afternoon drive.' He smiled. 'I'm well in there, being nice to the old girls.'

'Yeah, sounds like you. What about straight from school? That'd be dead easy. We could easy bunk off together on the day, meet you somewhere close . . .'

Old Man Penfold thought about it for a second or two. 'No, mate. You two go missin' on the day an' they've got hours to come round the yard, shoot over Stonelands, raise a real 'ue an' cry. Every East End trailer on the road'll get stopped by some nosy copper or other. No, we need a good couple of hours to get out the smoke, not someone harin' out after our tails. First date's the pre-Easter fair down Rochester way. An' we're movin' further out every stop. We'll get well lost once we're south o' London: but I must 'ave that good two hours. There's no way round a night-time job.'

Rose put her elbows on her knees and a sour face into her hands.

'What about you an' the painter goin' missin' then? Won't they come after you when 'e don't get back for supper?'

'I got plans,' the old man said. 'I know 'ow to play Stonelands along.' He flapped his cap. ''Ere, I got an idea . . .'

Rose looked as if she didn't believe him.

'Not very nice, though.'

Now she perked up. 'What you on about?'

'The old Diddakoi trick. The School Board stunt. What they used to do when the School Board went round the scrap sites . . .'

'Oh strewth, thanks very much.'

Simon saw her pulling her face from up his tree.

''Ow's that supposed to 'elp?'

'Get yourselves in the Sick Bay. Both of you. Just one night. You know the stunt – nothin' too bad for 'em to sit up 'olding your 'and all night or shoot you off to 'ospital. Just enough to keep you in the isolation. Be easy out o' there together, won't it?'

'Yeah, done it once before, I think. Windows open up there.' Rose shuddered. 'I don't fancy that! An' I dunno about 'im.'

''E'll be all right. 'E's desperate, that one. Try anything for 'is ol' man. It don't last long. Gotta be all over, mind – 'ow the diddies do it . . .'

Rose shuddered again.

'. . . Ideal round 'ere in these overgrown grounds. Now don't say you ain't up to that.'

She stood. 'Thank you very much. It ain't you got to do it.'

Old Man Penfold put his arm round her waist. ''S'important, Rose. As we are, if this paintin' stroke don't come off we're done for. It's the end after all them years . . .'

'Oh, shut up! Save your ol' soft soap. All right, I'll do it if I've got to. But will 'e? That's what I want to know. That's the million dollar question.'

The pair of them looked out of the window, as if they

might see the boy and read it in his face. But Simon was well hidden where he was, camouflaged up Little Lee's tree, getting in practice at fooling the enemy.

Rose told him, secretly, and he whistled through his teeth. There wasn't anything he could find to say which wouldn't make him sound chicken, so he kept his mouth shut. It was a good plan on paper, he thought. If you were reading about someone else doing it, it sounded great. But . . . A tingle ran down his back as he tried to imagine what it would feel like. A fight with Ear-ring would be a million times better – would certainly be over quicker.

'I'll tell you when. Soon as I get word from the ol' man. You be ready, that's all. 'Ave the things you want for the break all ready to put on quick.'

Simon did as he was told. He put his smoothest, softest jeans on one side, his loosest socks, his silkiest tee-shirt, and his leather bomber for a cold night. These he kept neatly folded in his locker. His emergency gear, he called it. He felt like a spy preparing, and every time he saw it his stomach turned with a sickening sort of apprehension. He checked the Sick Bay window from the outside, saw the sloping roof of the out-house beneath it. That should all be O.K., he reckoned. And then he went to the place Rose had chosen for them to do it, and he looked at what was there with a strange, mixed feeling of excitement and hatred. This would show him just how far he was prepared to go.

When the word came he thought he was going to be sick. It was after a greasy supper on the Wednesday, and he tried to put it down to that. But he knew what it was all right. He was scared stiff. It would be all right once he was up in the Sick Bay with Rose: he'd follow her then, he wouldn't even have to do any thinking and planning, and he'd be getting over it, on the way to getting better: but it was what had to come first. That could drive him out of his mind.

''Alf an hour,' she said, 'round the side be'ind the old laundry.' She looked him over, critically. 'Get your stuff on.'

His mouth was suddenly very dry. 'O.K.,' he managed. He wanted to ask more, about the rendezvous with Alex and the old man, about the transport, about whether she'd done this before and how long the pain would last. But he couldn't force out the words. Oh, God! Why couldn't he have been born a cat, or a rabbit, or a bird with free wings and an unfeeling coat of feathers?

He went off and changed quickly, fumble-fingered, and he left himself too much time to walk this way and that. Who would ever have thought half-an-hour could tick away so slowly? Was it like this before an execution, in the condemned cell? Waiting like this it was taking forever; and yet he'd have done it before the minute hand got up to the top of the clock. With a cold shiver he wondered what he'd be feeling like by then.

At last, when the time came – too soon now, he walked outside, his head up as if the eyes of the world were on him. He'd go bravely, wouldn't be found wanting, wasn't going to be chicken . . .

Rose was already there, her back against the old laundry wall as if all she was doing was having a quiet drag. It was a good spot, secluded, damp and dark as these private places are; definitely not somewhere anyone would want to go. But she wasn't taking any chances. She scowled at him as if she didn't want him there, just as if Ear-ring were following him. Only when she seemed to be sure he was alone did her look match his and show its apprehension.

No, he wasn't going to be chicken, but he had to have one last try to get out of it.

'Couldn't we just tell 'em we've got belly ache? Or a sore throat? Pretend to cry?'

''Course not.' Her voice was an urgent, throaty growl. 'It's a lot of bother opening up the Sick Bay. They've gotta think it's worth it, to keep us sep'rate from the rest.'

'Yeah.'

'You ain't gonna let me down, are you?'

'No! What d'you think I am?'

'Right then.' Her voice went even lower. 'You know what you got to do.'

She looked at the bed of nettles in front of them, where his eyes were already drawn and fixed, fascinated by the soft dark green of all those painful stings, tall, swaying in the evening air like so many snakes' heads.

'When I tell you, get your clothes off, quick, an' roll right over there. Then back 'ere an' get dressed like greased lightning. Make sure you get 'em all over – an don't forget your face!'

Simon drew in the biggest breath of his life to protest, but her hand was clamped tight on his mouth.

'You get food poisoning all over!' she hissed in his ear. 'Don' be bloody stupid! I'll show yer. An' if you don't foller on after me I'll kill you!'

She would, too, he reckoned. Or damned near.

'Quick – 'ave a last look round that corner. Make sure no one's comin'.'

His skull felt tight; his heart seemed almost to pull him to the corner by the strength of its thump; his legs were no more than two sticks of weak rhubarb. 'It's all clear,' he croaked.

When he turned she was ready, her clothes in a heap behind her, her arms and hands held modestly in front of her. Then urgently, she nodded at him. 'Come on, quick, straight after me.' She hesitated, looked at him with big, scared eyes, all the confidence suddenly gone.

He stared at her, saw the private, frightened Rose. He scrambled with his zip, his laces, his sticky socks, and she waited till he was past the point of no return, till he was ready, too. 'Oh, God! In for a penny, in for a pound!' and with a weird moaning sound in her throat she went, throwing herself flat like a nervous diver into cold water, rolling over and over like some kid in a secret summer game, thin and white in the rub of the nettles. Soundless after the first noise, just the crush of the nettles as she flattened them, within seconds it was all over for her – and then she was up, tight-mouthed and gesturing violently at him with her head as she dived for her clothes.

Simon stopped thinking about it. She'd throw him in them if he didn't go. He knelt down gingerly, took a very deep breath, and then he went. Cupping his hands over his groin, he rolled in the hollow she'd made – over once, over twice, found a sharp stone with his knee – and came back, shaking all over at the thought of what he'd done to himself.

Had it hurt? Was it bad? Apart from the stone, which he'd felt like a knife, he didn't know for a few seconds. He grappled with his clothes. It had hurt – hurt him like nothing he'd ever known before. . .

Rose was standing dressed and rigid against the wall. It had got her now, he could see. And here it came for him, rising up suddenly and spreading all over like someone turning up the heat.

It was total. It was Joan of Arc, Guy Fawkes. It was flame and heat and closing eyes and the hiss of tears and mucus as he tried to take his skin off with his nails.

'Oh, Jesus! Mary! Bloody 'ell!' Rose was crying.

'Help me! Mum, Mum, Mum . . .!' Simon mouthed. He clutched at the wall and tried to rub himself through it, his legs, his groin, his face, his ears. 'Please God, let me die . . .'

'Count 'undred! 'Old still an' count . . . 'undred . . . get used . . . then go in . . .'

They stood there, crouched there, rocked themselves,

cursed, blasphemed, and tried to ride out the burning, wealing pain with any movement a body could make, writhed to every low yell of protest they could lay tongue to – until at last with stiff, shaking legs and arms like scarlet twigs lumped in angry white, they staggered off in their separate directions to find the adults and report their excruciating condition as if nothing hurt really, as if they'd done no more than eaten something bad.

'Just a mild temperature,' said the doctor. Even after the cold relief of calomine there was still a welcome feel to her cool hands. 'No fever. And they go to the same school? Had the same lunch?'

'There weren't no choice today,' Rose said feebly from the other side of the screen.

'So what did you have?' The doctor was looking at Simon kindly, but with just the faintest air of suspicion.

'Can't remember.' Be weak. It was safer like that. Let Rose take the initiative.

And always the leader, she was ready for that. 'Some mince an' potato stuff, an' peas . . . an' choc'late pudding.'

The doctor was nodding, perhaps dismissing something from her mind. But Simon wasn't thinking about her. His mind was on Rose, lying there as burning and itchy as he was, and yet with her brain working fast to keep on top. She hadn't let them down: she'd been in with her answer almost before he'd passed the question on, alert in all her pain. Thinking of her made him catch a huge breath, like after crying; the opposite of a sigh.

'Cereal and an egg for breakfast? I think we can rule out food poisoning. Maybe just an allergy. Neither on penicillin? No. Shellfish perhaps, some sort of sea-food might induce a rash like this, but if you haven't eaten any . . .' She clicked her stethoscope. 'Anyway, one thing's clear: you haven't got the plague – you haven't got too high a temperature and the rash does seem to be fading.'

You didn't expect to see the doctor baffled. It was what the two of them wanted, but for Simon it still had the shock effect of finding out about Father Christmas.

'Some sort of urticaria – nettle rash – but I can't see why you'd get it together like this . . .'

Simon went rigid in his bed. He cried out – a sound of surprise at the mention of nettles. 'Ow! My . . . leg.' He had to pretend he'd shifted uncomfortably on a sensitive weal. He swore under his breath. That should never have happened, however bad he felt. He should have kept on top, like Rose. That was the difference between making it and being caught out. He moaned again, to emphasize his discomfort, hoping perhaps that he'd fooled Rose, too.

'Well, I'll leave some anti-histamine syrup and a prescription for some more; you can get it in the morning.' The doctor tore a scribble off her pad for Rick's deputy, Ruth. 'But if the rash persists or there are any other symptoms, call me in again and I'll inject. Meanwhile, I think we can relax. And you two mustn't worry about yourselves. It looks bad, but I don't think anybody's going to die.'

The doctor was standing, smiling and yet frowning, between the beds at the foot, where she could see the patients on either side of the dividing screen.

'Thank Gawd for that,' Rose managed. ''Ad me worried, I can tell you.'

Simon had to imagine what the doctor could see: the girl's face acting its relief at not being at death's door; a brave smile: Rose being Rose.

His stomach turned over. They'd still got it all to do, though, hadn't they? This was only the early hours yet. No wonder he felt all chewed up inside. But at least the worst the stinging nettles had done seemed to be passing. Now, as the doctor threw her things into a bag, he thought with the slightest sense of luxury of what he'd been through.

At first he'd thought he was going to die – be driven crazy by those furry, bladed fingers that were searing him red hot, white hot, all over his body, the gentle pain that had suddenly come on harsh like water from a tap turning to boiling, getting into the places where a rough touch always hurts, and then all over the whole surface of a prickly skin. As he'd dressed, walked stiff-legged and frantic into the house to be seen and loudly pointed out, he'd had only one picture in his mind: that of a smooth and empty pool where he could plunge and stay under, for ever if need be. Nothing else seemed possible to put out that total fire, to ease the savage burns.

'Don't walk like that for crissake!' Rose had said before they'd split. 'Don't bloody *look* like you've just fallen in the prickles. Walk normal, make it look like it's comin' out from inside.'

He'd tried, rash rubbing on rash with every step, until a bottle of calomine in the Sick Bay had spread some relief at last.

But it was definitely going off. Now he could think about other things: about the doctor going away till tomorrow, about Ruth's mention of milk before they settled for an early night, about Rose asking for the window to be left open a crack to give a nice cool draught.

The doctor went, with no mutterings outside the door, the screen was folded away, and Ruth went off to do a few other things. Simon turned his head to Rose. He managed a swollen wink.

'You all right?' he asked.

'Would be, if you din' try to give it all away every five minutes.'

'Sorry.'

'Didn't do no 'arm this time, I don't think. We'll soon know, if they're waitin' under that out-'ouse with a bloody great butterfly net.' She laughed.

Even leaders must feel relieved at times, Simon thought – even blank-faced Rose.

'Don' talk about it no more,' she cautioned. 'They wear special soft shoes in these places, I reckon. Keep your trap shut till I tell you. Where's your clothes?'

Simon nodded towards his bedside locker. They'd been lucky. There'd been no question of sending their day-time clothes back to their rooms.

'Right. Get yourself some kip, then, if you can. You're gonna need it.'

'Yeah.' And Simon tried; but there was never a hope of sleep coming. What with the itch of nettle-rash – fading, but still there to quiver the skin whenever his body stopped its constant moving and scratching – and with that other itch in his mind, irritating to get away, the last thing his body could give him was a nicely numbing sleep.

It soon became clear they weren't going to do anything but lie awake and shoot their limbs about, and they started to talk again in low voices, curses becoming conversation. But in the end Simon lay and stared at the ceiling while Rose told him what would be happening with the others.

''Course, they don' know who my uncle is, not your dad's lot. 'E didn't give 'em no proper name or nothing. Just said 'e's a friend of your ol' man's an' says 'e'll take 'im out for a drive. Then tonight 'e's gonna 'phone – cars broke down out Braintree way, 'e's gonna say: tell 'em they'll be back a bit late.' A sudden frenzy of movement and bad language turned her on to her front. 'Then 'e'll ring 'em again around eleven. A.A. can't do nothin', they're comin' back on a coach but they'll kip down round my uncle's. 'S'all worked out. Give 'im that, 'e's a clever ol' so-an'-so.'

'Yeah.' Simon was going through his own agonies. He'd need more calomine in a minute. 'And what's really happening?'

'They're down the yard, 'itchin' up two trailers to the tractor –'

'Eh?'

'The lorry, makin' their way out Whipps Cross, parkin' along from the all-night tea bar.'

'Where all the motor-bikes get?'

''S'right, an' the all-night fishers in the pond. You an' me get there 'bout one, straight in the second trailer on the floor, an' 'old tight till we're down the country.'

'Oh.'

'An' that's it. Out on the road right round till October time.'

'Yeah.'

Simon felt all choked-up for some reason: the thought of the time ahead with Alex, getting things right to prove to everyone; the sudden thought of his mum not being in on this time of his life; and the special thought of that Rose he'd seen to share it with. It was a powerful mixture, and the choking-up was for all of it, or some of it, or maybe none of it. He didn't know. Nothing was very easy to work out any more.

'Oh, you two are looking better.'

Ruth was back, on those soft shoes Rose had kidded him about, and she'd caught them very much awake. Please God she wouldn't suddenly decide to send them back to their own rooms.

But they were lucky – she had a tray of milk and biscuits in her hands.

'One more dab of calomine, and you can settle down,' she said. 'Now, who's going to be first?' She set down the tray and pulled the screen between them.

'Let 'im,' said Rose. 'Sort the kid out first.'

Ruth pulled back his sheet. Oh, yeah? thought Simon. Not so much of the kid. I'll show you who's a kid when we get on the fair. Or was she only acting for Ruth's bene-fit? That was the trouble with Rose. You never knew. She always made it very hard to tell over things like that.

But one thing he was clear about. Something that had been going round in his head. What she'd said when she was just going to do it. That old saying of his mum's he'd heard again in Rose's frightened voice. 'In for a penny, in for a pound.' Good old Rose. She wasn't so bad. There was definitely something about her . . .

Simon closed his eyes. For a few seconds nothing in the world mattered but the cool pink stuff coming from Ruth's bottle. It took all his attention. If happiness could be counted in such short dabs, then he had to be happy now. Let all the big things wait, just for a bit . . .

Midnight came, that special time which always seemed to Simon to mark the difference between early and late. If ever there'd been a few words beween his mum and Alex it would always be if she came in from dancing after midnight. A minute to twelve was all right, it seemed. A minute after, and Alex sulked. And tonight it was very special, it would mark the difference between being here and being away.

There was a clock in the room or they'd have been lost for time. No convenient town hall bells chimed the hours around here. As the hand jerked up to the top, Rose muttered something about it being an hour earlier than they'd really wanted for the break – but trailers parked at night drew suspicious coppers who thought everyone with a trailer was a gypsy and moved them on. They had to be away from the tea-bar by one at the latest if they wanted to be free of all hassle. The trouble was, and Simon knew it, there were some adults who'd still be awake in the Lodge at midnight – and it meant the two of them would have to be as silent as sleepers when they got out of that window and slid down the sloping roof.

The glasses of milk had been drunk and washed up, the biscuits eaten and the crumbs brushed from the sheets, the screen put back and a blue night-light switched on. They'd been settled for the night and told they were both miles better: whatever it was, Ruth had said, it definitely wouldn't have them waking up dead! The Sick Bay door, opposite Ruth's, was open, but so was the window, sucking the bottom of the net curtain out into the night. It was all very peaceful, like any going to bed early always seemed to be.

It was as if Rose had planned everything right down to the smallest detail. 'See them blankets on that cupboard. Roll two of 'em up together an' shove 'em in your bed. An' chuck two of 'em over 'ere to me.' Obediently, Simon moved his bedclothes to get out. 'An' put your feet on that floor as if they're made o' fresh air.'

He moved quickly. He'd done this sort of thing once, and he'd thought about doing it again for so long that fooling the adults at Darenth Lodge seemed to have been born in him. Of course, he was right in what he was doing, they were right, so hesitation didn't come into it. Rose said 'Move' and he moved. The rash was forgotten. They'd paid their price, now they were going after their reward.

While Simon fetched and rolled the blankets Rose dressed and set her shoes by the window; and while Simon dressed she saw to her bed. But as the two of them got ready every other move they made seemed to have an awareness of that open door, a continual check for the sight or the sound of someone coming.

The house seemed quiet enough, though. From what Simon knew of the programme some organized games out on the small lawn would have worn out the younger ones, and a new batch of records for the stereo would have given Ear-ring's lot plenty to leap to. So long as Ear-ring didn't suspect enough to try something on they oughtn't to be surprised by any unsuspected commotion. It was only the adults getting edgy that needed to worry him and Rose.

His leather top creaked like old stairs, and for a moment

he thought Rose was going to make him leave it behind: but while she frowned, she worked at the slow window, and suddenly she was ready.

'Close the door, slow an' quiet. It could easy 'a shut in the draught. An' put the locker be'ind it: give us a couple of extra seconds if they come . . .'

Awkwardly, but quietly, he did as he was told.

'An' put out that stupid light.'

Again he obeyed. Now they were working in darkness. And now, if anyone came, there'd be no use pretending.

His leather creaked again.

'Shut up! An' come straight after me.'

'Right.' As if he wouldn't! A lot easier, this would be, than following her into the nettles.

'Spread yourself out on the roof. You don' wanna fall through it.'

'O.K.'

'An' mind your stupid ankle when you jump. I can't carry a cripple all the way to Whipps Cross.'

'All *right*.' What did she think he was? A moron? He wasn't the sort to make the same mistake twice.

'Come on, then!' The net curtain was scragged aside and she was over the sill, one second filling the window, the next just a pair of hands and the top of a head as she let herself down onto the out-house roof.

Simon had a moment of panic as he realized he was the one who was left. What if someone came in now? She'd be off and he'd be kept behind under such strict control he'd never get away. He almost kicked her head off in his rush to follow: but Rose knew how to keep her mouth shut when she had to.

There was no moon, but enough light from the street lamps to see the sloping roof she was sliding down, the orange glow making it look like something from the titles of an adventure film. Like her, Simon slid like a spread star till his feet found the guttering. Only the scrape of their descent and the slight creak of asbestos sounded in the general rustle of the trees. And from above, nothing. Again, no shout, no slam, no sudden beam of light.

It was always the guttering that gave in the films, and Simon willed himself to stay light. He tried to feel like Anansi, the spider-man, all limbs and no weight as he levered himself over, balancing on his belly, his hands going where his feet had been. Then he was hanging, and she was hissing, 'Let go you berk! It ain't far!'

A drop into the dark, where the lights didn't reach. It was hard to let go, not knowing when you'd hit the ground. But Simon knew better than to delay, hanging there thinking about it. Just keep light, and be ready to buckle and roll. He let go and like in that blindfold party game, he was there before he knew it, dropping nowhere near as far as he'd thought. He didn't even fall over, just stood there – and he was ready to run.

'Come on, then! What you want, a clap for being brave?' She was away, swishing through the undergrowth, leading him, gaining speed as they found their feet and left the dark side of the house behind them. She headed for the back wall, the stretch which came out onto a quiet lane.

Here there were only weak pools of light, well-spread lamps which just about served to show where each one stood. It'd be ideal, Simon thought from the top of the easy wall, if it went like this all the way to Whipps Cross. But that was stupid, he knew that. There were main roads where kids like them would really stand out at this hour, and huge flood-lit roundabouts whichever way you came to the Whipps Cross all-night tea bar.

But this time he had underestimated Rose. He wasn't to know about her paper collection, her times on an open lorry crawling round the side-streets of Market Junction and Whipps Cross, her late nights out sorting some bit of business with Old Man Penfold. Her knowledge of the back doubles of this part of East London equalled the cabbies' – and bettered the police. He didn't know how well she understood which pubs turned out rowdy, where the racist bricks flew about after dark. But Simon could see she was as sure as hell about which way she wanted to go. Past the long terraced rows where people like Simon lived, that was the way she took him, well clear of trouble spots and the big smart houses where it paid a policeman to give a bit of attention. At one point, about to cross a busier road, she stopped him in a shadow and told him, in a voice which defied any joke, 'If I tell you to put your arm round me an' act all lovey, just do it – an' don't get no ideas. We'll just look nat'ral, bein' out late.' It didn't come to that, though. They went on undisturbed, cutting a quiet way across the borough like a rip against the weave. No one gave them so much as a second glance. A crowd of yelling yobs passed them a street away; but after a cautious slowing to be sure they didn't meet, Rose led him on, and the noise of the shouting faded.

It was all very well thought out: and not for a moment did Simon doubt that Alex would be there. While Rose was leading him, Old Man Penfold was looking after Alex. Enough said. With that pair in charge everything would *have* to go as planned.

The lights at Whipps Cross glowed like circus lamps from their gantries high up above the roundabout. Beyond them, darkness and infinity; beneath them, a steady stream of traffic going off in all directions. Rose led him to it along a side road he'd never noticed driving past, by a hospital as big as a small town: and as they boldly avoided the cars on the main road Simon found himself thinking not so much about the fear of the traffic or about being stopped by a police car as by the sudden shock of something Rose quietly said to him.

''S'where I was born, in there.'

Strangely disturbing, Simon found that. Rose was Rose, a bossy, couldn't-care-less female who knew all about making the world work her way. It was hard to think of her being a baby, being cuddled, having a mum. It somehow made her different again. He knew how he'd come to be where *he* was, doing what he was doing – how he'd changed from the kid he'd been once. Now he'd had a look at some other Rose *she'd* been once, a long time ago. Keeping close by her side as they waited for a container lorry to rumble its length, he linked that Rose for a moment with the Rose who had hesitated at the nettles, who'd said something very near to home, stood there like some undressed girl on the beach. It was a different idea of Rose, and he was thrown by it.

'Come on then – you want your arse cut off?'

He ran across the road with her, made it to the verge, and settled for the curt Rose he knew, the one who'd definitely got them here all right.

And there was no doubt about Old Man Penfold being here, either. He seemed to be taking up the best part of the East End with his transport. It stood there no more than fifty metres from the tea-bar and it seemed to stretch for ever: a big flat-fronted lorry with two caravans hitched up behind it. Simon had seen it all in his mind's eye, of course, gaudy, shining, fairground stuff: but nothing as long as this – and nothing as tatty. Even in the false lights of the highway the three vehicles looked flat, undercoated, dull. Obviously that was how Old Man Penfold thought he'd get away with it.

And Alex? Where was he? Lying down depressed in one of the beds, or sitting up straight in the driver's cab?

'Over 'ere.' Quietly, in a gap in the traffic's noise, Old Man Penfold called them from under the canopy of the tea-bar. And there was Alex, standing by the old man's side, sipping a carton of tea, and spilling it down his raincoat when he caught sight of Simon.

'Alex!' Simon ran at him and spilled some more. Rose watched.

'Hello, Simon.' Alex's free hand was round Simon's shoulder; but not gripping all that hard.

'You all right Alex? You look all right.'

'I'm O.K.'

Simon squeezed his arm. It was still the wrong way round between them, but Simon was used to that. If he was disappointed because Alex hadn't magically become his old self again, he didn't show it: he hardly felt it. You soon learned to get used to the way things were. Rose had had to, Simon thought, since she'd been that baby.

'You kids wan' a cup o' tea?'

'Yeah – an' I'll 'ave a couple o' doughnuts.'

Simon had a doughnut, too, and while the pair of them spread their faces with sugar they walked towards the trailers and told them how it had been.

'It 'urt like 'ell. But it soon wore off.' She scratched herself. ''Ad 'em well fooled.'

'The doctor wasn't hundred-per-cent, but she couldn't put her finger on anything.'

'Well, it's not a nice thing to 'ave to do, but it got you 'ere – an' 'ere *we* are so let's get off while the going's good.'

They had come to the trailers: Alex first and anxious. The longer one, hitched behind the lorry, was what Simon had imagined, apart from its looking so dull: it was a home on wheels, the sort you could live in. But the other one tacked on behind was much smaller, more like a garden shed by comparison.

'Dog's inside – given 'em 'is pills. Alex an' me are in the tractor, you two kids in the back trailer. But don't move about for Gawd's sake or you'll 'ave 'er over on the road.'

Old Man Penfold got them round a wheel of the trailer pretending to inspect a tyre, till the coast was clear.

'In you get, quick!' He pushed the rickety door open.

'See you later, Alex.'

But Alex was still staring at the tyre, and he'd hardly turned his head by the time the door was shut.

Inside it was dark and musty, smelling of paraffin and paper and recent paint. Simon could sense rather than see the stains on the mattress which filled the floor space. They both stumbled over it, and fell. It was cold and damp on there.

''E said there's blankets somewhere. 'Old on till me eyes get used to the dark.'

Way up front the diesel choked into life. Well, at least that was a real fairground sound. They lay where they'd fallen, and Simon suddenly felt exhausted. But he stayed tense till the first bump and jerk of movement told him they were under way. He blew out a long, tired sigh. At last. They'd started the next, the important part of the break away. From now on every rock and sway of this little thing meant a metre further out of London, a metre nearer getting lost for the summer somewhere down in the country.

And the trailer certainly rocked. But Simon slept. He woke, often: bracing himself for this corner or that, shooting his eyes open every time they stopped at a junction, and he discovered early on that he'd been covered by a blanket; but he hadn't the energy any more even to say thank you to the silent mound beside him. He went off to sleep again and the night journey went on, vague lights filtering through the curtained windows, the occasional roar of things going past them, till at one awakening much later a long stretch at a steady speed told him they were on some sort of a motorway. But it was all submerged and surrounded by sleep: a shallow sleep, but drug-like, and tonight it was without dreams.

7

What finally woke him was the backing and bumping over grass, and the daylight breaking through the windows. He was on his own in the trailer, rolling about on the mattress as if he were on some throw-about ride. But there was no music and no screaming: just the sound of men's manoeuvring voices: Old Man Penfold's and someone else's, commanding, full of Cockney confidence. Simon scrambled up to look out of the grimy window, just as the trailer was spun through a hundred and eighty degrees, and he was thrown back onto the mattress – unceremoniously put back to bed. He tried again, and this time as the trailer see-sawed beneath him he made it to the perspex and managed to see what they were doing. Alex and Old Man Penfold were bent double, manhandling the trailer by its tow bar round where the other man was telling them.

'That's got you. Square to your other one. Leaves room for your cables to come through to the front.'

Simon was all eyes for Alex. This was the first glimpse of his father working he'd had for ages: his first glimpse of him doing something outside himself. Next to Old Man Penfold he had a new, keen look in his eye, rubbing his hands with the effort of moving the trailer, and crouching to check it was on an even keel.

The keen look soon went; but it had definitely been there, and Simon had already started to race to the door.

A shout from the man in charge stopped him.

'Watch out! You wanna 'ave 'er over, son? Wait till she's anchored 'fore you start leaping about.'

'Oh. Sorry.' Simon mumbled the apology in his throat and stepped gingerly onto the grass.

The man was wearing a jaunty tartan cap and no more than a thin tee-shirt and jeans in the chilly morning; he was big built, and he looked as tough as nails. He had already moved away to where a big lorry was nosing across the grass, waving his thick arms at it and shouting instructions. Definitely the Boss, thought Simon: the Guv'nor, and this was his fair.

Simon walked over to Alex and punched him softly. 'Good, eh, Alex?' He looked out at the field for Alex's benefit, trying to draw him into the feeling he had. He looked up at the mottled sky, the only thing above their heads now. 'A bit of all right, eh?'

'Oh. Yes . . .' Alex didn't sound very convinced.

'We'll be all right now.'

The early morning excitement shivered him. The field – or park, or whatever it was – had that special Bank Holiday look about it, with high-sided vehicles and their trailers beginning to group themselves round an open rectangle like iron filings round a magnet. Vehicles which were quiet now in their maroons and browns and blue tarpaulins, all gave off their hints of pleasures to come: TUCKER'S FUN FAIR ON TOUR, HOUSE OF HORROR, FAMILY AMUSE-MENTS. Simon knew how the local kids would feel when they saw all this: it would be like waking up to snow.

There was no sign of Rose. But her trailer was only metres away and Simon could see the curtains drawn closed. She'd gone back to her own place to sleep, he reckoned, and he felt vaguely sorry about that. The things they'd done together had worked out all right for them: painful in parts, but at the same time a real change, when he thought how he was usually one on his own. But she'd be with her own sort of people now: she'd drift away from him, be all hard again: and perhaps he'd best forget that other Rose he'd seen . . .

The Guv'nor was striding back towards them, down their side of the field with a plan of some sort in his hand. Behind him a youth was unrolling a well-used marking tape onto the ground.

'That's where your side-stuff goes, Nick. Get it marked all the way round, then as they come in, get 'em off the road and send 'em over for siting. Make sure they don't unhitch without seeing me, right? An' watch Hargreaves and his Big Wheels 'specially. I want that deep, to pull 'em through: not by the gates where he'll want to put it. We'll start off the season as we mean to go on.'

'Yeah. All right.'

'Right then. I'll 'ave a bit o' breakfast myself in a minute an' we'll start building-up.'

'O.K.'

The man lifted his tartan cap to scratch his black hair. He stamped the ground beneath his feet, breathed in deeply through his nostrils, rubbed his hands. He didn't need to say a word for Simon to know what he was thinking. The fresh beginning started here.

Abruptly, he turned and walked over to them. 'Well. 'ere you are, then. 'Ope you fit in all right.'

Simon looked at the confident, commanding figure: blue eyes, an out-door face, not an ounce of fat on him, as strong as one of those Foden tractors: a man who could wear some silly cap and make it look the thing to do. A big contrast to the thin, uncertain shadow of Alex.

The man thrust out a huge hand. 'Jimmy Tucker. Junior. Everyone calls me Junior. Any problems, come to me. Any aggravation on my site, I settle. You're new, but you'll soon see.'

Alex nodded.

'An' who are you?'

'Leighton. Alex.' Tentatively, Alex took the big hand

and had his arm pumped twice, then dropped. 'And . . . Simon.'

The man looked hard into Simon's eyes. 'I've got a boy your age; an' a girl of fourteen. Both away at boarding school.'

Simon stared at the big, tough man. He hadn't quite expected that.

'Right, Alex. You get your trailer sorted out. Then you get started on my ride. We'll 'ave one rounding board off at a time, see 'ow you shape up. Give us an hour, then I'll see you over at the Dodgem.' He pointed to a spot in the middle of the empty space. Then, turning to go, he dropped his voice, very slightly. 'An' don't let Charlie Penfold 'ave you over a barrel. Any problems, come an' put a word in my ear.'

Whistling, rolling up his plan, nodding to an old woman with a bucket, he strode off down the line to a modest trailer fifty metres away. Fascinated, Simon watched him go. A bit gruff, he'd been: but putting some of it on, Simon thought, like a teacher with a new class. Everything Alex wasn't, at the minute; but they were in good hands with him. You could tell.

''Ere, mate, take the end of this, will you?'

Nick, the youth with the tape, was unravelling a tangle of muddy old knots.

'O.K. Will it take long? I've got to help my dad.'

'No, 'course it won't. Wouldn't've asked you.'

Simon went over to him. The kid was taller than he was, and dirty, with dried sleep in his eyes and blackheads round his nose.

'Gotta fetch a mallet. Get this undone for us.'

The tape was dropped in a heap at Simon's feet and the kid shambled off, round the back of a parked generator. Simon didn't fancy even touching the tape, but while he watched Alex wandering aimlessly in and out of the trailer he had a go at the stubborn knots. The minutes went by and the kid didn't come back, and Simon began to get anxious. They had to get organized, him and Alex. They had to get some breakfast off Old Man Penfold and get over to the Guv'nor within the hour. He couldn't afford to spend much more time on this kid's knots. He had other things of his own to do.

Simon looked all round the field – the recreation ground, as he began to recognize it, with its small pavilion at the far end, a couple of swings – and he saw the signs of early morning life on the fairground. The odd column of blue smoke was rising from a trailer top, shining churns were being carried from the tap by the pavilion to stand outside the small porches – and some kids, over by one of the lorries were leaning against its side and dragging on cigarettes, having a laugh. Squinting, he saw who one of them was: Nick, the kid who'd landed him with this little lot.

Good enough. Simon dropped the tape in its muddle on the ground and ran back to Alex's trailer. So, a bit of a con job, was it? Clobber the new kid. Hold the ends of this while I walk round the corner. If only he'd recognized it, it was the oldest dodge in the world. Well, up his! Like he'd always said, Simon Leighton was a quick learner. He wouldn't get caught like that again.

By daylight the trailer came well short of his idea of home. It had been kitted out for living in, but only just. They needed two cups and saucers, and there they were, all odds and not very clean: the knives looked as if they wouldn't cut cake, and the calor gas stove told its own history of what someone had once cooked in it. There was a salt pot without a top and a pepper pot which said 'salt'. The mattress he and Rose had fallen over was, in fact, two: one for each bunk bed. But one was the wrong size and overhung its frame: while the linen and blankets looked as if the first thing they needed was a good go in the sink. A right load of old tat, Simon thought, and it smelt like the first sorting at a jumble sale.

Meanwhile Alex was putting the crockery away as if it were Royal Doulton. Simon knew this phase in his depression: Alex had been through it all before. In this mood Alex only had to be set off in one direction and he went and carried on going, without a question. But it was a step in the right direction, it was always better than having him sitting and staring, picking at his fingers. The trouble came when he finished – because then you had to find him something else, or back he went into the depths.

Well, at least there'd be plenty to do on the fairground – if all the trouble of getting here was supposed to pay off for Old Man Penfold.

With a small kick of pleasure Simon noticed that the sign-writing gear was there; and it was Alex's stuff, not new. His leather-topped resting stick stood up in a jar like a brown flower in bud; the cleaned and oiled palette looked like a picture in itself, and the brushes were banded together like a thin bouquet, clean and shaped and shining. In a Woolworths box on one of the bed-seats were the special paints: tins of them, all new, and exactly what Alex used. Someone had done a good buying-in job, and gone to a lot of trouble to do it. Only one firm in London made those special signwriters' paints, those rich, thick pastes ground in turpentine, which Simon loved to handle and to smell.

'You're all set up, then?'

'Yes.' He was vigorously removing a tea stain from the handle of one of the cups.

'Got your brushes for the undercoat and the varnish?'

'Yes.' He was frowning at the stubborn stain.

'Go back home, did you, Alex? Back to the house?'

'Yes.' At last he was satisfied and moved on to a saucer.

'Everything all right there?'

'Eh?' Alex frowned at Simon as if he didn't follow.

'The house – it's all right, is it? No one's broke in . . . done the meter, or anything?' *Or taken our picture of Mum*

144

off the wall? Did you notice that big empty patch? Simon wanted to ask.

'No. It's all right.'

So. He hadn't noticed. Well, that was good; he wouldn't be all upset about that. Simon tidied some newspaper wrappings into a plastic ice-cream box which would serve as their bin.

Or had Alex noticed and he just didn't care very much?

What a terrible thing to even think! Simon felt so ashamed with himself he tried to knock his elbow or bang his head as a punishment. But he couldn't quite bring himself to do it, and in the end he settled for the memory of the nettles. He'd already suffered, hadn't he? But, God, between them all they'd really got at him to have him seriously thinking like that!

Doubt. Simon could only sense how it worked, feeding on droppings and growing like a killer disease: but he'd got it, had caught it over the months, and whether he liked it or not he had to face up to it.

Was that how Alex had got to thinking about his mum? Those doubts? Had he had his own unfair thoughts coming uncalled again and again, until he'd stopped seeing things straight that night?

Hell, no! What was up with him? Anyway, that was one of those things he was going to prove – for the Jacksons and Clarks and the two old turds at Parkside! Too right!

A bang on the side rocked the trailer, making him jump. Old Man Penfold pulled the door open and leaned himself in. ''Ere's a pint o' milk, fresh. Dairy's been round, comin' ev'ry mornin', so watch out for 'im tomorrow. Now, son – drinkin' water's over by them changin' rooms. 'Ave some cornflakes . . .' he threw in an opened, rolled-over carton '. . . an' I'll brew you up a mug o' tea. We'll get your gas sorted out when I've built my ride up. An' don't 'ang about, Alex, get over soon as you can an' get started on Tucker's boards. Show 'im what you can do . . .'

Still anxious, Alex immediately started doing as he was told. He took the cornflake carton from Simon and began pouring flakes into two bowls, swamping them in milk.

''Ere, steady on the milk, mate. That's got to do you all day.' Old Man Penfold turned to Simon, as if the boy would understand things better. 'Tucker's got three big rides 'e travels 'imself – 'is Dodgems, 'is Waltzer, an' 'is Ghost Train. Now, the scheme of things is, Alex starts on 'is Dodgems while we're down 'ere: an' if Tucker likes the work we go on with 'im an' get 'is other rides done. After that, it's word o' mouth – we shoot off wi' one of the others an' do a bit for them. There's tons o' work – tractors, trailers, all sorts if we show out well. It's a dying art, this paintin', an' we're cheap this year, sprat to catch a mackerel. But if we fall down on the job, son . . .' Dramatically, the old man fanned his fingers across his windpipe. 'Well, we ain't gonna think about that, eh?'

Simon nodded. He wasn't happy about the 'we'; it was Alex who was going to have to do it all, but he got the point. It was his job, Simon's, to keep Alex in line, look after him and see that he succeeded – like someone minding an unreliable drunk: then they could all travel round in freedom.

'We won't be long,' he said; and the old man went. They hurried, Simon for the occasion, Alex because he couldn't help it. The milk dribbled back into the plates, and for a moment Simon thought of those same sounds at the Lodge, and the prospect of another day at that school to follow, with Jackson and Clark hunting in the yard like hyenas, the other kids treating him like an immigrant, humouring or ignoring, and the waste of time in the classroom on things that had no bearing on his problems or on his life. And he looked past Alex and out of the trailer's window to the gathering of fairground vehicles, the laced and tarpaulined rides, the excitement of what was going to unwrap itself here in this recreation ground and in the weeks to come. Despite the gnawing doubt which he'd be carrying, till certain things were settled, he told himself that this had to be better. A million times better. A whole different life, with him playing a proper part again; with ways of going on which his previous narrow world had never even heard about. Jackson and Clark wouldn't last five minutes here. He spooned in a last mouthful of sweet milk. You had to look on the bright side, he told himself. Whatever else was wrong, this was more like what they wanted.

He took his plate to the shallow bowl and rinsed it, listening with fascination to the waste running through to the plastic bucket beneath. There was a small window here, from which he could see beyond the corner of Old Man Penfold's trailer right across the field to the pavilion where the tap was. A cluster of women and children were there, hobbling with plastic containers and shining steel churns. And Rose – Rose was amongst them, a familiar figure in the huddle of strangers, in the same old dress, the same straight, defiant back. A familiar enough sight to him, but much more like one of them, in the easy way she stood there with her bucket.

And Nick – tricky Nicky – was there. Jack-the-lad, walking across wiping his mouth, heading for a drink of water. Simon couldn't take his eyes off him. He was one of them, too. How well did he know Rose? The scruffy kid walked over to the front of the line as if he owned the field. And just as Simon knew he would, he stopped at Rose. He said something to her, and she answered. Did she laugh? Simon couldn't see from where he was. But he did see him put a grubby hand on her shoulder while he bent his head down and said something in her ear. And she didn't move off, or shove his hand away.

And now her neck! His hand had moved up round the back of her neck. And still she didn't do anything about it.

She listened to what he was saying, that was all, and let it stay there. And then he walked away. He dropped his hand, and swaggered off, over to point at a lorry coming in.

'Simon. Mind that water.'

Alex's voice brought Simon back into the trailer, where his foot had moved the bucket aside and the milky waste was dribbling onto the floor.

'Oh, yeah,' he said. And he went through the motions of putting things right before they both went out to work. But he was all mixed up. One part of him strangely upset by what he'd seen: and another part delighted to see Alex showing some normal reaction at last, even if it was over spilt milk. Like the fair itself, life just now seemed to be all swings and roundabouts.

Jimmy Tucker's Dodgem Ride was an impressive sight, even when it was only taking shape and in obvious need of a repaint. In a taped rectangle bang in the middle of the field, it was being expertly bolted together by a small team of men and boys: two working on the heavy metal plates which formed the ice-rink floor, and two on the pillars and balustrades over which the canvas roof would be spread. Jimmy Tucker himself was busy carefully dropping a heavy electricity cable into a shallow trench which had been dug from the ride to its generator behind the line of trailers. He filled-in as he went, topping it off by replacing the turf that had been expertly removed.

'Hard old ground,' the man said to Alex, scratching under that cap again. 'Still, it's dry – mustn't grumble.'

Alex made no response, and Simon wished his dad could find something to say at times like this: some small bit of chat to make these moments easier. But he stood there in silence, his battered suitcase of painting gear gripped tight in his hand.

'Right, I'll show you your start, then.' Tucker gave a final stamp to a turf and walked briskly over to the ride – a big metal space without its cars. 'You're new to this game, aren't you? I wasn't sure from Charlie Penfold's letter.'

Simon jumped in quickly to the silence he knew Alex would leave. 'Only new to fairs. He's not new to painting and signwriting.'

There was a long, appraising stare from Mr Tucker.

'Well, let's see 'ow you make out. See if it's worth giving space to Penfold's clapped-out old ride. Now – see up there?' He waved his tartan cap at the top of the ride, where the upright pillars met the horizontal battens along the top edge. 'Your top boards sit up there, all highly decorated with my name and the ride's and lots of fancy scroll-work. Sid Flowers 'ad it all winter, but 'e was a sick man at the end. Any'ow I 'ave touched it up and re-varnished the last couple of years, so it ain't as bad as it could be, but it's badly in need of a facelift. See, if your ride don't look smart it don't look safe in this game.' He turned to one of the gang who was bolting a stretch of marbled step to the side. 'Tommy, fetch us out a top board, will you? Get us twenty-one.'

Dropping his spanner, Tommy followed the dug-out trench behind the tractors and came back with a long, thin board, like a section of stage scenery. The back was battered and undercoated, with its place number painted crudely on in white. Along the bottom ran a line of empty bulb holders, and above them the dull and faded EMS of DODGEMS and a meaningless pattern of coloured scrolls.

Tommy laid it flat at Alex's feet. Instantly, Alex was down on his heels, picking at the paint with hard fingernails. Jimmy Tucker put on his cap again and folded his arms, as if he were waiting to see what Alex knew.

Alex seemed to take an age, inspecting – the long, careful look of the expert – but Simon willed him to say something quickly, before Mr Tucker started to think it was all bluff.

At last he straightened up. 'Two ways,' he said to the board on the ground. 'Rub off the worst from each colour, fill-in, put on a new face and varnish.' He looked briefly at Mr Tucker, then back at the board again. 'Or take off the whole surface, make good properly, and repaint from scratch.'

Now it was the Guv'nor who was staring at the board. There was a bit to think about, Simon knew. What if Alex rubbed it all down and then couldn't do a good job with the lettering? That must be in Mr Tucker's mind. That and the time involved, because a proper job was a longer job. But Simon's own reckoning was going on, too. Alex had seemed marvellously confident for those few minutes. That was great. But what if he went back, found he couldn't keep it up, halfway through? They'd all be in the cart, then.

The man kicked the board. 'You keep an eye on Charlie Penfold,' he said, out of the blue. 'All the same, I talk money with him, right? That don't come into it between you an' me.' He scratched his head again.

Alex shrugged. He didn't know about all that, he was saying. All he knew was that he was here, with a job to do. 'Last you longer if I do it properly.' He knelt down again and picked at the flaking.

'All right, do me a board from scratch,' Mr Tucker said suddenly. 'But show us your design first. We can be using the rest, leave one gap at a time – that's the beauty of doin' top boards. Then we'll see . . .' He had already turned away. Some toddlers were playing with his trench. 'Work behind your trailer – or inside Penfold's lorry if it's wet. An' don't forget there's twenty-four of these boards 'fore we even start on the pillars and the gates, so don't 'ang about.' He walked away, stopped, and called back to Tommy. 'The painter's got twenty-one. Put the rest up an' wire across the gap.'

Tommy stopped for a second to show that he understood; then he went on bolting.

The painter. Simon tingled at the sound of the words.

The painter. Suddenly it was as if Alex was back in the real world. He had a job again, a part to play, a place in things – that's what Mr Tucker had made it sound like. Simon picked up the twenty-one board. It was lighter than he'd thought; he could manage that all right. Now the only question was, could Alex manage what he had in his hands? *Could* he pick up his brushes again and paint for his living? That was the first question. And while they found that out, the really big question could be sorted. But first things first: one small step at a time . . .

Simon's neck ached with the twisting. There was so much going on. Across two trestles in front of him lay the top rounding board of Jimmy Tucker's Dodgems; while all about him the showmen's vehicles were moving in to narrow spaces and the build-up of their rides had begun. Between the long, hard rubs at the old paintwork, chipping at the layers of hard varnish, he turned this way and that and tried to take it all in. There was the big, dramatic stuff: the arrival of a modern metal ride that worked off the back of its own loader, the long arms opening out like spiders' legs from their nest on the vehicles' back, ready to whirl people all over the sky. Then there were the small circular goldfish and bingo stalls going up just inside the tape. Up in no time, they were. One minute a bare patch of grass, the next a gaudy attraction of Elvis mirrors and floating ducks. While the side-stuff, as Old Man Penfold called it, the line of rifle galleries, hot dogs and coconuts was going up where you'd expect it to: down the side, just in front of the trailers. And almost as fascinating were the domestic arrangements: the little sentry-box lavatories set in place, the washing hanging out, and the children being called in and fed and ticked-off, just like down any street. It was a new world, a magic, fascinating world – and real, hard work for everyone.

Old Man Penfold and Rose were slogging to get their

own ride up: and by contrast a right tatty old affair it was, too, Simon thought. No wonder their corner of the fairground was well away from the main way in. It seemed unable to make its mind up whether it was a children's ride or something for grown-ups. It was on the small side, badly in need of Alex's services, and all it consisted of was a circular track and a short string of uncomfortable-looking seats, going up a slight slope and disappearing into a stretch of moth-eaten canvas from which the old words TUNNEL OF LOVE were fading. The small seats had old-fashioned cars painted on their outside edges, out-of-date vehicles, not vintage, and across the entrance the uncertain, spindly, lettering said AUTODROME – *The modern thrill*. Well, it would be a wonder if many people paid good money to ride on that, Simon thought. If you wanted a quick kiss in that holey dark you'd bash your teeth out, sitting on those bone-shaking wooden seats. Against the other favourites going up – the Disco Waltzer with its revolving armchairs, the Demon Whip, the Big Wheel which was just pulling onto the ground – Penfold's Autodrome stood no chance. No wonder the Penfolds needed Alex to buy themselves in.

And Alex was doing his stuff. He hadn't said a word after setting Simon to work with the coarse sandpaper, but he'd pulled out of his case a big roll of signwriters' tracing paper, and organizing himself on a separate trestle with a paperhanger's board to work on, he'd started tracing a new design for the twenty-one board: the EMS of DODG-EMS and some fancy patterning. It was hard to tell in the soft pencil, but it looked all right from what Simon could see of it; and at least Alex was getting on. No jokes, like the old days; no radio playing through the morning; just a worried frown and an obsessive movement of the pencil arm. Relax, Simon wanted to say; take it easy; *enjoy* designing it. But the work went feverishly on, till the sound of hot fat from a nearby trailer told Simon that they had to eat sometime. He had no idea what time it was, nor what time they'd arrived, nor woken, nor started their fairground life. He didn't even know the day of the week for sure. But then time was for the Welfare's world not theirs.

All the same, he was ready for some food. He mentioned it to Alex, but Alex didn't respond, so he went over to find Old Man Penfold. The old man was supposed to be looking after them, wasn't he? So were they with him, or independent now? If they were on their own they'd need some money.

''Ow's it goin'? Alex made a start?' Old Man Penfold got his own anxiety in first.

Simon told him, and asked about the chances of something to eat.

'Good idea, boy, good idea.' He seemed pleased with Simon's report, relaxing on a balustrade to wipe his glistening head. 'I'll fix up the cookers tonight, an' Rose can do a bit o' shopping this afternoon. Don't worry, boy, we'll eat all right. Meantime there's a cut loaf in my trailer. You an' Rose knock us up some cheese sarnies, eh? Bit o' pickle on mine. An' a drop of water for now. We'll brew up later.'

As if from nowhere, Rose came out of the Tunnel of Love. She didn't say a word – just threw down the wrench she'd been using and walked off to the trailer, leaving Simon to follow. Without bothering to wash her hands, she scraped round a carton of margarine and covered eight slices of bread. She threw a lump of hard-edged cheese at Simon, who cut it and laid it on the slices, giving a spreading of pickle to them all. He kept his elbows well in, inhibited by the big dog which lay on one of the seats. It might look a bit drowsy, but all dogs were ready to bite you, he'd assumed that all his life. But making the best of it, he used the beast as a way in to the conversation he badly wanted with Rose.

'Nice old dog. What's his name?'

153

'Tempest.' She was as offhand again as ever she'd been. 'Bet he's travelled round a lot.'

No reply – just a rewrapping of the remains of the bread.

'Expect you know all these people, do you, from travelling round?'

'Some of 'em.'

'Who's that bloke, Nick?'

'Who?'

'That kid with the tape. Over by the tap.'

'Oh, 'im. One of the boys.'

'Old mate of yours, is he?'

'Never met 'im before. Trav'lin' wi' Tucker.'

Simon spooned a double spread of pickle on the last slice. Never met him before! And she'd stood there and calmly let him put his dirty hand round her neck? He was shocked. What was up with her, hadn't she got any pride?

''Ere y'are, these are your'n.' She scooped up two of the sandwiches on her dirty palm and breezed off out of the trailer. Simon picked his up under the suspicious gaze of Tempest and followed Rose out quickly, firmly shutting the door. In his own trailer he poured two cups of water from the plastic container and finally got the frugal lunch to Alex.

The paper design was coming on well. Alex had altered the styling of the lettering to give it a bolder, more modern look, but at the same time he'd kept it in the fairground tradition: familiar without being fussy. The new scroll, too, gave more of a feeling of speed to the design. It looked all right, Simon thought, and he said so. Perhaps it just lacked the real flair Alex could show at times.

Meanwhile Alex worked feverishly on, ignoring the sandwiches, which he left to go hard on the plate. And working out another of his own devils now, Simon matched him for effort. God, they'd get through a lot of work – and kill themselves – if they took the next six months at this pace!

But Alex and Simon didn't have a monopoly on hard work. Build-up Thursday, with the fair opening on the following night, wasn't a time for getting out deck-chairs, even if a showman happened to possess one. It was all go – not the frantic, feverish activity of the Leightons – but the steady one-job-after-another methodical routine of travelling showmen, where each trip between the transport and the ride was perfected for time and motion in a way that men with stop watches could never do. Their very walks seemed to say it was their own time, their own motion, and everything had its order and its place. Gradually, like this, the fair took shape. It wasn't gigantic – not the sort Simon would have often seen arriving for Bank Holiday on one of the London commons: more a country fair with four or five big rides, a few more children's roundabouts, and a scattering of hooplas. The side-stuff round the edge had one or two gaps in it, and some of the lorries had tarpaulined equipment on them which wasn't unpacked. But in the late afternoon, as the perimeter of tall trees gathered and held the gloom in their thin fingers, there was an excitement about it all as tangible as the diesel smoke. With his disappointment at Rose worked out through his muscles, Simon's stomach was stirred as the first flickering lights were tried on, and the first blare of raucous pop travelled across the ground. Local kids started cycling aimlessly round, and passed near enough with their big eyes to give Simon a professional feel of belonging to this other world.

The light was just beginning to be lost when Jimmy Tucker came over to Alex's trailer. Guv'nor or not, he hadn't stopped all day, either; he hadn't shaved or changed.

Simon stood back. His board was ready, rubbed down, the cracks filled-in with plastic wood, and one layer of a mixed primer and undercoat applied. Alex's design was almost complete, with just one or two areas left which needed their colours pencilled in.

When the man came, Alex stood off it and put his hands in his pockets. Mr Tucker crouched and looked along the surface of Simon's board. He ran a finger along a smoothed edge. He stood it on its side and eyed it for true; then he cuffed Simon lightly round the head 'Done well,' he said. Now Alex's design. Strange, Simon thought, how he'd come to him first. Strange, and pleasing. The man walked to the spread paper, squinting, and backed away again. Once more he approached it. 'Yeah, that'll do. Don't 'ang about, will you? Now, where's that Charlie . . .?' And he'd gone, on to his next worry. No overwhelming praise for Alex or his new design, no discussion about it, even. Just, 'That'll do.' But Alex didn't seem to be bothered about that. He didn't seem to expect more. Perhaps that's what it's like, Simon thought: people take it as read that you'll do a good job when you're a craftsman: just pay you and feel they've done enough. All the same, a bit of a good word for old Alex wouldn't have been out of order today.

'Paint it tomorrow,' Simon told him. 'You won't see the colours proper, tonight. Tell you what, though, we're going to need two boards off at a time, aren't we? One for you, painting, one for me, preparing, if we're going to get on.'

Alex looked at Simon's board. He nodded. 'Thicken up your undercoat with emulsion next time. Else this'll drink up the top coat.'

'O.K.' Like walking along a high, narrow wall, Simon felt shivery with Alex's show of interest in what he was doing. This was better than he could have hoped for, first off: but how long before there was a slip? How long before they came a cropper? That was the feeling. Could it possibly last long enough to keep these people happy?

Well, there was one way to help avoid unnecessary upset

tomorrow. 'I'll go over and get another board, eh? Before they get them all up: put 'em both in Penfold's lorry.'

'If you like.' Alex was rolling up his crackling design, fast and furious again, half-running to the trailer to put it inside.

Simon left him and walked, business-like, through a gap between two empty arcades, round a hoopla being fitted with neon strips, and across to the Dodgems in the middle. Mr Tucker's 'Done well' still rang secretly in his ear, and his longer paces measured his greater sense of belonging on the site.

With a slight falter of dismay he saw that all the top boards were up – LATEST CONTINENTAL CARS they read, JIMMY TUCKER'S MODERN DODG . . ., the gap was wired across, and a lone figure at the top of a pair of steps was already putting the last of the bulbs into the holders. Should he go back and leave this till morning? No, he decided – if he had it tonight he could start rubbing it down first thing, and anyway the next board had to come down sometime. And this bloke was up there handy with the steps.

''Scuse me, I'm from the painter . . .'

'Eh?' the figure twisted round. It was grimy Nick. He stared at Simon. 'Oh, it's you, is it?' Slowly and deliberately he came down the steps, something about his movement which Simon recognised, made him want to turn and run. 'Got me a ruckin', 's'mornin', you did, clearin' off. Dropped me in it, you did.' He stood there nodding his head.

'Sorry. Had to get back on my own job.' Even as he said it Simon was cross with himself for apologizing. But the kid was bigger than he was.

'Oh, yeah? What job's that then, big man?' He had that same open-mouthed, tantalizing look which Simon knew so well: Jackson and Clark, Ear-ring, they all had it. God, there was always one of these wherever you went.

'Painting. We're painting all these boards. For Mr Tucker . . .'

'Oh, for Mr Tucker.' He made the way Simon had said it sound very childish. 'Are you now? An' what's your name, baby boy?'

'Leighton.'

'*Leighton?* Christ! Leighton what?' He laughed without any hint of being amused: just the usual riling.

'Leighton nothing. Simon Leighton.'

The kid laughed once more, cuffing his nose. 'What's your old lady call you? "Simple", I bet a million. "Simple, you got a pimple"!'

'No!'

'So what you want, Simple Simon? What you over 'ere for, 'olding me up?'

'That next board.' Simon pointed to it. 'We need two at a time.'

'Oh, do you? That's news to me. Junior told us to fix it up the way it is. An' we've done it. Are you saying diff'rent?'

'No – it's just he wants them done as quick as we can, and I just thought . . .'

'Oh, did you? Well, don't. I do what the Guv'nor says, not some stupid little Simple Simon . . . An' any'ow . . .'

But Simon wasn't hanging around to be told any more by this character. He turned and ran back towards Alex while Nick spat loudly from the top of his steps.

Kids! People! Was the whole world like this, outside? Because it was a bloody rotten look-out if it was. Or was it him? he suddenly wondered. Was there something about him which seemed to rub people up the wrong way all the time? Had those months looking after Alex like the grown-up in the house turned him into some sort of horrible little know-all. A cocky kid everyone came to hate?

Cocky or not, though, he'd keep Alex in the dark about what had happened. There was no need to worry him with it. Fortunately by the time he got back Old Man Penfold had connected up the dirty little cooker to a bottle of Calor gas, and Rose had left some eggs and bacon on the table, so there was plenty for him to do without saying much to Alex at all.

And there was always something else to get used to, to occupy your mind. Now it was him and Alex being on top of one another the way they were. Back at the house, like at the Lodge, it had been dead easy to hide in your own private thoughts. Now Simon wished he'd nicked a paperback from the bedroom. He tried some uphill chat about the day's work and tomorrow's tasks, but nothing much lasted longer than a word or two, and neither of them went anywhere near the important issues, nor even over what they'd been up to, apart. The big question that had grown every day inside his brain would have to wait for a more favourable time to be asked, Simon knew. So it was as if nothing had happened to either of them between living in Market Junction and coming here. Meanwhile, he and Alex got in one another's silent way – cooking, eating, and washing-up – till in the end Simon yawned and grasped at the chance to suggest bed.

He silenced the hiss of the Calor light, and by the over-spill from other windows they stripped to their pants and slid chilly into Old Man Penfold's creased-up sheets.

'Night, Alex.'

'Night.'

But sleep was quite another matter. Only too well, Simon knew how Alex was lying there, staring up into the gloom; while his own agitated mind had a lot to sort out again before it was prepared to let his body rest.

That pig Nick – treating him like a heap of something nasty on the ground, and going round treating Rose as if she was one of his fairground tarts. And what about Rose herself – back with her own? Where was the special Rose he'd run off with? Where was the Rose who'd once come out of Whipps Cross hospital a new baby: or who'd been all nervous and natural with him when she'd gone into the nettles? And what had she said? 'In for a penny, in for a pound': just like his mum when she'd been buoying herself up: and looking just like his mum standing with her arms across her in the picture. That was a Rose who existed somewhere; someone special, just to him.

He was uncomfortable, suddenly hot in bed, and he had to scratch his fading rash. He tried to switch Rose off and think about Alex's small, unspectacular progress; about the big talk he knew was hanging over them. But he kept coming back to that moment by the nettles. There was an image there he couldn't dislodge: something he didn't want to lose. Until all at once, so that he didn't know it, like a toddler on a late night out, he went off – a kid in someone's arms at a Sunday night bus stop, awake one minute, unconscious the next – with a thumb not far from his mouth and one dusty foot hanging out from his bed.

8

Denny Adams sat back in a Darenth Lodge armchair like a man with the day off, released for a while from the round of school complaints, court appearances, and difficult home visits. Here, with most of the residents at school, a cup of coffee in the Warden's office was hot and uninterrupted – and Rick always seemed prepared to listen to the older man's stories.

'So I caught old Cowling as he came out of the house,' the Welfare wheezed, 'the old woman's claiming he's not living with her and there he was going off to work in her Escort!' He laughed and rubbed his chin. 'Tried to tell me he was picking it up to give it a service. That time of the morning!' He sipped at his mug, delicately. 'It's worth getting up early sometimes. That's one meals and clothing grant I can tear up.' His shoes shone in the middle of the room, his serviceable blue raincoat giving the impression of a Petty Officer in the Watch Room, relaxed but alert to duty. He could still spring to his feet quicker than most.

But Rick Bayne, up most of the night, looked ready to turn in. His tired moccasins flopped while his weary voice told its tale of the small hours.

'So they've gone,' he yawned at the end. 'No sign of them anywhere.'

'Neat little trick,' Denny Adams smiled. 'Got to hand it to them. Haven't heard of that one being used since just after I came out of the navy. One of these travelling people pulled it, when we were cracking down on the A13 gypsies.'

'Oh, so it's a known trick, is it?' Rick asked. 'I didn't know – thought they'd been poisoned by school dinners at first. Oh!' he was more awake now. 'That'd be Rose, then, wouldn't it?'

'You can bet your pension. Anyway, I've called at the Leighton house, no reply, and Penfold's yard is all packed up and gone off for the summer. I've been on the phone to Stonelands. No sign of our Alex. Went out for a drive yesterday with a bloke sounding remarkably like friend Penfold, 'phoned in to say they couldn't get back.' His mobile face creased in a hundred appreciative wrinkles. 'Well planned little run, eh?'

Rick wasn't so amused. 'Makes me look a right berk, though, doesn't it?' He lit a cigarette with a clunky lighter. 'There's a few who'd like to see this place closed as it is.'

Like passing a hand over his face Denny Adams became concerned again. 'Informed the police, have you?'

'Oh, sure. Soon as Ruth went in for a late check and found their beds with blankets in. Usually I give it a couple of hours, go to a few likely places with the Transit: but this kid's done it before – and his grandparents are a right stroppy pair. Wanted my guts for garters last time.'

Denny Adams put his mug down and wrote a note to himself in his pocket book. 'As far as I can see you've done all you can, Rick. You're not running a prison, are you? The Council don't provide you with bars on the windows and locks on the doors. If kids want to walk out they can walk out. Besides,' he winked, 'we know what they're up to. Gone off on the road, all four of them. We're not after two kids on their own legging it to Gretna Green to get married. And Old Penfold's no more a hardened criminal than our Alex is. Interim care orders for non-school attendance – we weren't exactly rescuing them from dens of vice. Leave it to me. I'll inform the court officer this afternoon. He's an old mate of mine . . .'

'O.K., Denny. Thanks. All the same . . .'

The Welfare got up to go. 'Listen, do you know how many people there are missing from home these days?

Salvation Army deal with six thousand. Kids disappeared on their own, parents frantic or couldn't care less, grown-ups done a runner ... Your two aren't going to cause much of a ripple. If we're lucky some lad in a Panda somewhere might just be in the right place at the right time, giving a fairground the once over.' He laughed at the improbability. 'But no one else is losing any sleep. If I were you I'd hit my hammock for an hour.'

'Wish I could,' Rick stretched.

'Well don't let this get you down. If you lose the sleep I shall over this, you'll have a good night tonight.' His face moved in a confident wink: then buttoning his raincoat and closing the door firmly behind him Denny Adams went out, back to his world of real parasites and children at risk.

Simon had rarely felt so much at risk as he did the next morning, walking across the fairground front to Jimmy Tucker's Dodgems. Alex had got up with the birds and the light, so anxious to make a start that he'd ignored food and drink, and would have ignored a wash if Simon hadn't pulled himself out of his own bed to persuade him. He still seemed tense and obsessive, and Simon hadn't bothered him about the other board; it hadn't been mentioned; he'd left Alex to it, setting up his trestles in the cold dew, and walked as confidently as he could across the front to Mr Tucker – and to Nick.

It was the usual mix of anxieties in Simon's stomach: a fairground ride of feelings of concern for himself rolling round with his worries about Alex. He looked at one of the big, modern rides: a huge revolve with four pairs of seats set to spin madly at the end of each of its three huge arms. That about summed up his inside, Simon thought. The Twist. The Cyclone Twist! Was Nick going to be there to block him, to put him down in front of whoever wanted to listen? Was Alex starting to miss his tablets?

And was Rose up and about yet – if so, who'd be making free with their hands round her today? Because it needn't just be Nick. For this new life to succeed, here or at any other place they'd run to, they needed work; and work meant people, and people meant lots of Nicks being about – in Wales, in Ireland, in Scotland – wherever. The Jacksons, the Clarks, the Ear-rings, the Nicks – they were all the same menace with lots of different, ugly, faces, and they were all over the world.

But that wasn't all. Wherever the two of them went, and this was the strongest inside twist of all, there would always be the nagging doubt about Alex and his mum to sort out. That had got to be done for both their sakes: and that could be the hardest thing of all.

Within a few strides, though, he found one consolation: there was no Nick to worry about just yet. Mr Tucker, yes; he was there, looking like yesterday, as if he'd slept in that cap, sorting something out in the Dodgem pay box: but no sign of Nick. Simon ran to get to the man before anyone else could get to Simon. The door at the back was open.

''Ello son. Up bright and early! Wish I could get my Jack-the-lads up, something like. Bang on their trailer before eight an' all you get for an answer is snoring an' wind.' He swivelled on his operator's chair. 'Put a budgie in there an' 'e'd die, I swear it.'

The man didn't seem in any hurry to find out what Simon wanted; he seemed happy enough to be passing the prime time of day, sorting out a leather money pouch, trying to slide an aluminium strip through a series of slits in the neck.

'Big eyes, son, big eyes. All new to you, all this, ain't it? Well – I'll tell you what we've got 'ere.' He sat back and cleared his throat, as if he were giving a television interview, and enjoying it. 'The dying skills of old England.' His hand rested on a big, brass arm with a cloth-wrapped handle. 'This is the 'andle regulates the flow of juice. Full on, half, and off.' He ran it round its shiny arc. 'Extension of me, this is. There's my record deck, up there, and 'ere's my mike.' Then he held up the bag in his hand like a fisherman's catch. 'This is where the day's takings go, for running down the bank after closing. Night safe. And this –' he took a stubby truncheon which was dangling down by his knee and smacked it hard into his palm '– this is what keeps my takings still my takings till I get 'em to our friend, Nat. West.' He flipped his cap and laughed at Simon's face, as if at knowing what had made his eyes so big; a glimpse at the secrets of fairground life.

'So, what can I do for you, son?'

Simon explained. He was quick to tell the man that Alex had made a start already, and how they'd be a lot more efficient from now on if they would have two boards over at the trailer instead of one.

'Makes sense,' Mr Tucker said. 'But just the two. Like I told you yesterday, if we don't look something near the mark we don't look safe. An' we wanna look safe, 'cos we are safe.' He got up and came out of his pay-box, careful to shut the door behind him. 'I'll get you this one down myself, won't 'old you up. Then we're right, eh? You only need one at a time after this.'

'Yes, that's right.' Simon watched him fetch the steps, unbolt the next board, and took it from him as he handed it down. And only when the light bulbs off it were back in their cardboard box did the moment seem right for the next, important, question.

'Where is this place, anyhow?'

'Where is it? Don't you know? Higham. Midway 'tween Gravesend an' Rochester. Nice little family date to start off the season. 'Ad the licence 'ere for twenty years or more, my family.'

Simon had only a vague idea where Rochester was, but he'd heard of it. It sounded a bit civilized: and he wasn't too happy about that. The idea they'd been sold on was being buried in the depths of country lanes, not setting themselves up in easy reach of the Welfare and some nosy policeman.

'Oh, Rochester. Here till Sunday, aren't we?'

''S'right. then a nice couple o' days to pull down an' over near Maidstone for Easter. That's traditional, too. Very good week-end if the weather's reasonable. They'll even keep Charlie's Autodrome a bit busy over there.'

Simon just nodded. This morning he didn't particularly want to be drawn into a talk about Old Man Penfold and his problems, because that could only lead to talk about him and Alex – and the two of them were still very much on trial.

'Well, let's get about it. Let's get ourselves a bit of work done. Come six o'clock tonight we'll 'ave to 'ave things really 'umming . . .'

Alex was busy already when Simon got back, and drawing a bit of a crowd. It made a change for Simon's stomach to flip with a thrill as he saw an old lady, a little girl and a dog watching Alex at work. The rich showman's colours were going on like oil-based velvet: a blue just deeper than royal for background, a flamboyant yellow, burning like the sun, for lettering, and a liquid black line to edge each area of colour. There was no 'What is it?' watching this artist at work: simply, 'Be nice, something like that, wouldn't it, Peg?' And Simon felt pleased. Other jobs would soon line themselves up.

A special time of day like early morning soon becomes everyone's to share, and by the time Simon was halfway through rubbing off the worst of the second board the whole fairground was about. He kept an eye open for Rose, ready to smile at her, to milk a smile back if he could; he even had a phrase running over and over in his head, ready to say to her. 'How you feeling? No more nettle rash?' Not serious, yet reminding her of their special experience together: something which might just re-open that closed door. But when he saw her at last she was in the distance, working on the ride, and only Old Man Penfold had the time to stop and throw a few words at them.

The chilly sun, like a light behind a white sheet, was spread overhead, dentist's bright, when the crisis suddenly came. One minute it was all sandpaper and paint, and the next a police Panda car, as quiet and as stealthy as a cat, was inching over the bumps at the rear of the trailers and stopping at a spot where people were neither up their ladders nor walking about with loads in their hands, where Simon and Alex seemed to be just who it was looking for.

The first Simon knew, concentrating on smoothing-in some filling, came with a quiet click of the car door. Unsuspecting, he looked up and saw the tall figure with the white winter face, the chequer-banded cap, the no-nonsense uniform and the black gloves. Simon's hand froze, his breathing stopped where it was for a second, his legs seemed to run into the ground like columns of water, all before he could fight his mouth into a smile. He leaned on the board; too much show of confidence, and only a warning crack stopped him from splintering it into halves.

'A busy lad. Well, well. Well, well.'

The same old cat with the same small mouse; but older, lawful, this menace. God, what did he want? Were they found out already – before they'd even got started? Simon looked across at Alex, who blinked at the figure in blue and calmly went back to outlining his speeding comets as if he'd merely glanced up at a lamp-post.

'This your dad, is it?'

'Yeah.'

'And where are you from, son?'

The Cyclone Twist again. Jesus Christ, what did he say to that? Tell a lie? Or would the policeman be expecting a lie, so he comes out with the truth?

Alex was carrying on his painting like a man with no

time to spare for anything, as if neither Simon nor the policeman existed, his concentration intense on the swift tip of the fine black brush. He could have been in an operating theatre doing something tricky, with ears and eyes for no one till he could stand back off the job. There was no help coming from him.

After what seemed an age Simon mumbled, 'London.' That was vague enough, he thought. See what the man asked next.

'What's your name?'

Simon stared at him suspiciously, desperately playing for time now; an obvious stare, though, the way he reckoned any fairground kid would react to a nosy copper. But he knew his name would pinpoint him surely enough, if word had been put out by the Welfare. What the hell was he going to say?

'Oh, come on, you can tell 'im Billy. You ain't never been ashamed o' being Billy Flowers before!'

It was Rose, sauntering round from her trailer, as composed and confident as someone telling the truth.

'Best fair painters on the road, an' proud of it.' She swaggered over to Alex and drooped an arm round his shoulder. 'Comin' on a treat, i'n it?' she asked the policeman.

The policeman looked at Rose long and hard, and then at the gleaming board. 'Yeah, looks all right to me,' he said. 'But then my cats always look like pigeons.'

Rose threw her head back and laughed. They all laughed, except Alex, who tried to keep on working under Rose's pressure.

'Any'ow, can I 'elp you? Who you lookin' for?'

'Mr Tucker?' He took a scrap of paper out of his top pocket and checked it. 'Mr J. Tucker, the licensee.'

'Oh, Junior. 'E's over there. The Dodgems. 'E'll be there, or there about . . .'

'Ta, love.' The policeman took a last look at Alex's work.

'Yes, very nice,' he said, and he strode off in Jimmy Tucker's direction.

Simon was overwhelmed with a mad desire to throw his arms round Rose then and there: but a freezing look kept him where he was.

'Get lost!' she hissed at him. 'Lose yourself in that trailer till 'e's gone. An' keep your 'ead down.'

There was going to be no second telling – and none needed. Simon bolted inside and shut the door on himself.

Rose turned on Alex. 'An' you keep on paintin', Sid Flowers!'

His heart thudding, but filled with admiration at the way Rose had dealt with the situation, Simon found a place where he could keep himself well back from the curtained window but still see the police car and the girl; and he tried to make his nervous, shaking reactions steady themselves. God, that had been a close call. He'd had such a ridiculous name in his head – his favourite other name for games where he played himself at something – Roger Watson, his own second name, and his mother's before she married Alex. A dead giveaway that could have been, too, to anyone suspicious enough to check. But as it was, Rose had made it all sound so natural – so right.

They weren't out of the nettles, yet, though. The policeman had to come back, and drive himself away. But Rose was still playing her confident, nothing-to-hide part, circling the man's Panda car and bossing into it like any normal, nosy, kid. As long as Alex didn't do or say anything stupid they still stood a fair chance . . .

There wasn't long to wait. Having checked on the licence, or delivered it, or whatever he'd been sent to do, the policeman strolled back to his car, his eyes still everywhere – but clearly bent on going. He'd got his car keys out.

Rose played her part to the full, though. She could have disappeared, too, by now, Simon thought: but there she was, leaning on the Panda's bonnet and looking at the policeman with her big brown eyes. She had nothing to hide, she seemed to be saying; quite the opposite.

'You comin' up the fair tonight?' she asked him.

He stopped with his hand on the door and gave her a knowing smile. 'Oh, I don't know about that.'

Rose waved a bare arm at the board Alex was still painting, and then vaguely at the rides on the front. 'We've got a ride an' all. I'll give you a free go.'

'Thanks very much, love. But I get sick on rides.'

'What, on the Tunnel of Love? Poor ol' you!'

'That specially.' He laughed.

God, she was chancing her arm! What the hell was she up to now?

'Now, if you'll move out the way, young lady, I've got work to do.'

Rose stood off the bonnet and put her hands on her hips, looking for a moment like a gypsy dancer. 'Oh, you spoil sport!'

Smiling at her, the policeman got into his car and shut the door. He wound his window down and called out at her. 'Come on, game's over. Get out of the way, I'm going now.'

Rose pouted at him like a bad loser. But she didn't move, and the policeman turned his key in the ignition.

He had left it in gear. Trying to go, it jolted him, jerked forward and stalled, centimetres from Rose. She jumped, and laughed. The policeman swore – and Rose ran off, waving to him cheekily before she disappeared behind her trailer. Red with confusion, the policeman looked all round and pulled very carefully away, over the tufts towards the gate of the recreation ground. But Simon's relief at seeing him go wasn't what it should have been. As usual these days it was eaten into by something else. What about that Rose, flaunting herself at him like that? What did she think she was up to? Was she ill in the head or something

– or was she just one of those girls who had to flirt at a uniform – pushing herself at him till she nearly got run over for her pains? And what about Alex? How was he? Almost as quickly as he'd bolted in, Simon rushed out the trailer to see how Alex had taken the drama.

Not well. He was hunched over the board with a pool of black spreading itself as thick as an oil slick over the smooth blue background.

'Quick, Alex! Turps!' Simon moved fast, he swamped the black, dabbed and wiped, and by moving fast he prevented too much damage from being done. Quickly, he put the board near enough back to rights, ready for a fresh touch-in of background blue as soon as it had dried.

But the damage to Alex was of another sort, not likely to be made good with any sort of speed.

'What's up, Alex?'

Alex was hunched over the trestle-end like someone at a desk, staring at his own ruin set out there before him. His long hair, his stubble even, seemed hang-dog; he was breathing in and out like a choking case on a respirator.

'What's up?' Unable to reach his shoulders, Simon put an arm round his waist, and beneath the droop of a scruffy pullover Simon felt the sobs in the thin muscles.

It was a long time before Alex was prepared to say anything: it was as if he was fighting not to make his misery public. Why? Because it might hurt? Shock? Because no one would understand?

'What's up, Alex?' Simon walked away, came back, squeezed him again. 'Tell me. You can tell me.'

And then at last Alex was prepared to give. Shaking, he twisted inside the arm around him and pointed at the spot where the car had been, and Rose.

'The c . . . car,' he said. 'Nearly hit her.'

Simon soothed. 'Yeah,' he said. 'I saw, Alex . . .'

'Like . . .' And Alex had gone. He'd brushed Simon

aside with a bony strength and yanked the door open to get into the gloom of the trailer.

So. That was it. Like with Simon's mum, the car had leapt. And Alex had taken it bad. Simon sighed, body deep. He looked down at the drying board. He looked over at the trailer, and wondered whether it was just his imagination or was it really rocking? He looked up – and there was Mr Tucker striding over towards him.

Not now! Why couldn't he leave them alone? Now was just the moment to go to Alex. Now was so dead right for their crucial conversation it wasn't true. But nothing worked out, did it? Not even after a disaster like this.

Whistling a tune he neither knew nor felt, Simon picked up a medium brush, and quickly started to apply a covering coat of blue to the accident.

The first coloured lights like indoors out, the diesel drone of generators out of sight, the competing rhythms of roped-up speakers with eerie shrieks and siren wails – this was the fairground Simon prowled amongst the early visitors. All around him were the sights and sounds of normal people: small hands ringing fire-bells, clutching candy-floss; bigger hands cocking rifles and pinging at little metal men; and old hands simply holding, guiding and pulling back. He saw fathers finding forgotten skills, cautiously eyeing remembered thrills; saw youths standing up where they should have sat and bumping instead of dodging. And drawing every other glance, taller than the spire behind the trees, the Big Wheel spun its excitement over the village and pulled the people in.

Simon felt lost and useless in this crowd. He wasn't strolling round with his mum and dad; he wasn't mucking about with a bunch of his own, dawdling past the girls and making remarks; and he wasn't working one of the rides. Not that he fancied what some of the fairground kids his age were doing: standing cold and bored in front of rows of hanging goldfish, or offering a hand of darts to anyone within reach. No – what would really have taken his mind off Alex tonight was a bit of the real Jack-the-lad stuff, balancing on the up-and-down boards of the Disco Waltzer, spinning those seats and making the girls scream: or hanging on the backs of Dodgem cars, taking fares and getting them back to the pay-box like a bullfighter. Some job like that might help him lose the thought of Alex, hunched up in the dark trailer, picking at his fingers again. He needed something. This run to the fair had been the last resort, was supposed to be the answer to all his problems, a time to set the right mood for their vital talk. Instead of which, here they were back where they started. So what did you do? Simon asked himself. Where did you go from here? Was this the stage where adults turned to drink?

The Dodgems were getting busy; just a few cars left with their plastic covers on. But Simon's first look was up at the boards, where the first of the finished jobs was already in place. Like the first strip of new wallpaper it looked nothing without another to match it, but there it was, the new end of DODGEMS, fresh and shining beneath its hardening varnish. Mr Tucker had liked it; this time he'd said so, looking over Simon's shoulder as Alex's accident was covered up. But just as you'd expect out of this rotten life, Alex had been nowhere near to hear it.

Nick was at the Dodgems, of course, lounging against a pillar while a ride neared its end, giving all his attention to a cigarette.

What was up with him? Simon wondered. What made him the way he was? He'd done Nick no real harm, only shown him he wasn't a soft touch.

He kicked his feet on again, over towards Old Man Penfold's quiet corner. It was embarrassing by the Autodrome. If anyone gave the ride a second glance all they could see was its uncomfortable tattiness. The old man stood ready to help people into seats, but no one went, the scratchy music jumped, and Rose sat smoking in the pay-box looking bored out of her mind. Was this really what she lived the rest of the year for? What was she all about? What had grown that hardness on her like a shell? Why the sudden shameless behaviour with the policeman? What had changed her from being the real Rose he'd seen into this dead-eyed creature? He suddenly stopped walking. Would he go the same way, too? Would a few more weeks of this start the change in him, begin the hardening that seemed to happen to everyone else?

Someone bumped into him, bought him back with a silent swear. Anyway, what to do tonight? Old Man Penfold didn't need a hand – he had thought he might offer – and he couldn't face the prospect of the rest of the evening cooped up in the trailer with Alex, not yet. So that left just mooching on round the fair, envying everyone he could see: the kids with families, the kids out with friends, even a kid in a wheelchair, the centre of a cluster of attention. He felt himself frowning, biting at a fingernail. God, he was getting in a state!

By some strange magnetism, or perhaps by the cunning of Jimmy Tucker's fair plan, Simon found himself back at the Dodgems. The cars were grinding down to another halt.

'Next ride, please. Pay in the car. One way only, no bumping.'

Well, there was something he could do to take his mind off everything. Impulsively, Simon stepped onto the metal floor and climbed into one of the cars. A green, number twelve. He squeezed his fingers into a tight pocket for one of the crumpled notes Old Man Penfold had given him for food. One go, he'd have. A little bit of fun. Well, he'd earned that, hadn't he? He saw Nick looking at him, and he was ready with an answer for when he came over to get his money. But Nick didn't. He went to someone else, and another big kid came for his pound and brought the change back from the pay-box.

Had Nick decided to call a truce, then? He could easily have made something nasty out of collecting his money.

There was a small tingle of excitement in the waiting to go. Simon looked around him, saw where the other cars were, and made his mind up where he'd go when they all started. He was going to try to miss everyone, see if he could get through the whole ride with less than ten touches. That'd test his skill, give him an aim. Straight ahead first, he decided. There was a nice gap between two others he could just squeeze through, a man with a little girl in one car and two kids about his own age fighting over who was going to steer in the other. He gripped the wheel like a Monte Carlo starter: round the houses. Any second now and the sparks would fly at the top of those poles and he'd be off, into the first corner. In spite of himself he felt a small thrill. It had been a long time since he'd played at anything.

'Fasten your belts for safety and comfort,' Mr Tucker crackled. Simon fixed the loop of leather under his right armpit. He took up his grip on the wheel again. Hold it dead straight for two metres, then throw it to the left. Go into the first corner with a bit of room to spare. He pressed the easy accelerator right down to the floor, ready for the power to surge on. Looking over at the pay-box he saw Mr Tucker hand out some change to Nick, then reach down to his right where the big brass handle was. Ready. Steady.

Go! There was a crackle of sparks. Everyone jerked forward. And Simon, holding his steering wheel rigid, shot sharp to the right and thudded the car into the side. Smack into the sprung surround. What a show-up! The wheels had been left hard locked to the right by the last driver and Simon had assumed they were set straight ahead.

Blast! And who was coming over to push him off with a casual foot and a cocky leer? Nick!

'Wassup, Simple? Want 'and with your steerin'? You *are* old enough to be on this on your own?'

Simon swore at him, and Nick laughed: the start of the tensest, bumpiest, longest ride in a Dodgem car he'd ever had in his life. Not even as a little kid had he longed so much for a ride to finish. And when it did, after crash upon crash, he was out of the car before it had stopped rolling, legging it over the creaking marbled steps before Nick could shout anything else after him.

It was rock bottom. The big show-up. Five minutes of public embarrassment, all because he wasn't thinking straight any more. And why wasn't he? he asked himself as he fled. Why wasn't this run to the fair working the way it should? Was it because nothing could?

The fairground was in full swing now, there was no walking in a straight line any more. The generators were pulsing full pelt behind the front, revving up hard when their different rides began, and the air was thick with diesel. There was light everywhere, and the shrieks and shouts were the sound of the fairground breathing.

The trailer was claustrophobic, warm with Alex's long presence. Simon made him out, lying weak and awake on his bed, and at first he tiptoed about, keeping up a pretence. Then all at once, damn it, that seemed to be just about enough! Shaken and upset himself, he was more concerned with his own feelings than with Alex's tonight. So he came out with it, just like that. He'd waited a long time for this conversation, and now it was happening right here, this minute – and because it was coming out of the blue, starting it wasn't nearly as hard as he'd imagined.

'It was Mum, wasn't it? With that car today. That's what's getting at you.'

'Eh?'

Alex was pretending to come out of sleep. Playing for

time! God, Simon was beginning to get fed-up with this self-pity.

'You know what I mean. You saw Mum there, didn't you – instead of Rose? Only Mum got hit, and . . .'

'Stop it!' Alex covered his face. He was crying, his body was jerking on the bed with his sobs. But Simon couldn't bring himself to go over and comfort him. Outside, the blare and the laughter went on, and he had to raise his voice above the noise, but even that helped him to feel less sentimental tonight, made it easier for him, somehow.

'Tell me how it happened. Tell me again. I've got to know, Alex. She was at the back, wasn't she?'

'I can't.' Again, the pathetic sobbing: but still Simon kept his distance.

'You've got to! It's the same for me as it is for you, you know. I've lost her an' all, Alex!' He was shouting it while the Ghost Train siren wailed. 'Can't you see you *owe* it to me to tell me?' All his own aggression was there now: his frustration, his aggravation at what he'd been through – the hatred of the bullies, the sting of all those nettles, the Cyclone Twist of Rose. 'You tell me, Alex, or I'm clearing off. I've got to get it clear in my head.'

Right or wrong, it had stopped the grizzling. Alex was sitting up and trying to control his breathing. 'You know . . .' he started to evade. 'You know, don't you?'

'Tell me again, then.' Simon had never known he could be so hard. But all right if he *was* changing, this was just how he wanted to be right now.

'It was . . . it was just like today. That policeman – he was all confused. She was getting him upset.' Alex took in a deep breath, like life itself. 'He forgot, didn't he? Forgot he was in gear. She'd made him forget.' He turned his head and stared at Simon, quivering with intensity. 'But he missed her. She ran off . . . laughing . . .'

'And Mum got hit, and fell under . . .' How come he was able to say it tonight without breaking down himself?

'Hit . . . hit her head. Chance in a million.'

Simon sat on his own bed, close to Alex but still a distance away. All right, perhaps he could accept that. It had happened to him the same, hadn't it, on the Dodgems? He'd been all mixed-up tonight, not thinking about whether he was straight or not, and he'd run the car into the side. It sounded right. But he was sure there was still a lot more to know than he had ever been told – perhaps because he was only a kid. On the other hand, if he was grown-up enough to be going through all this for Alex, he was grown-up enough to know *all* the truth. And if ever a time was right, now was the time.

'So what got you all upset, Alex? Rose was bumping up that copper. Was Mum doing that to you?' Simon could hardly believe he was saying such a thing. But there they were, the words hanging between them in the trailer like a line of dirty washing.

And they'd stopped Alex shaking, anyway. Now he was staring Simon straight in the eye with an adult look that suddenly put the age gap back between them. It was like being about to be ticked off for something; and for a moment Simon thought that he might have gone too far. It was a father's look that Simon hadn't seen for eleven months.

'All right,' Alex said, softly. '*All right!*' he shouted. 'I was mad. Angry mad. She made me mad. I got in a temper. Reversed the car like a maniac without looking. And she was there.' He was bolt upright now, feet firm on the floor, arms stiff by his sides, his manner at once confessional and defiant. 'I ran her down, didn't I?'

Against the terrible strength of these words Simon felt himself weaken: but he managed to clutch at his determination desperately, a last grasp before it went.

'What . . . made you mad, then?'

And as he watched, Alex started coiling up again, began to rock a little, his foot tapping out of rhythm on the trailer floor. 'You want to know?' he asked. He laughed, explosively. 'I'll tell you if you really want to know.'

Simon nodded. He couldn't be too certain how any words of his might come out right now: too brash or too prying: or his voice simply sounding too young for him to be told anything.

'Well, she never meant any harm by it. That's definite, that's for certain; no one's got any doubts about that. But she was . . .' Alex twisted his head painfully 'she was a good dancer. Sparkled when she got on the floor; went like a pattern of bright colour. Me, I'm hopeless, got two left feet. I could never dance well enough for her. Then this Georgie Jones came along, and he was good, too, tons better than me . . .' Alex stopped, very finally, as if he had just decided he wouldn't go on. He closed his eyes, and swayed a little. For an instant Simon thought he was going to faint, and he went to reach forward, but suddenly, very calmly, and in a different, conversational tone he started speaking again. 'The pair of them joined a dancing class, up at the Astor. That was all, nothing to it. Always good as gold, she was. Loyal. A good mum. But she liked the dancing, made a lot of this Georgie Jones when they started to win things. Always seemed to have her hand on his shoulder. Don't think she knew she was doing it. She definitely didn't see any harm in what was going on . . .'

Simon had never listened so hard to anything in his life; and as he listened he tried to match this description of his mother with what he knew of her. No, she'd never neglected him; she'd always been a terrific mum, the other kids used to envy him having her; beautiful, immaculate clothes, laughing a lot with him. Their mums were like grans compared to his. He knew about her dancing all right; he'd met Mr Jones a lot when he'd brought her home and Alex had made the coffee – Alex all scruffy, his mind lost in a picture or a job, her looking like a model out of one of the magazines. But she'd never seemed to mind. And neither had Alex, really. Just a bit quiet some-times.

Or had he? Wasn't this what Alex was trying to tell him now? He *had* minded over something, because that night she'd got him angry mad.

'That night,' Alex was rocking again, telling it to the floor, his head in his clutching hands. 'She phoned home from the Astor. They'd won something special. She was over the moon; you know how she went. Told me on the phone she'd be late. Did I mind?'

Simon stared at Alex's twisted face as his father remembered: the memory that must have been running round inside his mind ever since.

'I minded like hell, and I told her. I said Georgie Jones could bring her home and we'd open something special, celebrate here. If they liked they could bring some take-away in for me as well. And she said no. She said . . . she said it was special that night. She was going with Georgie Jones . . .'

He stopped as if it were all too painful in one go. Like a dentist giving a patient a breather. Except he was the dentist and the patient was Alex.

'"I'm . . . I'm not having this," I said, and I drove to the Astor to catch her before she could get in his car.' He stopped again, a long stop, the flow ended. He coughed nervously. He was coming to the part that was hard to tell.

'I caught them in the doorway. Arms round one another. No music playing. No dancing excuse. When they saw me they jumped apart like they'd had an electric shock. All smiles. Came to talk to me, make it right. I was . . . *that angry* with the two of them. He walked round the front of the car, she walked round the back, as far apart as they could get. But I didn't see her step off, didn't realize. I wasn't thinking. All I knew was, I wasn't going to hang around there to be humiliated. Let them get on with it. I threw the car into reverse to miss him, and, oh my Christ . . .'

All the racket of the fair made only a long, long silence. No other sounds existed in the world now beyond what hung between Simon and Alex.

'Poor kid. It wasn't her fault, it was mine, never trying hard enough to get away from my stupid paints. If I'd only gone to watch her win some of her medals. It wasn't Georgie Jones at fault, either, it was me . . .'

Simon sat where he was. He knew he should have been helped by the explanation, but he was more confused than ever now. He'd never thought of there really being such a strong husband and wife reason before. If this was what Jackson and Clark had got hold of you could even understand what they went round saying.

With a deep and agonized groan Alex, not the man-to-man any more, threw himself back on the bed, twisted himself face down and started to weep like a baby: tears and dribble.

'And . . . worst . . . of all . . . Simon! She's gone!' He hit at his head violently with his fist. 'Even out of here! I can't even see her in my head any more!'

Simon stared at him, suddenly shocked and ashamed at himself; because even after what he'd heard, at this moment he found he couldn't do so much as put out his hand. All he was capable of doing right now was watching Alex, like some outsider looking in, and think about what he'd heard. This talk was supposed to have made things better. But somehow it had made them worse.

9

Alex slept on the next morning, deeply enough for Simon to suspect he might have some tablets with him after all, so he didn't try to rouse him. Instead, from the security provided by Alex being unconscious, he looked for a while at the peaceful face. It was a lot younger with those troubled eyes closed; it almost had a baby's open-mouthed look of innocence; and Simon had the feeling that he was seeing a glimpse of the *person* – the baby, the boy, the man – which had always been Alex, the essence of him that could never change. Quiet, sincere, serious, loving. Perhaps too loving.

Could he have done that terrible thing deliberately? Was it in his nature? In the clear light of day it hardly seemed possible. Could you be so wrong about someone after living all your life with them? Simon stood and looked, and drew back from shaking those shoulders – one part of him not wanting to reawaken the pains of the night before, another just wanting to keep his distance till he could feel a lot more sure of where he stood himself this morning. Mind, half a night's sleep seemed to have sorted some of that out for him. He could see where some of the others stood. With sadness he could see what his mother's position had been, wanting more than just sitting still for Alex, modelling or watching him paint: he could see why she'd had to have her dancing and some of the success that went with it. He could see Alex's final jealousy – but still not the truth of his actions. He could even see, although he couldn't accept it, his grandparents' disappointment in Linda Watson choosing Alex for a husband instead of some go-getting, smart man-of-the-world. And, clearest of all, he could see his own position, right here in the foreground. Like a Dodgem, he was, someone bashed into from all angles, from Alex on one side and the rest on all the others, and he was going to need to do some pretty clever steering to keep himself from getting hurt. Because – and this was the big thing the night had taught him – it was him who mattered now. He'd tried to do all he could for Alex and that just wasn't enough. So, without a mother to worry about, it was going to have to be him who counted. He might get the truth sorted, or he mightn't. Somehow it just wasn't so important to prove anything any more. The night had worked that out, too. Knowing more had upset him more: and had somehow left him caring less.

He made himself some breakfast, the noisiest bowl of Rice Krispies ever: loud enough to snap anyone awake but Alex. Another breakfast. It was a good job there were nights and days, he thought – a small fresh start every so-many hours, after rest – because otherwise, if life just went running on and on without a break, everything would get to fever pitch and nothing would ever have the chance to calm down and change. A night-time break away from everyone else, with things just going on inside your own head, with time to think and change your own position, had to happen if you were ever going to talk to people again. Like with Alex. After that night's break, however uncertain he was, he'd at least be able to go through the surface moves of eating and working with him again.

Outside his window the fair was settled. The frantic activity was over, they were all set up. Now some sort of routine had taken over. Children were playing, fresh washing was going up on the improvised lines, groups of showmen were talking shop, looking at one another's problems. But there was certainly work for the Leightons to do; and plenty of it.

Simon burped on his cereal, and shook Alex awake.

Immediately, Alex sat up and stretched and yawned at the day. His eyes were clearer than Simon expected to see them, and his voice was firmer.

'You let me go on.'

What was he saying? Was he referring to the sleep, or to what had been said the night before? Simon couldn't be sure, so he replied in the same vein. 'You needed it, didn't you?'

Alex grunted and got out of bed. He washed, and ate his breakfast, and neither of them spoke about what had happened; only about the chilly, dry weather and the next board. Perhaps Alex had dreamed, Simon thought. Perhaps after talking about her he'd dreamed of Linda Leighton and found her in his head again. But Simon didn't ask. This morning he didn't really want to know.

'You've got your next board ready to start. I'm going over for another one.' It was too early again for Nick, he reckoned: and somehow he wasn't so worried if it wasn't.

He was right. Once more it was only Mr Tucker about.

'Saw you last night,' he said, cheerfully meeting Simon more than halfway. 'Didn't pay, did you?'

'Yes . . .' Of course he'd paid. There'd been no question of not paying, had there?

''Ere,' Mr Tucker flipped a fifty pence at him, ''you're part of the fair, son. Don't want to make my money out of you.'

'Thanks.' Well, that was nice, Simon thought, but it put paid to Dodgem rides – because he wouldn't be able to get on and actually tell Nick or one of the others that Mr Tucker said he went for free. And a good job after his performance last night!

'Any'ow, I was going to say to you, d'you want a job over 'ere when we're busy?'

Simon's eyes said 'Eh?'

'I need five lads when we're busy – when five colours

are workin' – an' I lost one to the Army. See, the quicker we get 'em on an' the cash in, the more rides we do . . .'

'Oh, yeah?' That made good sense, Simon thought. But couldn't the others move a bit faster and collect from one more car each?

'I've got this system, see. Twenty-five cars, five colours. Four colours on till we're busy, then the five. Last night I kept the yellows off – but around seven tonight we'll be usin' the lot if it's dry.'

'Yeah?'

'Five colours, five cars, five lads. It stops any confusion an' makes the money easy. You collect fifty pence a car from your five – say it's greens. You bring to me whatever the punter gives you, pound notes, fivers, the right money, an' I reckon up. Five cars at fifty is two-fifty. I take two-fifty off you and give you change for whatever you've give me – notes and silver. You give 'em their change, get off the floor, an' off we go. It's quick and easy, but you do 'ave to move fast, or I'm not saving time and money.' He looked up at Simon. 'This ain't just because I like you.'

'Yes, please!' Simon's answer was immediate. This was more like it! This was a bit nearer the mark! And surely he could find a way round Nick if he was actually working with him.

'None o' that Jack-the-lad stuff, though. Get your money, give your change, an' get off the floor. Leave the sorting out of the cars to the others. From what I saw you wouldn't be too marvellous at that . . ' Jimmy Tucker laughed, and Simon smiled. Well, at least it had made someone feel good!

'All right then, come over 'round 'alf-six an' I'll give you a start. What did you say your name was?'

'Simon.'

'Si-mon.' He wrote it down in a scruffy notebok from his back pocket. 'Fair enough, Simon. Two quid a night all right?'

'Sure.'

'Right. And now I s'pose you want another board. 'Ere y'are then, son, it's all ready for you. Go on, then, don' 'ang about. Tell your ol' man to pull his finger out. See if we can't get two out of 'im today.'

'O.K., Mr Tucker.'

'"Junior". Gawd, you make me feel old.'

'O.K. . . .' But Simon couldn't quite say it. He picked up the board and went. 'See you later then.'

He went back across the front like a Flymo, his feet just off the ground. This was better, wasn't it? More like it? This was what being a fairground boy was all about. And what a nice bloke Junior was. Someone who *liked* him. All of a sudden things seemed to be taking a slight change for the better.

And Alex seemed to be going well, too. Already he'd got his design pencilled on to the second board Simon had prepared and a glistening coat of smooth blue was swirling round the outlines. His head was in the air, and he was even looking round from time to time as he worked. Simon wouldn't have been too surprised to hear him whistling. But he made nothing of it, not in his own mind nor out loud to Alex – perhaps because he didn't want to tempt fate, or perhaps because he didn't want to go along with Alex's ups and downs so closely any more. Whatever the reason, he got stuck into his own job instead.

There was a lot to be said for hard, physical work. Your fingers ached as they were held rigid on the coarse sandpaper; they slipped off from time to time and you hurt your knuckles, your arm began to feel as if it would never straighten out again; but it was satisfying seeing the fading flakes come off as you rubbed away in wide sweeps and short pushes, because you could see the board changing in front of you. You were having an effect on something. That hadn't happened to him for a long time.

But after an hour or so he had to have a breather, and

with nowhere else to go he wandered over to see how things were shaping with Alex. There was a definite improvement. The painting was better than yesterday, with more life about the scroll-work, more movement across the board. Alex's hand seemed to have more flow – the lines went running on where yesterday they had stopped short within his pencilled outlines; today they were like musical notes that were held on, instead of being cut-off by a lack of breath. The devastated Alex of last night was the creative Alex today.

It was a good time to tell him. 'I've got a job tonight,' Simon said. 'Helping on the Dodgems.'

'Have you?' But Alex didn't inquire what it was: he was busy mixing a paste of new colour. Simon looked hard at him, and said no more about it. Was that the reaction his mother used to have, late at night, when she came in with Georgie Jones and a new dancing medal? If it was, who could blame her for wanting to celebrate that last time, to share her pleasure with someone who was involved in it? Who could blame her for letting him give her a hug? And then again, with someone as deep as Alex, who could wonder that he'd got jealous and suddenly wanted to hit back?

Simon made another snack meal from the carrier of food Old Man Penfold brought over late in the morning: but they ate while they worked, and early in the afternoon Simon handed his board to Alex while Alex's was set aside to dry. At this pace it wouldn't quite be two a day, Simon reckoned, but three in two days wasn't bad, and Mr Tucker would be well pleased.

They worked on until the light began to fade. Casual, inquisitive visitors came and went: a fairground was like that, Simon found. There was often a presence being felt at his elbow, but he rarely looked up straightaway. Well it might be Nick, he reasoned, and he didn't want to be caught out with the wrong reaction: smiling if Nick wanted trouble, or scowling if he wanted to make friends. They'd be working together that night and that'd be time enough to try to make a truce. But he knew without looking who it was when Rose came and stood behind him. There was no telling how – it was just a knowledge – and his working hands began to quicken with his pulse.

'You're a fast worker.'

'Yeah?' Not as fast as you are, he thought. He still held the policeman against her. But she was different again now, leaning towards him with a look on her face that could almost have been the beginning of a smile.

''Ow's your ol' man?' Alex was well within earshot but she had the directness of an infant.

'All right.' Simon looked across at him and Alex looked back, frowning at Rose.

'An' 'ow are you?'

'All right.'

She squinted at him. 'You ain't still worried about bein' caught, are you?'

Was that a slight sneer, or did she really want to know? He just shrugged. Being carted back was always on the cards, but today the threat of it didn't chill him as it had.

'You don' wanna. I saw that copper off good. Made 'im go all goosey an' cock-up 'is drivin'!' She laughed and showed surprisingly white teeth. ''E won' wanna come back!'

'No.' Somehow Simon kept his voice all casual. So that's what she'd been on at! Frightening the man off – even a policeman! So she hadn't really been pushing herself – just the *idea* of herself. Well, that put things in a bit of a different light.

'I 'ear you got a job tonight . . .'

'Yeah. On the Dodgems.' Word got round quicker here than down a small street.

'Might come over after we've shut up. Y'can give me a free ride.'

188

'Can I?'

Rose shrugged her thin shoulders. 'Up to you. Any'ow, see you.' She sauntered past Alex's dark eyes and slammed into her trailer, singing something recent.

'I wouldn't get too thick with her.' Alex had come across to rub a finger along Simon's filling-in. 'Keep a little bit of distance,' he muttered.

Simon decided not to start sulking. 'I do,' he said, shortly, and he turned back to his board.

But Alex didn't go. There was an awkward silence, ended by a long drawn-out sigh. 'I still can't see her,' he said as he turned away.

Simon's immediate reaction was to look at the closed door of Rose's trailer. Nor can anyone else, he thought, she's gone inside. And then he realized who Alex was really talking about. His mum, Linda Leighton.

Another ride on the Cyclone Twist. So, telling him about things had helped Alex for a while, then, but nothing was better for long. How much longer was he going to keep on needing help? And how much more could Simon give to him? That was the big, new question. It was all getting so heavy, so involved. Simon started rubbing. No, running away like this wasn't solving much for either of them.

At least Simon's evening started off well enough. Those two boards were done and drying nicely, with Mr Tucker well pleased with Alex's work. It was getting faster and freer all the time. And the local kids who came early gave Simon a boost, staring with their big eyes at the fairground people, at him and at Rose. He felt like a real pro then, and the feeling was good. He washed himself in the trailer and smoothed his hair. Suddenly he couldn't wait to be one of the lads busy on the Dodgems.

One by one the generators started up; the wandering kids came in bigger, older groups; the shouting started;

records began thumping; and the rides took on more and more patrons every time they restarted. By the time Simon came out of his trailer only Old Man Penfold's Autodrome was rattling round with more space than riders. If he hadn't been hurrying to the Dodgems Simon would have felt sorry for Rose, stuck there smoking herself to death in the cash desk.

He'd deliberately held off for half an hour and he was about right for Jimmy Tucker. The four sets of Dodgem cars were busy, with people waiting to rush on when the music stopped, and when he arrived the covers were coming off the yellows. Simon went straight up to the cash desk as the Dodgems bumped and jarred all round him.

'All right, son? You timed that nice. Now remember what I told you. All your money comes to me – an' any aggravation an' all. Don' argue with no one, whatever you do.' He smiled at him. 'I got the truncheon, not you. You're just my 'and out there, taking the money.'

Simon nodded. He remembered where the truncheon was hanging, out of sight of the public. He'd be more than happy to let the man deal with any problems.

'I'll give 'em a bit longer this ride, give the lads a couple more minutes to get them covers off. Then you're on the yellows.' He pushed his cap up and scratched his head, humming to the music. Simon leant on the cash desk trying to look bored, too.

'So you like the fair, do you?'

'Yeah, it's all right.' The man was smiling at him again, as if he were proud to be offering him this special life. Suddenly Simon wanted to sound more enthusiastic for him. 'It's great!'

'It suits some. Them who don't want to be stuck in the same place all their life. Them who want a bit of freedom, a bit of variety.'

'Yeah.'

'You'll do all right, if you keep your nose clean, play it by our rules.'

Simon smiled sheepishly for him. He was all right, Jimmy Tucker. He was the sort you could get on with; certainly the first bloke for a long time who seemed really to like him, who wasn't just paid to be pleasant. He could get on with Jimmy Tucker: someone strong and sure of himself.

''Ow's your dad? 'E's doin' all right, eh?'

'Yeah, not bad.' It depended how you looked at it, Simon thought.

'It's Charlie Penfold who must be over the moon. As it stands that ride of 'is ain't worth the space it takes up. We've all be tellin' 'im for years. It needs modernizing, making the cars more comfy, a good paint up. Now your old man could do a real good job for him!'

'Yeah.' Simon stared across at the Autodrome. But for the minute he wasn't thinking about Alex or Old Man Penfold. Alex was busy with a coat of clear varnish in the trailer, and that was all Simon needed to worry about him at the moment: and Old Man Penfold certainly didn't seem to matter. It was Rose he was suddenly thinking about. After all these years Jimmy Tucker must know her well. What could he tell him about her? Could he tell him what had made her what she was – how come she'd got two such different sides? And could he give him just a clue to getting to her soft side when he wanted, instead of having to wait for those rare glimpses?

Desperately, still looking bored, Simon fought with the words of an innocent question – but he'd already lost when Jimmy Tucker suddenly threw the big switch in front of him and called 'Next ride please' into the microphone.

Now! Forget about Rose and get into this job. Keep Nick happy if he could, and out of his way if he couldn't.

Let's enjoy a couple of hours out of all this, he told himself.

Get it all in a cupped hand and pile it on the counter for Mr Tucker. It was really very easy, he decided – simply a question of remembering which cars needed change. Perhaps it was just good luck, or beginner's enthusiasm, but he was finished first: and of course Nick had to draw everyone's attention to it. What else? 'Speedy Gonzales hits town!' he nudged at the others; but it was mild enough, and Simon could live with that, he reckoned.

Time passed quickly. It was hard work, but good fun – and you learned fast. Like you soon learned the trick of telling them what they'd given you if they had to have change; then they relaxed and didn't watch you like a thief all the way to the cash desk and back. And you soon lost the beginner's smile, just shoved out your hand for the money with a stare elsewhere, and leant bored on a pillar while the ride ran for its record and a half. And you learned what you might do another night, kicking the jams free – or standing on the backs and steering for the girls who liked it. Simon watched how Nick and the others did it, how they quickly cut their losses and cleared off when the girls objected. Nothing seemed to go deep with them – there was another ride in a minute. He picked up a lot, just watching. And he was pleased to be treated like the rest by Jimmy Tucker, nothing special done for him: yes, he liked that. The man had a few words now and again, like with the others, and Simon kept busy like them, and he managed all night long not to make himself look stupid in front of the people on the ride. He enjoyed it, as much as he'd enjoyed anything for years, and the time flew like lightning. It could have gone on all night for him, but when the end came, it came suddenly. One ride everyone was thronging for cars, and the next there were several empty Dodgems. It was as if some secret signal had sounded in the village, time to come home: like when all the ants everywhere knew to fly at the same time. Simon gave his change out and helped to push the empty cars to the side. He looked round the fair. The Big Wheel was still spinning, but all the other rides and hooplas were running down, and the lights were off already on the Autodrome. He guessed at the time. Ten o'clock? Half-past? It had been the fastest four hours of his life. He wondered if Mr Tucker wanted all the yellows taken out, the reverse of starting, and he decided to go over and ask him.

But he didn't get a chance to show his bit of willing.

'You still gonna give me a ride?'

It was Rose, leaning on the next pillar. He hadn't seen her come.

'Yeah. 'Course, if you like.' He knew he could do it now, knew Mr Tucker wouldn't mind when there was space.

'Good ol' Simon. I'll 'ave this number six.'

But the car she'd chosen, the one standing empty in front of him, was red. It was one of Nick's; and it wasn't down to him. She obviously didn't know how the Dodgem boys took their money here.

'Have a yellow car,' he told her. But for some stupid reason he couldn't bring himself to tell her why. Somehow it made a sort of rivalry between him and Nick, made his link with Rose too important to him if he told her it wouldn't be him giving her the free ride. 'They're faster, yellows,' was all he could say. He tried to smile. 'Honest!'

'Nuts! Is this one broken?'

'No . . .' Still he couldn't find just the right way of saying it, of getting it across all casual. 'Take my word for it, leave this one. Go for a yellow. Look, twenty-four. Four times as fast as six!' Now he managed to laugh, acknowledging his make-believe, hoping he'd been emphatic enough.

'You're up the twist!' For a second she sounded as if she

were beginning to have serious doubts about his sanity: like father like son, sort of thing.

And then it was too late. The cars stopped and Rose was behind the wheel of her red number six before Jimmy Tucker could say 'Next ride please' or Simon could throw out a word to stop her. She looked up at him.

'Don' ask me for no money, will you?'

'It's not up to me . . .'

'Oh, big man!'

Simon had to move quickly to collect his own fares, but not before he'd seen her toss her head away. The next he saw of her was with Nick leaning all over the car, and her being one of the girls who didn't object. A tough knot of jealousy gristled inside him. Nick could do more with one hand on the wheel than most could with two, spinning the car round, stunt-man stuff, avoiding all the crashes, squeezing it through gaps which he seemed to make ahead of him. And Simon could only stand and watch them, churning again, the Cyclone Twist inside. Rose made sure Simon saw them every time around, screeching with false pleasure at the next near-miss, letting him know what he was missing. This could have been you, she was saying, if you'd wanted. This was supposed to be you.

It was supposed to have been like the last waltz at a dance, this last ride of the fair, everyone with their proper partner. And now Simon knew how Alex must have felt sometimes. And like with Alex, not being positive enough, it had been his own stupid fault . . .

Without a second chance, Jimmy Tucker closed it down. The lights went out and Simon missed the going of Rose as he joined in to line up the cars and put their covers on. His throat was big with disappointment. Choked. They were right, that's just how you felt, he decided. Right *choked* at times like this.

Nick was in some sort of a rush. 'Don' 'ang about now, Gonzales,' he said as Simon struggled with a reef-knot and an eyelet, 'else 'e'll wanna start pullin' down tonight. 'Urry up, and make yourself scarce.'

Moodily, in his own time, Simon finished what he was doing. Pulling down was their business, not his; he wasn't being paid for that. And good luck if Nick did have to work another couple of hours! All Simon had ahead of him was another depressing night shut up in the trailer with Alex.

Like thieves into the night the others disappeared. Simon secured the cover on the last yellow car, half waiting for a word from Mr Tucker. But the man was busy with his money, and Simon was left on his own. There wouldn't be another friendly word from anyone tonight. Well, at least there'd be two quid in his pocket, he tried to cheer himself. A bit more in the kitty. He pulled up his collar and hunched off.

What took him round the back of the generator he didn't know. It wasn't the quickest way back to the trailer. Perhaps he was just delaying being shut in again with Alex for a few minutes. More likely, he thought afterwards, it was just the same bad luck that had dogged him for the past twelve months. But whatever it was, bad luck or some horrible turn of fate, it still hit him just as hard.

The two of them were round there, in the shadows: Rose and Nick, her leaning against the door of the tractor's cab, him with a foot on the running board and an arm round her shoulder, his face close to hers while she stared blankly into the dark.

'Oh, no, it's Speedy Gonzales.'

Rose said nothing.

'Time you was in bed, i'n it?'

Simon wanted to turn and walk away: except Rose didn't look all that delirious about Nick pressing so close.

'What you come snoopin' round 'ere for?'

'Not looking for you!'

'Oh, lookin' for 'er, was you?'

'No.'

''Cos she's wi' me, ain't you?' Nick pulled Rose closer; but still she said nothing, just stared ahead for a bit. Then she turned her eyes to Simon, and for the first time in a long while, just for a second, he saw that other look on her face. Or he thought he saw it, and then it was gone: a glimpse of that other Rose – by the nettles, in front of the hospital at Whipps Cross – that sudden look of uncertainty, of not being so sure any more. What would she say next? 'In for a penny, in for a pound?'

'Tell 'im, Rosie!' Nick commanded. 'Tell the little creep to clear off!' Rose's silent stare went on. 'Tell 'im who you want to 'ave with you . . .' And as Nick said it he pulled her head round to him and kissed her on the mouth; then looked back at Simon as if to enjoy his reaction.

For several seconds Simon stood and watched, and heard the coarse slip of Nick's hand on Rose's dress. Rose giggled, and turned her head away from both of them, staring into the darkness again; but she made no other move.

He'd better stop doing that! And why didn't she make him stop? She could if she wanted to. Simon's head felt that old lightness, his own hands started that twitching and knuckling. It was now, now that he had to go. He had this moment to walk away and leave them to it. Turn away nonchalantly, and walk back to his trailer. That was what he ought to do. But something else, the stupid, secret way he felt about Rose, somehow stopped any chance of that. He stood facing them, blazing-eyed and angry, while Nick stared back at him, his mouth open in a sneer. And slowly and very deliberately he went for one of her buttons.

Rose still didn't move a muscle. What *was* up with her? was Simon's last rational thought – before he threw himself at Nick's head, determined to bash that cocky sneer into the side of the generator, to give him something else to do with those hands, to punch both fists into his face, to kick him in the crutch like he'd done to Jackson in the playground – all the things he'd been ready to do to Ear-ring, what he'd do to anyone who asked for it.

But Nick's first boot dead-legged Simon in the calf and told him it wasn't going to be like that tonight. His second went into Simon's side and, hurting like a broken rib, sent him rolling back, bleeding and eating dirt.

'Stop poncin' about you two!' Rose hissed. 'You'll 'ave Tucker round 'ere. I don't want no trouble with 'im!'

But Nick wasn't listening. He was singing an obscene song at Simon, and looking as if he might put his words into action.

Simon charged forward again, bent double, his head leading like a battering ram, his hands scrabbling at the ground for balance. He'd nut him! Anything to get at him and stop him. It had worked before, his temper! But Nick was bigger than he was, and stronger, and what Simon's head met wasn't Nick's belly or his crutch but a hard knee raised up to crunch into his left cheek. The force of it, and the hard-grazing denim which went up into his eye, brought tears to the surface like stamping on hard sand, and Simon was bowled back again – humiliated and stung into an anger now which he *wouldn't* control.

'Come on, Simple Simon, my little sister can do better'n you!'

'You – !' Without any care for the cost of himself so long as he could hurt this creature, Simon hurled himself once more at the big kid, bodily, like a dog tackling an ox, clawing at him, biting at him, kicking. But nothing got home. Nick threw him back again with casual ease and Simon's breath was thumped out of his chest as he crashed flat on the hard, stony surface once more.

'You bastard!' Simon screamed. 'I'll kill you! I'll kill you!' Nick was no more than a swimming of blood and dirt and tears. 'I'll bloody kill you!' And he would now. Or hurt him bad. *Something* had to be done to that great heap of filth who was pawing again at Rose.

And suddenly Simon knew what. He was smaller, he was younger, he needed something else. He had to have a weapon – and he knew just where that weapon was.

Scrambling to his feet he ran off to the sound of Nick's triumphant laughter, to the sound of the yob who thought he'd won. But let him wait! God, let him wait! Round the generator he flew, back to Jimmy Tucker's Dodgems, straight for the cash desk. Even if Junior was there he'd get that truncheon, if it killed him he would!

But the cash desk was empty. The light was on and the flap was up. Over the top he went, reaching and groping. His fingers wriggled at the thong, and he had it. He had it! Heavy. Hard. Just what he wanted for Nick's filthy, gloating face. In a great lift he pulled it over and he spun on his heel to run full charge back across the plated floor. The pig'd be all over her again by now, thinking he'd won, but just let him wait . . .

The truncheon was up, in full view. Mad and determined, he couldn't have disguised his intentions even if he'd wanted to. With his rage roaring in his head, he ran full out for Nick: to get him for good.

To be stopped. To be caught round the middle by the biggest, broadest arm on the fairground.

'What the 'ell are you up to?'

'Get off!' Simon wriggled, struggled with Jimmy Tucker, tried to take a swing at the man with the truncheon.

'Give that 'ere! What the devil d'you think you're doin'?'

'Let go! You let me go! I'm gonna kill 'im!' Crying and screaming, lashing out blindly with his arms and his feet, Simon's frenzied rage tried to get him past the man. He didn't care who this was, there wasn't anything in the world now that mattered more than getting to Nick. 'Get outta my way, you! Let me go, you big git!'

'What? You . . .'

Simon's weapon arm was yanked, twisted – broken, it seemed. The truncheon spun away and clanged into the side of a trailer. Then the arm was hard up behind Simon's back and Jimmy Tucker's temper was surging over his own, engulfing it.

'I don't take that from no one, boy.' He shook Simon this way and that like the beating of a doormat. 'Not from no one!' He snorted, growled, breathed angry hamburger in Simon's face and held him up, a whipped puppy. 'Don't you ever dare . . .' He pushed Simon to the ground for his third faceful of grit, and he retrieved the truncheon. 'I ought to give *you* a dose of this! If this is what one night o' workin' for me does for you . . .' the man threw the truncheon down and groped angrily in his back pocket . . . 'then I can do without you, boy!'

Two crumpled notes came out and were flung at Simon's head.

'You stick with Penfold an' your ol' man in future. Just don't cross my path. There's things you do an' things you don't round 'ere. You break the rules, son, an' I'll break you!' Jimmy Tucker breathed in heavily, picked up the truncheon again, and stamped off towards the cash desk.

For a full minute Simon didn't move. He lay there panting like an injured cat, with a body which wondered whether it could ever move again, and a mind which questioned whether it ever wanted to. But when it became clear that Jimmy Tucker wasn't coming back, not to go at him any more nor to find out what had gone on, Simon pulled himself painfully to his feet and shuffled the darkest route back to his trailer, his head hanging fit to fall in disconsolation and disgust. His body, all his left side, felt raw and swollen: he could feel the hot wet blood on his face; his jerky breathing hurt as if a rib were really broken, and his right arm ached where it had been wrenched up his back. He was defeated all ways round, and he pushed himself in through the door of his trailer only because it was the one place he had to go right then. He'd just as soon have died.

The light was on inside. Well on; Alex had turned it up high. And through the blood and the tears Simon saw why. Alex was working, hunched over a sheet of paper on the table. His hands were smudged black with charcoal, and his face was, too, where he had worried at his brow. Even in his own terrible condition Simon could see all that. Yet Alex seemed to see nothing in him. He glanced up, and away again, and back to that troubled piece of paper.

It was a woman's face. It was no one Simon could recognize, but he knew only too well who it was intended to be.

Suddenly, Alex screwed the paper up and threw it to the floor, the charcoal after it. 'I . . . can't . . . get . . . her . . .' he whimpered. 'Still . . . can't . . . see . . . her . . .' He banged his fist against his head as if it were some television on the blink. 'Been thinking I could . . . all day . . . like this . . . But . . .' He started to cry.

Simon said nothing. He didn't even try, didn't even *think* of a reply. He just found a wet cloth, scrubbed it rough around his face, and threw himself onto his bed with his back turned on everything and everyone.

10

It was just too bumpy for sleep in the Green Line bus. The seats were comfortable enough with high neck-rests, and there was plenty of room; but the narrow road was in poor repair and the wide bus lurched and swayed, knocking Simon's head on the window when he tried to relax. So he was forced into taking a passing interest in the distant river and the grey hedges of the cement factories.

'You never been down this way before?' Rose asked him. 'Gawd, what a life, breathin' in all this muck all the time . . .'

'I can think of worse,' Simon muttered to the hard glass. And he could. His own existence wasn't too clever these days. The bus went over another bump and he winced. His rib still hurt like hell, but not quite as badly as the night before, so he guessed it wasn't broken after all. A puffy face and a cut lip was all he had to show for that big show-up after the fair – on the outside, that was. A lot else had happened in his mind. What about the way Alex hadn't even seen his injuries – he'd been better than that back at home – and the way the only friendly voice he'd heard in months had turned all angry against him? What hope was there for a kid like him at the fair if he'd fallen out with Jimmy Tucker and no one cared?

'Bit o' luck, just catchin' this, weren't it?'

Simon was a long way off in the might-have-been region where worry and steady movement takes you.

'You don' 'ave to talk. But I did tell you I was sorry, din' I?'

'Yes. *Yes*.' He made an effort. 'Sorry.' He turned back. He'd better not lose her help now: he'd be stupid to throw away his one piece of last-minute luck. He looked at her and tried a small, puffy smile, which she acknowledged with a nod and went on staring ahead; leaving Simon free to let his mind wander till she wanted to talk again.

It was funny, the way it had worked out: him making his big decisions during the night, then Rose turning up this morning full of apologies and all ready to help him work them out. If he'd believed in God any more he'd have thought there was some purpose being worked out.

In she'd come when Alex had gone, not so much as a knock, and shut the door hard behind her.

'You all right?' she'd asked, keeping her back to the way out.

'What do you reckon?' He'd been in no mood for kiss and make-up.

'Well, are you?'

'Well, I'm not exactly over the moon!'

'You was mad last night!'

'*Was* I?' What the devil did she think she was doing, causing everything, then coming in here to talk it over like the morning after a party?

'I shouldn't'a let it 'appen. I didn't know about all that colour stuff with the cars. I'm sorry about that. I thought you was bein' snobby.'

'Oh, cheers!' That was typical of Rose, he'd thought, winding things up and then casually saying sorry afterwards as if all she'd done was make him spill a drink. What was she up to? Was she frightened he'd up and off with Alex – and leave Old Man Penfold without his ticket for staying with the fair? Yes, that was about the size of it, he'd decided. In fact, the old man had probably put her up to coming over in the first place.

'Gonna let me off then?'

She'd smiled at him; but he'd hardly looked at her – hadn't let a smile from her affect him the way it might have done once. 'I told that Nick to get stuffed. I was just gonna when you went mad.'

'Oh, yeah?'

'Yeah, straight up. You'll see.'

'Oh, will I?' Simon had felt himself going tense with annoyance. 'Well, that's where you're wrong, because I ain't going to be here to see anything, thanks!'

'Oh?' She'd sat down then – and Simon had kicked himself for saying too much. 'Why, what you gonna do?'

Simon had stared at her at first, tight-lipped and determined to give nothing away, then he'd turned his back on her and gone on looking for the money he'd put in the food cupboard. But after a few seconds he'd thought, no, to hell with it, let her see what she's brought on herself; and slowly, like untangling Nick's dirty tape, he'd started to tell her something of the idea that had come to him during the long, painful night. He'd told her how he was going off to get something for Alex from his grandparents' house: but he'd been careful not to tell her why or what, because that was private, and what chance did a character like Rose have of understanding how a picture could put a person back in someone's mind? And he hadn't breathed a word of what was most difficult of all to explain – how free he'd feel of everyone after that last service to Alex. 'So I'm going up Market Junction today, and I'm coming back with what I'm after tonight.'

'What for? What is it you're gonna get? Money, is it?'

'No! It's a picture, if you must know.' There; she'd got it out of him easy enough; but he hadn't wanted her thinking he was a common thief. And he'd definitely drawn the line at telling her whose picture it was – and the significance of getting Linda Leighton back to Alex. She'd only try to persuade him a photo from home would do instead – and miss the point of him reclaiming it from those two.

'They've got it all ready for you, 'ave they?' she'd asked,

all disbelief. 'Wasn't they the ones who shot you back the Lodge that night?'

A good memory, she'd got. Put two-and-two together pretty well, Rose did. 'They don't know anything about it. Nor won't till it's over. I'll get in and get it out somehow.'

Now it had been Rose's turn to think for a bit. Then: 'D'you know your way 'ome from 'ere?' she'd asked, all matter of fact.

'No, but I can find it. I'm not daft. Get a train or something. We're not all that far off.'

'You get a bus. Green Line goes from Gravesend.'

'That's all right, then. I'll be back by tonight, before you push off from here.' He'd looked at her hard, at that point, for some confirmation on the one part he'd been a bit unsure about.

'Yeah. Prob'ly. We ain't in no 'urry. The ol' man 'ad a good drink last night. Feed the dog's about all 'e'll do today.'

'I've got a couple of quid . . .' There'd been nothing in the food cupboard; perhaps they'd spent it. But Rose would know if two pounds was enough.

'I got some money.' And suddenly, Rose had ruffled Simon's hair like a sister and told him very firmly. 'An' I'm comin' with you an' all. Show you the way an' give you 'and. I know a trick or two might 'elp at the other end. Owe you that much, don' I?'

Yes, you do, he'd thought: but a cautious alarm had started tingling inside. Is that really why you want to come? it had asked. Isn't it more like you can't afford to let me get lost? But he'd said none of that. Just, 'Nothing to do with nettles, these tricks, are they?' He'd take up her offer all right. She was good at this sort of thing. And why not use her, like Old Man Penfold was using Alex? He could definitely do with all the help he could get to bring that picture back.

The two of them had gone soon after that. Simon had

told Alex he was going to Gravesend, shopping – Alex no more knew it was Sunday than he knew about anything else – and within the hour they'd been in Gravesend, running for the 701 Green Line at the Clock Tower.

The driver was a thin, miserable-looking man who gave you your change as if he was giving up his life's savings: but appearances were deceptive. Rose had taken the lead, of course, and as soon as she'd asked for two tickets to the nearest stop for a bus to Market Junction he'd laid out the route for them. 'You want two to The Standard, Blackheath, then. Hop off there and get the 108 through the Blackwell Tunnel and pick up a 15 the other side.'

'Ta.'

And when they'd looked at the tickets he'd only charged them half fares. So much for appearances! And so much for him and Rose being the big grown-ups: it came as something of a shock to be reminded how the outside world saw you.

They went past a church turning out, all handshakes and bibles, and near the end of the journey the pubs turned out, too, all laughs and bottles tucked under the arm: but in between they looked at very little through the same window. They might be doing this together, but it was for totally different reasons – Simon to get the picture back, Rose to get Simon back – and it seemed as if neither of them was bothered much about the other any more. The plan was what mattered, not the people, and their minds were too busy for talk.

It was getting on for three o'clock when they made their cautious approach to Parkside; and only when Rose had seen the big double-fronted house, squinted at its position behind the high hedges from across in the park, did she start to talk about why they were there.

'You say it's a picture, what we've come for?'

'That's right.'

'And they ain't gonna give it you?'

'No way.'

'Big one, is it?'

'Not all that.' Simon traced its size in the air. 'Goes over the fireplace.'

'Valuable? Family treasure, sort o' thing?'

Simon looked at her hard. He supposed she'd got to know enough to make it work: besides, she'd be helping him to carry it back to Alex; she'd see it then. 'Alex did it. It's . . . a lady. They won't have it wired up against burglars or anything . . . It's ours, not theirs, that's all. Once we've got it back they won't be able to make any big fuss about it.'

'An' it's important, this picture, is it? To you two, like?'

She was looking at him and frowning. Was this some last minute doubt? Was she scared all of a sudden, and ready to back out – leave him to it, or go back without it?

Well, she'd better know it was as important to her as it was to him, he decided. They were in this together. One lose, all lose.

'If I don't get that picture back God knows what's going to happen to Alex. It'll make a real big difference to him.'

She took it: she blinked, and she understood. 'Which room's it in, then?'

'Downstairs, the living room: back of the house.'

'An' who's in the 'ouse?'

'Only them. My grandad, he's about fifty or sixty; but he's quite strong.' Would Simon ever forget being pinned down by the old so-and-so? 'And she's the same, but she's all nerves – all her strength's in her mouth. She'll shout the roof off if she sees a gypsy in the street.'

Rose gave him a narrow look. But he hadn't meant that, hadn't meant her. He'd meant anyone a bit different – it could have been a tramp he'd said; or a painter . . .

'Can you get in round the back?'

'No, no chance. They've even got a lock on the telly. It's being opposite the park makes them nervous.'

'Dead right. Quick get-away, that is, 'cross the park. Brings you out to the 'Igh Street, an' there's three gates an' all.'

She knew her Albert Park, did Rose. She'd been around, hadn't she? But it was useful; it was going to be very useful, he could see that.

'Any dogs or anything?'

'No. She's got asthma.'

'Any alarms?'

Simon had to think about that. There certainly wasn't a painted box on the front of the house to say so. 'I don't reckon. Just the telephone.'

'An' 'er loud voice . . .'

'Right.'

They were on a park bench now, staring across at some boys as if they were discussing their pick-up game of football, not a break-in over the road.

'An' livin' 'ere they don't like no fuss, right? Nothin' common to let 'em down in front of the neighbours?'

'Dead right.' It was uncanny how Rose sorted out a situation, Simon thought. That was *just* how they were, especially after all the publicity and talk when his mum had died. Even him going to the house had been too much for them for the past year.

'All right. Well, I've got a bit of a plan. A sort of idea . . .' She sat back on the seat looking casual: but while she spoke her sharp eyes were all over the park. 'I reckon we'll do the ol' broken wing. That'll get them out, an' you in. Any bushes in the front garden?'

'Yes, plenty. Not prickly, neither.'

Rose passed over that, and Simon let her. All that stupid nonsense about a soft Rose was over for him; the nettles business was all finished with, bar the odd scratchings on his body.

'All right, well I'll tell you what we're gonna do.' And in a few urgent words she told him her plan, how the picture was going to be got out of the house and back to the fairground by nightfall. It was simple and daring. Simple enough to work and daring enough to be difficult. But as Simon heard it he realized it was miles better than the no-plan he'd had – his vague idea in the night of crashing in and out and running away before they knew what had hit them. If anything was likely to work, this was.

And it had to, just had to . . .

'Come on!' she said. ''Fore we think about it an' get scared!'

'O.K.' Too right, he thought. Better than that half-hour wait for the roll in the nettles.

And almost before he knew it the raid was on.

Simon had to make the first move. Cautiously, he waited till the road was clear about fifty metres along from Parkside, and when the moment was right he ran across looking like any kid hurrying home for a late Sunday dinner. But once over, he brushed himself close in to the hedge and made his way slowly along to his grandparents' house. His left shoulder was dirtied by the dust in the privet, he had to press his top gum hard to stop a gathering sneeze, and he kept himself on his toes to take off at any moment things looked like going wrong.

But it was all peace. The occasional car and the soft fall of his trainers were the only sounds to compete with the football in the park. Sunday in London was more like the country than the country, he thought: it was *too* quiet. If only there was the clatter of a combine, or the sound of a fair pulling down to cover the squeak of the gate when he opened it.

At the gateway he stopped to tie his lace, and from knee level he spied through the fancy scrolls at the front of the house. It was just as he'd expected, as he'd hoped. There was no one in the garden and no eyes at the diamond-paned windows. This was their afternoon nap time under two sheets of the *Sunday Express*. And they were in, he knew that. All the small windows upstairs were open the regulation two holes, and the hall light was off (whenever they went out, day or night, they left the hall light on, both habits Simon had learned in years gone by when he'd been tolerated here); but they wouldn't have changed, not this pair; they never would.

Urged by that blind stare from the house, Simon pressed the latch and swung the gate inwards, going with it, leaving it open once he was through, and running fast for the cover of the first big bush on the left. He dived for it, and panting, he wriggled in and lay there in the alien territory. But the next bush up was the one he had to get to, the one to the left of the front door as he faced it. It was a big rhododendron, and close, and once he was well hidden under that he'd be in position, ready to make his run for the front door when it opened. Another careful look at the glinting windows, making sure there were no eyes glinting there, too. All clear, he reckoned – and he scrambled on his next dash, up a line of the lawn to his cover. He was a Commando, the S.A.S. – except this was no Sunday game with Little Lee.

Flattened and concealed, his inside rolled with another Cyclone Twist of anticipation. This was for real, and a hundred times worse than the last time he'd been near that front door, coming here in cold blood like this. It had helped before being up the wall with worry about Alex . . .

Now it was wait for Rose – and hope like hell that her broken wing routine worked as well as the nettle trick had.

She didn't keep him flattened there for long. He couldn't see her, but he heard the faint dry squeak of the gate quite clearly. She was coming in. Over the road in the park the football shouts went on; and for a moment that was all he could hear above the thud of his own pulse: just a moment's stillness when it would almost have been pleasant to cradle his head and forget the whole thing: and then suddenly the sound of Rose tip-toeing up the garden path became the only movement that mattered in the whole of Market Junction. Let her make it! he willed. Let her make it to the door and get this thing started!

She was level with him now. He could see her plastic shoes and her bare legs.

All at once, she sprinted forward and there was a loud thump and a rattle. He jumped at the movement and the sudden noise. She'd bashed the door with her two flat hands, by the knocker; and a scrape of feet and a swish of legs said she was pelting for it back down the garden path. Hardly daring to breathe, Simon raised his head to where he could see the door.

He waited, muscles trembling. It seemed an age before the door opened; for a while he thought it never would; but at last he saw it move a cautious centimetre, then it was suddenly thrown wide open, as if to catch a knock-down-ginger coming back for more.

'What the devil's going on?' It was his grandfather, red-eyed and unfocussed with sleep.

'Oh, gawd, me ankle! Oh, 'elp, I've done me ankle!' It was Rose, down by the gate.

'What? What?' The old man looked at his door, bewildered. How could someone hurting their ankle by the front gate make a noise like that on his door?

'Sorry, mister. Football come over. I come to get it an' I done me ankle chuckin' it back . . .'

'You want to be a bit more careful with your ball games. It could have hit a window.'

Rose started to whine. 'Oh, gawd, I can't put me foot down.'

'All right, there's no need to blaspheme.'

But he was going to her. He'd moved out of the porch and he was going off down the garden. Simon twisted himself under the bush to get a view. So far, so good, he thought. But now for the hard bit: now she'd got to get the old lady out.

'Give me your hand, I'll help you up.' But the old man had suddenly coughed, and stopped, and Simon, squinting through the rubbery green, could see why. Rose had sprawled herself on the path with her dress caught up under her back, showing all her legs, the sort of sight his grandad would soon turn his eyes from with his old lady just indoors.

'Yeah, give us 'elp up – an' a sit down somewhere for a coupla minutes?' A pause. 'You look big and strong.'

Simon couldn't see her face, he could only imagine the look on it: but he had a good idea what it was like: from the sound of her voice, Rose bumping up the policeman at the fair would be about right.

'Just wait there, young lady. I'd better get my wife to you.' Simon's grandfather hurried back up the path, got to the door and called urgently. 'Ellen, Ellen, here a minute . . .'

Simon flattened himself again, but now he lay there tensed and ready for action. The move after next was going to be his, into the house.

Almost immediately, he heard them coming out. '. . . Someone I want you to see,' the old man was saying.

'Eh? What's going on? It's Sunday afternoon . . .'

They went past the bush, down the garden path, the old lady protesting all the way. Now for it. This was where he had to move fast. With his heart pounding again and that old feeling in the pit of his stomach, he pushed himself up into a crouch and edged himself to look cautiously round the bush. They were both down by the gate, standing over Rose. 'And what's the matter with you?' his grandmother was saying. Both their backs were to him; and to his left there was the door, only metres away, wide open.

'It's me ankle, missus. I gone over on it.'

A quick double-check. They were both bending over Rose.

She suddenly whined loudly, 'It's that one. Oh, it 'urts! Look!'

Simon went. Lighter than he'd ever run, lending his weight only briefly to the ground for each step, he ran doubled-over to the porch. He jumped the step and landed silently on the surface of the deep-pile carpet. A quick look back to check again before he got himself trapped inside. They were helping Rose heavily to her feet, her being as awkward as she could. All right. Now, don't panic, he told himself. Do what she said. It could all be very important.

The telephone was first. It was in the hall on a little table-seat, next to a pay-for-your-calls piggy bank. Feverishly, he traced the cream instrument cord down to the skirting board. Just as she'd said, it went into a small plastic box. Gripping the cord in both hands, making sure he had space and wouldn't knock the whole lot over with the force, he yanked at it. Nothing: just a pain in his palm. It was held firmer than he'd thought. They came away a lot easier than this on the telly. Quick, one more go, then he'd have to leave it. With a renewed effort he tugged again – and this time it suddenly came, two copper ends shining at him like his own stripped nerves. He was panting, his hands shaking. He was well trapped in here if they came back, and guilty as hell now in anyone's eyes.

'Oh!' he heard from the front garden. ''Old on a minute . . .'

Finish it off properly. Don't let them even suspect, she'd said. With scrambling fingers he tucked the telephone ends down behind the edge of the carpet.

'Ouch! Wait a minute – I don't reckon I can make it . . .'

She was still holding them off, but it couldn't go on for ever. Get the picture! Hurry up and get what this was all about. The living room door was open; but he had to be very quick; he'd got to come back through this hall again before he could get away. He was in a real dead end now.

In he went, still on tiptoe, across onto another pattern of carpet, his muddy trainer prints like a hooligan's trail behind him . . .

And almost before he realized it, there she was: his mother, staring down from an alcove, young and beautiful and calmly apart from all this frantic villainy. And it was Linda Leighton herself, the way she'd been; and not looking a bit like Rose, really . . . It was weird what tricks his mind had played.

But he couldn't stop to think of all that. In seconds he had the picture off the wall. A simple lift and he was back across the room with it as if the swirls on the carpet were landmines. Into the hall again. A quick listen. 'All right, I'll get a chair, then.' His grandfather was losing his rag. Simon ran on through to that treacherous kitchen, to the back door with the key in it, locked but convenient, as Rose had said it was bound to be. He turned the key, pushed through it, and remembered just in time to steady it against slamming in the front door's draught. Good old Rose. She's had all the possibilities worked out. With a great tremble of relief he stood there, his back against the pebble-dash, and listened. Still so far, still so good. He was out of the house and he hadn't been seen. Now all he had to wait for was for the front door's slam, and then he could make his break round the side of the house and out the way he'd come in. But not too soon. Don't be too quick, she'd warned. We don't want to be chased. Don't let them even suspect, till they notice the space on the wall. So, try to calm down; listen for the door slam, the signal that Rose was away – had made a quick recovery when she'd put her foot to the ground – and he could start to count a hundred.

He stood as still as he could. Nothing yet. God, it was murder waiting, doing nothing . . . But hold on, wasn't there something he was supposed to do while he was standing here? Get the picture out of the frame, she'd said. Stop it looking like a picture – make it so it's more like a piece of hardboard or a roll of paper.

Simon crouched by the dustbin and turned over the glass to the smooth brown paper sticking down the back. Quickly, with a steady pressure, he slit along the back with his thumb nail, and pressing it against him to stop the crackle, he carefully eased the hardboard out. He did it with infinite care: the last thing he wanted now was the sound of breaking glass at the back of the house.

Out she slid, Linda Leighton, her shining, layered oils exposed to the afternoon: very vulnerable now, someone who had to be held close to him.

Still no sound of the door closing. Rose really was giving him every chance in the world.

What else could he do while she was playing for time? He knew, hide the frame: keep as much of everything Hidden as he possibly could. He looked around. There were bits and pieces stacked between the dustbin and the kitchen wall, an old tray, a polystyrene shape which something had come packed in. He'd tuck it in there. Gently, Simon slid the empty picture frame between the two. They'd need to be really looking to spot that. And just for a moment he trusted Linda Leighton to the hiding place, too – an easy grab for him, but protected against the scrape of the pebble-dash – while he took the quickest of peeps round the side of the house. It had all gone very quiet out the front, he thought: and what if Rose had already left and they'd shut the front door quietly?

Clutching at the pebble-dash with his free hands, like someone on the face of the Eiger, Simon inched his face up to the corner. Perhaps he'd be able to see from round here. Slowly, very slowly, shifting his weight with care and caution he put an eye to the corner of the wall.

'Got you!' It was his grandfather, looming centimetres away round the angle, pouncing at him, shooting out a big hand and grabbing him by a fistful of hair. 'You little devil, you!' The front door slammed, and while Simon tried to struggle without having his hair pulled out, punching and kicking as best he could, he heard the old lady's voice calling as she hurried through, 'All right, Ernie? Wasn't anything, was it?'

'Wasn't it, just! It was this little urchin!'

Simon put everything he knew into getting away: he twisted, he pulled, he gave ground, he ran at the corner to push the old man off balance but he couldn't get near him with only that long, tough arm from halfway round the angle to get to grips with. And being held tight by the hair stopped him short in every other move, like a steer ringed through the soft of the nose. Shrieking and shouting, the old woman was out there, too: and suddenly it was all up. The two of them together, furious like that, were tougher than he could cope with: and he was marched unceremoniously into the house, to the living room where the door was locked and the key thrust deep into Ernie Watson's trouser pocket.

'Clever little tike, aren't you? Or are you? Whose idea was that play-acting bit in the garden? Alex, was it? I wouldn't put that past a criminal like him!'

Thrown into a corner of the low settee, Simon said nothing. He wasn't even listening, really. All he was aware of was his own crushing sense of failure. It had all gone wrong again. Everything had gone wrong, all the time, and even this last act for Alex had ended up a screaming mess.

What was it, then? Was it him? Was he just doomed to fail at everything he did?

Or was there some other explanation? Could it be that Rose had pulled some devious trick on him? He gripped at the grooves on the settee, his arms rigid. Could she have had something secret of her own worked out for some reason?

'Showing all that leg did it,' the old man was saying –

as always, not above showing off his own cleverness. 'All those marks on them, lumps and scratches. Just what you'd expect from someone who'd been in the nettles . . . Just enough to make me think, especially when her ankle miraculously got better all of a sudden. So your grandmother locked the front door and I took a quiet look round the back. You have to get up early to catch me, son.'

The nettles! Simon's head twisted to stare up at him. So, it was just bad luck: nothing traitorous. That was some relief. But those diabolical nettles! He could almost shout with the irony of it.

'Well of course we knew all about the nettles. First people they told, we were. Next of kin.'

'Next of kin?' Those words hurt worse than any sting had. 'Some bloody next of kin!' Simon shouted. 'I wouldn't ask you for a drink of water if I was dying of thirst!'

'Oh, very cutting.' His grandfather bent down at him, and suddenly shouted in his face. 'You're in no position to be rude to me, boy! I know what your game is, what you're after, Sonny Jim. You've properly shown yourself up this time – and you can guess where you're off to in a minute. And I tell you, that picture . . .' he waved a hand towards the wall as if he were about to underline his possession – but the words were left clawing at the air, and none of them was ever to know what the end of that sentence was going to be.

The old man seemed to see the empty space, ignore it, then see it again. And with the arm he'd stuck out for waving confidently at it he landed out and scragged Simon roughly to his feet.

'Where is it, you little villain? What have you done with our picture?'

Simon clamped his mouth in a firm, determined line. Let them find it, he thought. There was no help he'd ever give to them.

'Where the devil . . .?' Ernie Watson turned on his heel and rushed over to snatch at the door: but he'd locked it, and Simon took a gram of consolation from the berk he looked, jerking at it. 'Keep this door locked!' he warned his wife. 'I'll lock the hatch. He's hidden it outside.' Deep red with a profound anger, the old man slammed the door shut and locked it from the outside. He rushed to the kitchen hatch and he shot the bolts on that, and muttering furiously he rattled at the back door.

Well, it was all up now, Simon knew. He stared ahead at the artificial logs on the fire, his eyes averted from the old lady who was supposed to be his grandmother. There was nothing either of them had to say to each other right now, and neither of them tried. They sat in silence in their mutual dislike and listened to the dustbin scrape, and the back door going again, and the loud unlocking of the lounge. Simon watched his grandfather come in, still spluttering with fury, the violated frame in his hand, and waited for the shouts of 'Vandal' as his mother was waved at him. But the other hand was empty. He hadn't brought the picture in.

'All right, clever – where is it? Where've you put it, you little thief?'

Simon's open mouth was no indication that he was going to speak. He was dumbstruck. He'd put the picture by the dustbin. Anyone seeing the frame was bound to see the picture. You couldn't miss it, once you were down there.

'If you've harmed it – if you've hurt a hair of that head –!' He raised his hand. But he was too far away to hit. 'Where the hell is it?'

Simon shrugged, and threw himself back on the settee. 'I dunno,' he said. And he didn't. But he could guess. Rose had got it, hadn't she? She had to have it. There was no way it could have disappeared. When he hadn't shown up she must have crept round the back to hurry him, and heard the voices, and seen the picture . . .

217

'Well, you'll soon start talking to the police!' the old man threatened. And when Simon folded his arms and firmly shut his mouth again, he went through his unlocking and locking routine once more and started shouting in the hall. 'Hello? Hello! *Hello!*' The receiver was pounded to the accompaniment of a string of curses, and finally it was crashed down. 'Just the right bloody time for the phone to pack up!' He slammed out of the house, and then all that was left was the long, awkward wait for the police, the lavender atmosphere hazed with hatred. But with every minute ticking by, Simon could picture Rose putting a few more metres between herself and Market Junction, and a few metres less between the picture and Alex in the country.

When the bell eventually rang, it wasn't the police but Denny Adams who stood blocking the Parkside doorway. With a look of disappointment and an air of standing on no ceremony he walked into the guarded room.

'Well,' he said, his small half-hooded eyes focussing seriously at Simon. 'I think you've got more than a bit of explaining to do, young man. Me first, then the law . . .'

Simon said nothing: just watched the man sit down to a flap of raincoat. What was there to tell him? The Welfare didn't expect him to give Rose away, did he, or say where Alex was, or help these two here to get Alex's picture back off him? Surely to God he didn't expect that. And what else was there to say? That he'd had enough? Wasn't so sure of Alex any more? That he'd fallen out at the fair and had nowhere special to go from here? He stared sullenly at the wall. None of that was anything the Welfare would care about. All the Market Junction authorities wanted to know was that he'd soon be getting an education again. The real facts of life meant nothing to them. Simon looked at Denny Adams from the corners of his eyes: eyes that were filling with tears again. What would he put in his stupid notebook if he told him he'd done the best he could

– right up to this afternoon – and now he was beaten? Defeated? He blinked the tears away. No, there was nothing he wanted to tell the Welfare . . .

'Well, son, I can't help you much if you don't help me . . .'

'*Help him?*' Ellen Watson sounded as if she would explode with indignation. '*Help him?*' she wheezed. 'He wants locking up, that's what, the same as his wicked father. Putting away, that's what they want, not *help*, for God's sake!'

'Well, that's not for you or me to decide,' Denny Adams said, diplomatically. 'But right now he's coming back to Darenth Lodge.' He got up, as if, like Simon, he knew he'd get nowhere with these two.

But the old lady hadn't finished. She got up, too, and stood shaking in front of Simon, fighting angrily for every noisy breath, her fat jowls trembling, a white, ringed hand pointing in accusation at him. 'What your sort needs is teaching lessons, not – *sympathy*.' She said it as if it were a mouthful of medicine. 'Decent people live by decent laws. They don't go breaking them when it suits.'

She was screeching now, beside herself again; and both her husband and Denny Adams stood there speechless, as if they weren't sure whether to lead her off quietly or let her get it out. But the way she was, it would have taken a brave man to risk laying a finger on that shaking frame.

'They don't go killing people, and then pretend they're round the twist!'

What? Simon wasn't sitting silent under that, if they were! Whatever Alex had done, he'd put nothing on.

'What you saying?' he shouted back. 'Come on, I want to hear! Say it in words, not in spit!' He was angry, too, could feel it rising inside him again, like last night: unstoppable, like milk past the boil.

'I'm saying, you rude little tike, that your father – ' she gave everything for the next breath – 'your father killed our Linda with his car. *Killed her!*' she screamed. 'And then put on he was mad to fool the stupid police!' She blazed round at Denny Adams as if he were one of the gullible idiots.

'You liar! He never!' Simon was gripping the settee to hold himself down, fire heaped on his anger now by having his own unworthy doubts suddenly made public in those terrible words. He grasped for something to say: but before he could get another word out she changed her tone, and a condescending baby-talk twisted from her lips. 'Well, smart little Sonny Jim, you can *call* me a liar if you like, you can *say* he never; but you were going to *prove* those words, once upon a time, weren't you? I remember, I remember.' She nodded at him to show emphatically she hadn't forgotten. 'That's what you promised last time you pushed yourself in here!'

There was nothing, *nothing* Simon could say to that! She was right. He hadn't proved a thing, going off with Alex. And since Friday night, knowing the motives Alex could have had, his secret doubts had grown bigger. And this ugly, twisted old cow was throwing it at him, grinding his face in the muck of his own failure.

'Well? We've suddenly gone all quiet, haven't we?' She stood off, her head on one side; the smug victory hers.

'You!' Desperately, Simon threw himself forward, grabbed for her middle – a physical explosion fused by frustration and defeat. But Denny Adams had him in one swift movement and pinned him as the tears began to burst.

'Oh! Hit a woman, would you?' she scoffed. 'Like father, like son! Is that how you got your face, bashing at women?'

'No!' he blurted. But what was the use? He couldn't make anyone here understand. Nor anyone anywhere. He'd got his face like that because he *hadn't* gone for a woman, he'd not hit at Rose – however much she deserved it last night. If he had you could bet your life Nick wouldn't have been half so bothered. No, he'd got his hiding because he'd gone for the big guy: been just as angry at both of them, but gone for Nick. Not because Rose was a female, though. Oh no! Not like that. If he was going to tell the truth he'd gone for Nick because he was stupid for Rose himself, and he had been since the nettles.

He cuffed his nose, pawed at his tears; and came back to the strong, no-nonsense grip of the Welfare on his arm.

It was over. All over. They were going.

But what else had she said? What was it she kept saying? Like father, like son? Well she was right there, anyhow. He was. He knew he was. There was so much likeness between them that he'd stuck with him, tried to help him, mixed the paints, worked on the boards, taken everything the rotten world had thrown at him.

And wait! Wasn't there was one more likeness when he thought about it, when he made the thinking come? His back stiffened, his eyes stared – and like a long, complicated problem the last equation came out, there in that hateful house. Nick and Rose. Georgie the dancer and Linda his mum. Anger at the two of them: frustration, upset, real aggravation. But then, something special about the way he'd felt for Rose – and Alex for Linda Leighton. It was all the same, wasn't it? The situations were dead alike. Now he could see. *And who had he gone for, against the odds?* Who had he wanted to take it out on? Only Nick. Not even a swear at Rose.

So now he knew – or reckoned he did. Somewhere between the low settee and the vandalized telephone in the hall it came to him with all the certainty of the worked-out truth. If Alex *had* gone for anyone, if it hadn't been the accident the police had said it was – the sort of accident the policeman at the fair had had himself – then he'd have gone for Georgie the dancer, wouldn't he? Like son, like father. He'd have slammed at him, not at Linda Leighton. Not at his wife, the one he'd gone to bring home.

Simon was by the front door now, on the path, with the Welfare gripping him like a hooligan at a football match. He took a few more paces, debating within himself: and then he pulled himself to stop, and Denny Adams stopped with him, ready for tricks. But all Simon did was turn round and call at the couple in the doorway.

'I don't have to prove nothing to you!' he shouted in triumph. 'Nothing at all!' And he led the Welfare to the car, as quiet as a mouse, because now he knew he really didn't care about them any more.

The car moved speedily through the quiet Sunday streets. Denny Adams didn't speak, gave his concentration to the road and to Simon's movements, and allowed a peace and silence for Simon to think and work out the mystery of what might lay ahead.

Till almost the end he'd given Alex the benefit of the doubt: and thank God he had, he thought: because while Alex was shown a bit of faith, on the road with the fair or back in Stonelands – or even at home – there was a chance he'd make it one day. But without that bit of faith who knew? How could he manage? The family picture wouldn't be enough for ever: and once Linda Leighton was back in his head he'd need to start filling some other spaces. So Simon still had a big part to play. And one thing was for sure – that mysterious Rose wouldn't always be around to make things happen.

And more's the pity for that, Simon thought, as the car turned swiftly into the overgrown grounds of Darenth Lodge.

Suspicion, then recognition, followed by a deepened look of distrust: Alex's face showed a life that had been absent for so much of the past twelve months. He frowned when he saw Rose at the door of his trailer, he registered what was in her hand – and only then did he stare out beyond her into the dark for some sign of Simon.

'Simon, he's been back home?' He looked hard at Linda Leighton's shy smile.

'Yeah, but we got a little problem . . .'

Alex put the picture away into a dark and private corner. 'What? Where is he?'

Rose, the accomplice, the messenger, but never the diplomat, told him what had happened in a few blunt words. 'We nicked the picture, an' they nicked 'im,' she finished. 'Like as not 'e's back up the Lodge till we can get 'im out.'

'Eh?'

'We'll get 'im. We done it once, we can do it again.'

But Alex wasn't listening any more. He was rocking the trailer with his frantic striding, fumbling here for his mac, there for his brushes and his battered signwriter's case.

'What you doin'? 'Old on, what's the rush? We won't get nothin' done tonight . . .'

But it was like reasoning with a single-minded cat bent on going its own way. He grabbed the hardboard picture again. 'I'm taking this back home where it belongs.'

'What, back to them old cruds? Gonna let them win you, are you?'

The look on Alex's face said he didn't want to know anything about any old cruds. It said he had a purpose and that his ears were quite deaf to reasoning or to explanation. Feverishly, he wrapped the picture of Simon's mother in a sheet of paper with DODGEMS traced upon it and he clutched it under his arm.

'But what about . . .?' Rose's waving arm took in the fair, Jimmy Tucker, Old Man Penfold, and all the boards and balustrades that had yet to be painted.

'I'll settle all that later. I'll tell the man. He'll understand. He'll give me directions. I'm on my feet now. I'm getting my boy back, soon as I can.' And in the same draught of activity Alex left the door swinging and went striding off towards the family trailer behind the Dodgems.

Rose looked down at his light luggage: his mac and his case of artists' gear. But her stare was glazed and unemotional again. If she felt she'd done her best, and failed at it, she didn't show it in her expression. She simply shrugged her shoulders, found half a cigarette in the pocket of her cardigan, and set about looking through the empty trailer for an unused match.